CAUGHT

With a slow smile, Nicholas glanced over her head at the torch.

Noelle turned to see

then she saw the red

dangling from it.

"It would seem tha

job of decorating,

caught," Nicholas saic

his head.

The intensity of his gaze made Noelle tremble. She should do something. It was the custom to kiss whoever you caught under the mistletoe, but she was promised to another. But this kiss wasn't really important—just a tradition, she thought to herself, as Nicholas's lips met hers.

After all, it was Christmas.

Nicholas's arms went around her. He was going to end this attraction he felt for her once he gave her a thorough kiss. Her arms slid around his neck, and he shook with a raw need that shot through him like a spear.

When he pressed his mouth against her lips, she parted them slightly and let him delve into the sweetness of her mouth. God, she was pleasing. She responded to his touch, and when she molded her body to his, he thought that what little reason he held on to had surely deserted him.

Where was the strong discipline that Nicholas prided himself in?

Evidently, he'd left it on the battlefield.

Good thing she wasn't the enemy. Or was she?

CHRISTMAS IN CAMELOT

BRENDA K. JERNIGAN

ZEBRA BOOKS
Kensington Publishing Corp.
http://www.kensingtonbooks.com

ZEBRA BOOKS are published by

Kensington Publishing Corp.
850 Third Avenue
New York, NY 10022

All Kensington titles, imprints and distributed lines are available at special quantity discounts for bulk purchases for sales promotion, premiums, fund-raising, educational or institutional use.

Special book excerpts or customized printings can also be created to fit specific needs. For details, write or phone the office of the Kensington Special Sales Manager: Kensington Publishing Corp., 850 Third Avenue, New York, NY 10022. Attn. Special Sales Department. Phone: 1-800-221-2647.

First Printing: October 2002
10 9 8 7 6 5 4 3 2 1

Printed in the United States of America

In memory of my mother, Bonnie Dittman, who died much too young of breast cancer. A portion of all the proceeds from this book will be donated to HOSPICE, so they can help those who can't help themselves.

This book is dedicated to my husband, Scott.
To all the Christmases past,
to the Christmas present,
to all the Christmases to come,
I love you.

Special Thanks

To the Harnett County Library for all the research materials that they provide. Melanie Collins, Director, handed me my first romance novel, and I have been hooked ever since. Now if they would just quit charging me all those late fees.

PROLOGUE

The Great Hall of Camelot stood silent.

The two men watched each other warily.

They waited.

Who would be the first to speak?

Both were Pendragons . . . a stubborn lot.

"Do you know why I have summoned you?" King Arthur finally asked as he leaned on the arm of his chair, gazing evenly at the only knight present at the Round Table.

"Aye, sire," Sir Nicholas the Dragon, and cousin to the king, replied, neither flinching nor casting his gaze away from Arthur. Nicholas was, however, thankful that his king had chosen a private audience to discuss these matters.

"It is a difficult decision I have to make," the king said, waiting for Nicholas to explain his actions.

Nicholas was in no mood for any of this. He did not make a habit of explaining himself, but since it was the king who'd asked, it was probably prudent that he answer him.

Stalling for time, Nicholas glanced at the beautiful wooden table which had been a gift to Arthur from

Lady Guinevere. Letters of gold marked the place of each knight, with Nicholas's seat directly across the table from the king. No knight could claim himself to be better than another, for there was no "high" or "low" table, simply the Table Round, where all men were equal.

Of course, King Arthur's seat was a bit higher, which wasn't really necessary, for none of his knights doubted that Arthur was in charge. All had sworn loyalty to their king, which brought Nicholas to the problem at hand.

He turned a baleful eye on the king and finally asked the words Arthur had waited patiently for. "Would you care to hear the truth, sire?"

Arthur nodded slowly. "Aye."

"I have never pretended to be other than I am with the Lady Clarisse. She knew from the start that it was not marriage I would be offering, merely a liaison for a while. Nothing more."

"What is this nonchalance that you have for women?" Arthur asked. "Do you think they are mere amusements?"

"There have always been damsels, sire. Everywhere. I have many times climbed into bed at night to find I was not alone. I did not bid them come. So why should they be treated as special?"

"I see," Arthur said. "As to Lady Clarisse . . ." Arthur paused as a serving maid, Matilda, appeared to refill his gold chalice, clumsily spilling the red liquid on the Siege Perilous seat. "God's teeth, will you ever learn to hit the goblet and not the chair?"

"Sorry, sire. My vision, you see, is not what it used

to be," she explained, paying absolutely no attention to Arthur's reprimand. She moved over to Nicholas and filled his chalice, giving him a brilliant smile. Matilda had been at the castle so long that she had grown bold in her old age, and she more or less ran the household. She was truly Arthur's favorite and, for that reason, he put up with her insolence.

She looked at Arthur. "Would you desire anything else, sire?"

"That will be all, Matilda." Arthur smiled fondly as she shuffled from the room, then he turned back to Nicholas. His smile instantly faded. "As I was saying, Lady Clarisse claims she is ruined."

"I can truly say that I have never ruined any woman, including Clarisse. I was not her first and will surely not be the last." Nicholas paused and then decided a bit more was needed. "At the moment, I have no desire to marry. When I do, it will be to someone of my own choosing.

"I saw with my own eyes how my mother destroyed my father and drove him to his death. I want none of that." Nicholas paused, taking a swallow of wine to wipe the bitter taste from his mouth. "I am not certain that the woman for me exists. You are fortunate to have Guinevere, sire."

"Aye. My queen is a rare gem indeed," Arthur said with a smile. "But I felt the same as you not so long ago," he confessed as he watched his favorite knight. Nicholas was favored not because they were cousins, but because he had saved Arthur's life twice in battle, earning his place at the Round Table in spite of his inauspicious beginnings.

Nicholas lost his birthright when his mother burned their castle to the ground. She perished in the fire, leaving Nicholas to fend for himself at ten. How the boy had survived, Arthur didn't know. Maybe Nicholas's ability to feel nothing had allowed him to persevere.

Since Sir Nicholas had stormed into the king's life, proving his bravery over and over again, Arthur had had little peace. An aura of excitement surrounded the knight wherever he went. Nicholas feared nothing, so it seemed, except love. He had broken at least five hearts that Arthur knew about and probably countless others.

King Arthur finished his wine before he spoke. "I want you to take your men and pay a visit to the King of Ireland. There are heathens there who do not support us. They must be convinced otherwise." Arthur paused, noting the excitement and anticipation in Nicholas's eyes.

It was apparent that Nicholas looked forward to the challenge, so the task was little punishment. A bit more was needed, Arthur thought.

"I also want your promise that you will not look at another woman for three months. I will relieve you of your promise on December first."

Nicholas's eyes narrowed and his brow wrinkled; then he said, "It is a bit harsh, sire."

"You said yourself that women meant little to you. I conclude, then, that you will not miss them. Perhaps they will mean more after you have done without a fair lady for a while. I wager you will have a different opinion upon your return."

"And what would you like to wager?" Nicholas challenged with a sly smile.

Arthur thought for a moment. "How about the two white warhorses you have been wanting?"

Nicholas nodded. "Agreed. And if I lose?"

"I want two of your black ones."

Nicholas rose to his feet with a triumphant smile. "As you know, sire, I never lose." He gave his I-am-already-the-victor smile, then picked up his chalice and raised it in a toast. "To God and King," Nicholas said, then drained the wine from his cup and left the room.

Arthur stared at the door long after it shut. Would Nicholas ever find the peace he sought? He was a man who feared nothing, a man who served Arthur faithfully, but cared not for his own welfare. Arthur hoped that one day Nicholas would find a woman he desired above all others. However, if the conquest were easy, he would tire and turn from her.

But what if the woman was unattainable?

"That would prove interesting," Arthur said to the empty room. "I believe we need a miracle in Camelot."

He rose and looked at his glorious table, a plan forming in his mind.

It would be difficult to accomplish.

And it could be for nothing.

But it would make for an entertaining Christmas season, he thought. Arthur smiled as he went to seek his queen.

This year Arthur couldn't wait for Christmas in Camelot.

ONE

"Not on my life!"

Lady Noelle Mallory's voice echoed around the Great Hall of Cranborne Castle. She gripped the back of the tapestry-covered chair. The Great Hall seemed to be closing in on her.

Were her brothers daft?

They didn't look daft.

But there they sat in the carved oak chairs reserved for the head of the table, apparently thinking that she'd be happy to do their bidding as if she were some simpleton. Well, they were not talking to a maiden of twelve years.

"Be reasonable, Noelle," her eldest brother said. "You should have been married long before now as you are older than most by some six years. If not for our father indulging your whims, you would be long married. But you were always waiting for that special knight with his polished armor to carry you away. What nonsense! Merlin put foolish notions into your head when you were but a child." John Mallory paused then sat back in his chair and leaned on the arm. "Tristan and I have tried to be patient, but our patience has worn thin."

"As has your coin," Noelle spat. "Should I point out that neither of you is married?"

"It is different for men," Tristan said.

"God's wounds!" John slammed his hand on the desk. His face was as red as his surcoat. "Don't you remember the men you have rejected? Good proposals all." Their wealth would have helped Cranborne thrive.

Noelle tightened her grip on the chair. "Aye, I well remember." She shrugged. "They were not to my liking."

"We have come to the conclusion that you know not what you want, so Tristan and I have chosen for you."

"It is so nice of you both," she said in as sarcastic a tone as she could muster, then looked at Tristan, who had always been her confidante. "You are a traitor."

"Nay." He shook his head in denial. "This time I must agree with John. We have not chosen a peasant for you. He is one of King Arthur's knights."

John faced his sister, noting her hellbent stare: one that could freeze him to the chair if he were to pay her any attention. He'd been living with her temper all his life and, thankfully, had learned to survive, as had Tristan. However, Tristan was of little help. He had contributed to her wild ways. He'd even gone so far as to let her pose as his squire.

John sighed. His attempts to reason with his sister were apparently getting nowhere.

The problem with Noelle was her beauty. With her flaxen hair and creamy skin, she could wrap any man around her finger. Upon doing so, she'd merrily send them on their way. She required a challenge. And this time, John had found somebody he was certain could handle her. They had been forced to throw in twenty acres of land because her stubborn disposition was well known. Praise the Lord, Sir Gavin was willing to try, and John wasn't sure that even Sir Gavin would be able to tame Noelle. But Cranborne needed a knight of his stature, and his army for protection. The evil Prince Meleagant was always on the prowl for weaker holdings. John admitted he had not done well managing Cranborne, but with a little help he would do better next time.

"Today is December first, your birthday, and you are one and twenty. It is time that you come to terms with the idea of marriage."

"Some birthday present," she said. Her eyebrow raised. "Wait until you see what I get you in return."

Tristan chuckled and John gave him a withering look.

John rose and braced his hands on the table. "No matter, Noelle. You will marry Sir Gavin on Christmas Day in the presence of King Arthur and his court."

"You cannot force me," Noelle declared. She squared her shoulders, then asked, "What if I refuse?"

"There will be no refusal!" John shouted.

"But I do not love him." Her voice matched his tone.

"You don't know him!"

"Precisely," Noelle shouted to both her brothers; then she turned and jumped down from the dais. As she ran past the large hearth, a log fell, shooting sparks up the chimney. Ignoring the colorful display, she headed for the front door.

Noelle could hear John and Tristan shouting for her to stop, but she jerked the door open anyway. Not bothering to pause or acknowledge that they were shouting, she slammed the door behind her.

She raced to the stable where her horse, Thor, had already been saddled. She had intended to ride earlier when the summons had come from her brothers.

The marshal, who had been pitching hay, straightened as she entered. "I still have Thor saddled, milady," Phillip called to her as she dashed past him. He leaned against the pitchfork, watching her. "Is something amiss, milady?"

"Everything is amiss," Noelle said as she stepped up on the mounting block. Grabbing the reins and the pommel, she mounted her horse, her skirts swirling down the stallion's side. "I am going for a ride."

Phillip took the stallion's bridle and walked him through the stable. "You don't have a cloak. It is cold outside," he said as he let go of the bridle. "Here, take my surcoat." He walked over to a peg and retrieved the heavy garment. "It is not as nice as yours, milady, but will keep you warm."

Noelle leaned down and smiled as she took the jacket. Phillip had run the Cranborne stables for a long time. "I will be honored to wear your garment."

She slipped the brown surcoat on over her head. "You should get someone else to pitch the hay."

"I like doing things myself, milady."

"You always have." She smiled at him. "I will be back shortly."

"Not without an escort," Phillip called after her, but she'd kicked Thor into a canter and was long gone. "No one will be able to catch her now," he said to himself.

He turned around and looked behind him. "Nigel," Phillip shouted.

The young groom stuck his head out from behind one of the stalls. "Ye want me?"

"Aye. Saddle a horse and try to accompany Lady Noelle." Phillip sighed. "If you can catch her, that is." He stood at the stable door, watching as the tail end of the mighty Thor disappeared through the gate. Noelle was so reckless. Phillip always feared for her safety.

Freedom. That was what Noelle sought.

Freedom to do just as she pleased with no one telling her what to do. If her father were still alive, her brothers would not be pressuring her into doing something she did not desire. Of course, they could not force her to marry against her will, but they could make her life hell if she didn't at least agree to consider the idea.

Her father had always treated her as an equal to her brothers. She could outshoot and outride both of them, and right now the thought of shooting them appealed to her a great deal.

Leaning low over Thor, she let him take her to their favorite place: a well-hidden lake that only she knew about, a place where she could find peace and escape her brothers for a little while.

The cool, crisp air chilled her body, if not her soul, and she was thankful for Phillip's kind gesture. He had been around all her life, and he was the one who had taught her to ride.

Noelle knew it would take a long time for her rage to cool down. If it cooled at all.

Some Christmas this would be, she thought as she neared the woods.

When she came to the grove of trees, thick with evergreens and oaks, she guided Thor to the small opening and ducked to avoid a low-hanging limb. Thor made his way along the familiar path to the first clearing where he stopped as he'd done many times before. Noelle dismounted.

Since it was wintertime, there wasn't much grass, but Thor would be able to find a few blades to munch upon. Noelle patted him on the side of his neck. He was a beautiful black stallion with a white lightning bolt running the length of his nose which was the reason she'd named him Thor.

She reached into a sack that had been tossed across his rump and drew out a handful of oats so the stallion could graze in his favorite spot.

Noelle followed the narrow path to the lake and sighed upon catching a glimpse of the sun shining on the calm water. It was breathtaking. A gust of cool wind blew her hair away from her face as she came to the end of the path.

As she neared the water's edge, a splash caught her attention and made her forget her anger as she wondered what animal she might see. Carefully, she eased down the final few steps of the path and stopped behind a bush. She hid there so she wouldn't frighten the creature. Ever so quietly, she inched her way up until she could see over the top of the bush.

Her eyes widened.

It was not the kind of animal she had expected to see.

No, indeed.

Emerging from the cold water was a man. A gasp escaped her lips so quickly, she had to clamp her hand over her mouth to silence it. Then she ducked back down behind her cover.

When Noelle felt it was safe, she rose again and, this time, kept her mouth shut. That didn't stop her eyes from widening as she gazed upon the backside of the man who was just emerging from the water . . . and . . . and he was completely naked.

Did the fool not realize that it was winter?

She knew any proper lady should blush and look away. However, she thought with a wry smile, who would know? Besides which, she was most curious. So, why not satisfy her curiosity just a wee bit? Aye, what could it hurt?

What she saw pleased her a great deal. A well-muscled back and a firm backside proved this one wasn't lazy. He looked more like a warrior than a peasant, but a warrior would have many soldiers around him, and he was alone. His rich, dark hair brushed his shoulders, and Noelle wondered what the front of him looked like as she leaned to the side to get a better view.

It was a mistake. She lost her grip on the hawthorn bush and fell sideways. Quickly, she put her hand out to catch herself and hastily resumed her position, peeking through the bushes.

A falcon in a nearby tree called, and the man swung halfway around to see it.

Noelle did have the decency to cover her eyes, but she couldn't help the cracks between her fingers that allowed her to view the finest specimen of a man she'd ever seen.

He must truly be a god.

"Oooooh," she sighed. Upon realizing she had actually made the sound, she ducked farther behind her protective bush and waited for the heat in her cheeks to cool before standing up again.

When she eased back up, he was gone.

Disappointment washed over her, and Noelle decided he truly must have been a god or a strong figment of her imagination, because no man could be *that* perfect and then disappear so quickly. She frowned as she swept her gaze over the lake, trying to catch another glimpse of him.

He was gone.

Noelle stepped from her hiding place. Why couldn't her brothers find someone like that man for her to marry? She still might not like the idea of marriage, but at least she'd have something fine to gaze upon in her misery. With her last pleasing thought, she turned to check on Thor.

And hit a tree.

Funny, she didn't remember a tree right behind her. When a pair of hands clasped her arms to keep her from falling backwards, she gasped. Something was amiss.

"Have you been enjoying the view, wench?" a rich voice sounded above her.

She stiffened. She'd been caught.

"Unhand me, sir." Noelle tried to sound furious, but to no avail. He did not loosen his grip.

So much for intimidation.

She stared at the spot where the ties of his kirtle lay opened at his neck. Slowly, her gaze traveled up until she could see his face.

Aye, he was truly a god.

The strength of his features overwhelmed her. Power, strength, danger were all she could think of and her gaze had only reached his chin. She shivered. Did she dare look at the rest of him? Noelle clasped his forearms as she tilted back to see all of him. The man was huge. He looked down at her with the most unusual, predatory amber eyes that she had ever seen.

Hopefully, she wasn't the prey.

"Pray tell, what are you doing here, sir? For you are trespassing," she finally said.

"Is that so?" he said in a tone not in the least bit cowed. "Since when does a peasant claim to own land?"

She stiffened in his arms. "And when does a peasant speak thus to a lady?"

His expression darkened at the insult. "I see before me a woman dressed in a well-worn and, I might add, ugly surcoat trying to act like a lady. Do you take me for a simpleton?"

"Nay. But at least I have clothes." She looked down and blushed at the sight of his bare legs. He hadn't put on his chauses. "I-I borrowed this surcoat," Noelle sputtered. "Wh-what is your name?"

"Nicholas."

Noelle laughed, wanting to insult him and get that smirk off his face—a face filled with dark arrogance that would be burned into her memory forever.

"Nicholas? It is a commoner's name to be sure," she flung at him as she tried to squirm out of his grip. "You are probably from some nearby village."

Instead of accomplishing her goal, she was suddenly jerked closer to her foe. She could now *feel* the muscles she'd only glimpsed earlier and see the rugged contours of a jaw that was now tense, telling her he hadn't cared for her comment.

"Do I look like the people in your village, wench? Excuse me, *milady,*" he sneered.

"N–nay," she managed, a little stunned by his closeness. She struggled, needing to put some distance between them so she could think straight. He smelled so clean and fresh. "Release me at once."

"Why should I? It is you who intruded, not I."

"It's not proper. It is my land that you have intruded upon."

"Let me make sure I understand." Nicholas chuckled. "You are out here unchaperoned, and you are trying to convince me that you have proper manners."

He looked at her for a long moment. "Do you know what I think?"

She shook her head. This man had the most beautiful eyes she'd ever seen. And she really shouldn't care what he thought of her, but she did.

He took a step closer.

She didn't retreat.

"Methinks your mouth says one thing, and your body another." His whispered voice hovered just above her mouth, his gaze fixed on her lips.

God's wounds. She felt as if she were melting. "I–I—" Noelle never finished her sentence because his mouth silenced her. His arms circled her waist, and she was suddenly very close to him. His lips were warm, caressing. She loved every minute of his kiss, but she pushed hard against his chest. She was, after all, a lady.

He wasn't a gentleman.

He only tightened his hold, so she couldn't move at all. He drew back slightly, giving her the chance to say something. When she opened her mouth to speak, he took advantage and plunged his tongue into her warmth.

Noelle was so shocked with the flood of heat that flowed into every part of her body that she forgot to struggle.

She also forgot that she was alone and could be ravaged by a man she didn't know.

It seemed she had forgotten everything . . . except the lips that moved with such expertise. Suddenly, Noelle was lost in a world she'd never known.

She clung to Nicholas like the simple maid he'd

claimed she was. And worse, she liked this new feeling, enjoying every minute of his embrace.

She had been kissed once, maybe twice, in her lifetime but never like this . . . no, nothing like this.

He wasn't a god. He was the devil.

Nicholas knew the minute the woman responded, and suddenly he lost control of the situation. He had meant to teach her a lesson, not seduce her. But her young, firm breasts pressed next to his thin kirtle were intoxicating indeed. The sweetness of her mouth stirred a passion in him much stronger than he could ever remember . . . and something more. A feeling he couldn't quite put his finger on.

Shyly, she followed his lead. Her tongue began to explore his mouth, giving him a new meaning to kissing.

By God, she was passionate.

Again, there was the oddest feeling, some unnamed thing he could not recall. Lifting his head, he gazed upon her face. Her eyelids fluttered open, and he saw so many mixed emotions in her eyes that it took his breath away. Then he knew what he felt for her . . . tenderness.

A feeling he'd never felt toward *any* woman before.

He used a wench and sent her on her way. He had never wanted attachments.

A man who cares becomes weak.

He becomes careless.

So Nicholas had always been careful not to let his emotions get in the way.

But here they were.

He felt tenderness, and he didn't like it.

He needed to get control of the situation and do it now.

Nicholas pushed the woman from him. He saw the raw desire in her eyes before reality set in, and she remembered she wasn't supposed to be kissing a stranger. She slapped him. The sound shattered the stillness of the lake.

"A bit late for that, milady," Nicholas growled as he rubbed his jaw.

How he'd had the luck to run into such a creature out here in the middle of nowhere, when he'd sworn off all damsels for at least a month, was either dumb luck or misfortune. He wasn't sure which.

But he was certain that she was a treasure, and he was sorely tempted to forget his vow and take her here and now on the cold, hard ground. That cold swim had frozen his brain, but it hadn't done much for the rest of his body, which raged with fire. And she had to be a commoner. Look at the way she was dressed. A plain cotehardie and shabby surcoat.

If she knew his identity, she'd probably be more than willing to share what was hers to share. How many times had he gone to his room to find some maiden in his bed? They had hopes that he would marry them so they could obtain a position and wealth. Greed! That's what drew most women.

But this one . . . this one could very easily satisfy the raging urges she stirred in him.

Just as he was thinking of acting upon his lust, something stopped him.

By all that was holy . . . he had no idea why all of a sudden he had a conscience.

The scent of roses floated up from golden hair that swirled around her shoulders. Her skin was flawless except for a tiny scar across her chin. He unthinkingly ran his fingertip over it.

"How did you come by this?" he asked ever so softly.

"My brother shoved me because I wasn't moving fast enough, and I fell and cut my chin," she said. Then she smiled as if she recalled that day, and Nicholas saw that she had twin dimples, one in each cheek. "He paid the piper when Father found out. Aye, he couldn't sit down for a week."

"And I see that pleased you."

"Aye, it did."

"Lady Noelle," a voice came from the other side of the trees.

"Lady? Who, pray tell, is that?"

"It is my groom," Noelle replied.

Nicholas gave her a doubtful look. "Or your brother. Nonetheless, I bid thee farewell. Mayhap our paths will one day cross again."

He stared at her for a long moment, and then strolled off, wondering who she was. On second thought, it was perhaps better that he never know, for he had the strangest feeling that she was trouble.

Aye, this one was trouble to be sure.

Noelle watched the stranger walk away, his strides powerful. He seemed so confident that it made her wonder who he really was and how he had happened upon her lake.

When he reached the other side, a falcon followed him until they both disappeared into the forest.

Then a long-ago memory began to crystallize in her mind. Merlin had come to visit Cranborne Castle when she was twelve, and she'd immediately become fascinated with the wizard. They had become friends.

Back then, she'd wanted to grow up and marry a knight on a magnificent destrier, so she'd asked Merlin to tell her what her future held. After all, he was a wizard, and he knew such things.

"You will marry a knight who is bigger than any of the others. He will be brave and bold," Merlin whispered and then drew back with a frown. "But . . . but he will have a cold heart. And only you will be able to give him the gift of love. However, making him want such a gift may prove too much for you."

She'd frowned and looked at the wizard. "And what does that mean?" she'd asked.

Merlin picked up her small hand in his. "That, my child, is something you will have to figure out for yourself when you are older."

Noelle had clung to his words and her childhood fantasy. True love. Was there really such a thing? Or was she the hopeless daydreamer, searching for something that didn't exist? She sighed and started back for Thor.

Just maybe she would go to Camelot. At least there she could find Merlin.

Merlin would have the answers to her questions. She just knew it.

* * *

Nicholas shook his head.

Even out in the middle of nowhere, women seemed to find him.

What had started out as a cold swim to wash away the many battles he'd been in had become much more. He hadn't expected to find a woman unaccompanied at the lake.

Nicholas slipped his tunic over his head. He welcomed the cool, crisp air after his brief encounter with the very desirable woman, but now his senses had returned, and he didn't want to catch his death.

He smiled. So far, he'd kept his promise to King Arthur and had not touched a woman in three months and a fortnight. But today was December first, so his vow had ended and Arthur owed him.

Nicholas looked back to where the woman had been. Why had he turned away from such a beautiful woman? He had seen the desire in her eyes, and with a little coaxing he'd have enjoyed an afternoon of pleasure.

An afternoon he needed desperately.

So why didn't he go back and satisfy his needs and be done with it? He didn't have the answer.

Mounting his destrier, he gave one last look at the lake, then jerked his mount around. When he reached Camelot he'd satisfy his urges, and this time he'd choose a wench who had no thoughts of marriage. Then he'd collect his wager with Arthur.

As Nicholas approached camp, his first in command, Dirk, met him. And he wasn't smiling.

Though Dirk was one of those muscle-bound Highlanders, he had become Nicholas's best comrade. Dirk had reddish-brown hair and a fiery temper to go with it. His size made men walk carefully around him.

"It is about time ye be returning ye sorry hide back to camp. Just how long does it take to wash ye filthy hide?"

Nicholas grinned. Something he rarely did. "So you were worried about me?" he asked as he dismounted.

"It is not worry I be doing. It is more like concern that some fool would take revenge on ye, and then I'd have to hunt the lazy cur down and lay him low."

"I see." Nicholas rubbed his chin. "The concern was not so much for me, but for the inconvenience of the fight."

"Aye," Dirk said with a nod. He laughed. "The last battle was a long one. We need to rest for a while."

"I can remember when you never complained about a battle." Nicholas pointed out.

"It was those Irish heathens, a slimy lot. Every time we thought we had the bad ones routed out, another bunch would show up."

"It was a long battle," Nicholas agreed with a smile. "We will rest here for a few days, and then return to Camelot for the Christmas season. How does that sound?"

"Very appealing." Dirk smiled. "There are a few wenches who have been heartbroken since I left. I'm sure they need consoling by now."

"Good. Then so be it. Three days hence, we ride to Camelot where we will find a peaceful time. Good food, good friends . . . who could ask for more?"

TWO

Noelle sighed. Maybe Merlin had been wrong. She had never met anyone to fit his description of the man in her future, and now she doubted that she ever would.

"Lady Noelle."

Noelle heard the groom's voice as she took Thor's bridle and walked him down the path toward the opening to the meadow. The leaves had all fallen from the birch trees except for a few stubborn ones which still clung tenaciously, but the branches were thick when combined with the many blue-green juniper trees, so her path was still hidden.

"Noelle!" Tristan called, forcefully.

When she emerged onto the open field, she saw her brother. It was apparent that he didn't trust the groom to bring her back. As soon as Tristan spotted her, he nudged his mount around and trotted toward her. "You have been told not to ride alone," he scolded.

"Aye." Noelle nodded. She felt weary from the day's events: first her brother's announcement and then the stranger who had her emotions so stirred up she didn't want to think about them. She glanced up at her brother. "You have told me many things I choose to ignore. However, you should know better than most how I feel about marriage."

She regretted the words the minute she'd said them, for that dead look immediately entered Tristan's eyes . . . the same look he'd worn for a year after his wife died in childbirth. A child, she'd confessed just before she died, that belonged to another man. Didn't her brother remember what it was like to be joined with one he did not love? "You, my brother, have betrayed me."

Tristan dismounted. "Nay. I have not."

His brown hair was windblown from his brisk ride, giving him a boyish appearance. He was a handsome man and had always been the one to protect her. There was no anger in his blue eyes, only guilt, and Noelle would make certain that guilt did not go away anytime soon.

"I have not betrayed you, sister," he said again.

She shot him a skeptical look.

"Not the way you think," he hurried to add. "Sir Gavin is a good man. I ask that you go to Camelot and meet him. If you have not changed your mind by the time your wedding arrives," Tristan paused and ran a hand through his hair, "I will think of a way to release you from my pledge."

Preparing to mount, Noelle grasped Thor's reins. "How can I trust you?"

Tristan helped his sister to her seat, then climbed up on his horse before he looked at her again. "I love you. But I want you to realize that King Arthur is in favor of this union. It will strengthen the Cranborne alliance."

"Then let the king marry Sir Gavin," Noelle snapped as she jerked her mount around and galloped off.

When Tristan finally caught up to her, he said, "By the saints, woman, be reasonable. Do you not care for your own people?"

"More than anything else," Noelle declared.

"Then do this for them. I will accompany you and your ladies-in-waiting on the morrow. Merlin has returned to Camelot. I know how much you like him."

"Aye. I want to see Merlin," Noelle said.

And for more than one reason.

The next morning dawned cold and crisp. The sky was dark gray and bleak, making Noelle wonder if it might snow. Snow would be perfect for Christmas, she thought, though she'd never seen a Christmas with snow.

Thor had been saddled and a small wagon readied, she noticed as she walked down the steps from the Great Hall to the bailey. Her ladies-in-waiting would have to ride in the small cart since most of the extra horses had been sold. Blankets and cushions had been placed in the bottom of the cart to make the ride comfortable.

She barely glanced at John, who stood by the wagon.

"Godspeed, Noelle. You will thank me for this one day," John called to her.

"I think not," Noelle replied as she mounted Thor and adjusted her cloak. She looked at her ladies as they settled themselves in the cart. It would be a long time before she'd forgive John, if ever. She knew this arrangement had been his idea. Why would King Arthur do such a thing? She'd not seen him since her father's death. Why would he remember her now?

It was the money, plain and simple.

As the procession started forward, she saw that Tristan rode in front. He was wise to ride with the guards and steer clear of her. At the moment, she could burn his ears with her displeasure.

"Are you not excited?" Isabelle gushed as soon as the wagon lurched forward.

Noelle rode beside the cart so she could talk with her ladies-in-waiting. Glancing over at them, she admired their beauty. Isabelle had long red hair and devilish blue eyes; Carolyn had shorter black hair and light blue eyes. They had been a joy to Noelle because they made her laugh often, and were constantly doing things they were not supposed to do.

As for herself, she was plain in comparison, but she cared not. She had never been one to fuss with her looks. She would rather be riding or shooting bows and arrows. Since her mother had died at her birth, Isabelle and Carolyn had been her only female contacts, and they hadn't happened along until after her twelfth birthday. So she had been at the mercy of her older brothers and had developed many unladylike habits.

For a time Lady Guinevere would come and visit, and they had developed a close relationship. But

Noelle had not seen Guinevere since she went to Camelot to marry King Arthur.

"Are you all right, Noelle?" Carolyn asked, concerned that Noelle had yet to answer them.

Noelle sighed before answering. "Alas, I may never be all right again."

"But we are going to Camelot," Isabelle said. "Have you not always wanted to see the city? I have heard that nothing compares to the splendor of Camelot."

Carolyn laughed. "You have always wanted to see Sir Lancelot."

"Aye, and does he not reside in Camelot?" Isabelle smiled. "I hear he is the bravest of knights, but 'tis another who is the most feared."

Carolyn nodded at Isabelle. "Aye, I've heard some tales about him."

"How, pray tell, do you two know so much about knights you have never seen before?" Noelle asked. She shifted the reins to her other hand. "Neither of you has left Cranborne that I can remember."

" 'Tis the soldiers, of course." Isabelle giggled. "They bring back wonderful stories of battles and the men who have fought with them."

Noelle smiled at her two companions. At least they were keeping her mind off her problems. Finally she had to ask, "So, who is this bold knight?"

Isabelle leaned forward as if she were going to tell a deep, dark secret. "He is called the Scarlet Knight and is feared by everyone. 'Tis said that he is nice to gaze upon, as well," she added with a giggle. "Or so I have heard tell."

"Why is he so feared?" Noelle asked, smiling at her gossiping ladies. She made sure she gave the impression that she was only mildly interested.

" 'Tis said he leaves a trail of blood in every battle he's ever fought. He saved King Arthur's life twice. He's ruthless, he is," Isabelle informed them.

"I am sure all of King Arthur's knights are brave."

"Such as your knight, milady?" Carolyn added.

"He is not my knight," Noelle quickly pointed out.

Her denial didn't stop Carolyn. "Have you ever seen Sir Gavin?"

Noelle frowned. "Nay."

Carolyn pulled the blanket up higher to protect her from the cool air. "I hope he will capture your heart, and then all this fretting will be for naught."

"Let us hope," Noelle said.

"I have always looked forward to your marriage, milady. A Christmas wedding would be special indeed," Isabelle said.

"As have I, but to a man of my choosing. Not one chosen for me."

"Let us not be hasty in our judgment," Carolyn, the ever-faithful optimist, pointed out. "Sir Gavin could be the very one."

"I agree. And I have promised to keep an open mind until I have met him. Does that satisfy both of you?"

They nodded.

Noelle glanced out at the tall oaks as they proceeded through the forest. The sun was breaking through the clouds, streaking the forest floor with sunlight. They had traveled a little ways past Cadbury when they came to Arthur's bridge.

The clicks of Thor's hooves echoed on the stones as they crossed the bridge. The beautiful gray stone archway stretched over the River Alham in the woodsy section between the little Somerset village of South Cadbury and Sutton Montis.

They were traveling up a hedge-lined path, when suddenly the procession burst out into a clearing and Camelot loomed in the far distance. Noelle's first glimpse was overwhelming for the castle was much larger than she'd ever imagined. "Turn around and look," she called to her ladies.

Sitting in the middle of a lake, on a very impressive hill, was a pristine white castle. The square corner towers were enormous, stretching up to the sky with multi-colored banners flying from each. There were eight towers in all, and a gigantic gateway led to massive walls where the king's banners flew.

Camelot was twice the size of Cranborne Castle, so tremendous that it encompassed the entire hill. A lower wall and a higher wall surrounded it.

"Why do they have two walls?" Isabelle asked. "We only have one."

"For protection," Noelle said as the wind tore wisps of hair from her braids. "The archers on the inner wall can shoot over the heads of those on the outer walls."

"That makes sense, but who would be foolish enough to attack the king?" Isabelle said.

Noelle took a deep breath as she stared at the castle. Her hands were trembling, but her expression remained inscrutable as she answered, "No one, I hope."

"Did you see all the banners?" Carolyn asked as she turned to sit down in the cart. "Are they not lovely?"

Suddenly trumpets began a fanfare as the coach started across the long road, leading over the moat and to the gates of Camelot, the only entrance into the castle. The chains and winches creaked as the drawbridge was lowered, landing with a loud thump. Once again the procession started forward through the gatehouse, which was larger than most. It had three portcullises, their sharp points hovering just above the riders' heads as they swept under them.

There were several murder holes in the ceiling of the gatehouse between the portcullises. From there the archers could fire arrows, drop rocks, or pour hot liquids on intruders.

The procession came to a halt once they had moved across the bailey. A moment later, a young page ran over to them. He bowed with a sweeping gesture. "Miladies, welcome to Camelot."

Noelle smiled. He held Thor's bridle so she could dismount, while another page helped Carolyn and Isabelle out of the wagon.

"Who is Sir Gavin?" Isabelle boldly asked the page.

Noelle sent a warning look to her lady-in-waiting for being so bold. "Isabelle."

"He is yonder, standing by King Arthur." The boy pointed.

"Oooo, he's a fine one, Noelle."

"Isabelle. Remember we are at court and should act as ladies of our station," Noelle whispered to her. "Behave yourself."

"Well, someone must ask questions."

The knights and the king dispersed and went in different directions. Arthur strode inside the castle.

"Are you ladies ready to meet the king?" Tristan said as he came and took Noelle's arm. "The page just informed me that the king wishes to see you right away. He awaits us in the Great Hall."

The page led the way to an outside staircase next to the stone wall of the keep. As they carefully climbed the narrow staircase, Noelle noticed that the shutters on the windows had been thrown open so the air wouldn't be so stuffy inside.

A guard stood by the single door that led into the Great Hall. He shoved open the door and bade them enter.

The large one-room structure was much bigger and grander than the one at home. The lofty ceiling had beams stretched across a ceiling which was at least forty feet high. Welcoming banners and tapestry hung on the walls, providing bright colors. So far everything about Camelot was beautiful.

The floor was strewn with fresh rushes which smelled of the lavender, roses, and mint that had been sprinkled on them.

The king and queen sat on a raised dais of wood at the upper end of the hall upon massive chairs with a blue canopy overhead. Usually there would be trestle tables set up for the soldiers, but they had been dismantled during the day to give more room.

The knights were missing from the room, and Noelle realized she'd been holding her breath, which she promptly let out. At least she had a little more time before she had to meet her future husband.

King Arthur nodded with a smile. "Noelle, you have grown into a lovely woman."

Noelle blushed as she came to stand before the king. She curtsied. "You are most kind, your majesty," Noelle said as she studied the kind face of the king. He had gray hair and a matching beard, but his eyes were the vibrant blue that she always remembered when he'd visited her father.

"Tristan, I hope you will join my knights in training. They are preparing for the joust and games we will be having for Christmas."

"I would be honored, sire."

"Good." Arthur nodded and turned his attention back to Noelle. "I believe that you and Guinevere are old friends." He reached over and placed a hand on the queen's arm, and Noelle could see in his eyes the affection that he had for Guinevere.

Guinevere smiled. Her two ladies-in-waiting were dressed in gay dresses, but Guinevere's beauty surpassed all around her. With dark brown hair that swirled past her waist, she looked every bit the queen and not the young girl who used to ride with Noelle. A gold chain was wrapped around her forehead. Her complexion was flawless.

"Your majesty." Noelle curtsied.

"It has been much too long, Noelle," Guinevere said, then stood. "I have looked forward to seeing you again. Come." She extended her hands to Noelle.

"You have been traveling a long way," Guinevere said as she took Noelle's hands, then called to a servant. "Ruth, please show these ladies to their chambers."

"This way, if you please," Ruth said to Carolyn and Isabelle.

"I will walk with you for a while," Guinevere said to Noelle.

As they started after the maid, Noelle said, "It is so good to see you, your majesty."

Guinevere raised her brow.

Noelle laughed. "You look so much like a queen and not the girl I once confided all my secrets to," she explained.

Guinevere chuckled. "I am still the same. Only the clothes are different. It's tiresome to be constantly surrounded by big, husky men, so it will be a pleasure to have someone near my age at the castle. Maybe you and your ladies would like to accompany me on the morrow to collect greenery for the castle."

"I would like that."

They traveled down a long hallway, then turned to their right and continued down another long hall. Wainscoting that had been painted green spangled with silver stretched down the hall. Her own castle did not have hallways—one room led to another—but she'd heard that King Arthur had especially designed his castle to be like none before. Wall hangings of painted wool adornments were on every wall.

"There will be a feast tonight where you will meet Sir Gavin. I imagine that you are excited about that," Lady Guinevere said.

"Nay," Noelle admitted.

"Really?" Guinevere said in an odd tone as she stopped in front of a door, then opened it. "Here are your chambers, and your ladies will sleep beyond in the smaller solar." Guinevere pointed as the servant took Isabelle and Carolyn to their solar. "I will have someone bring your trunks," Guinevere said.

"Thank you," Noelle said, then thought about her earlier comment. "I didn't mean to be so abrupt, but this marriage . . ." she sighed, "was not my idea."

Guinevere took Noelle's hand and squeezed it. "I know, but you might be surprised and fancy Sir Gavin. Were you not the one who was always looking for that special knight? Sir Gavin is a fine knight."

"I might like him, but the point is I love him not. I would marry for love."

"Love. What we all hope for." Guinevere sighed wistfully. "But love is not perfect, my dear," she said as she walked over to the window. "Sometimes love can be confusing and can hurt." She glanced back at Noelle. "What if you loved someone who cared naught for you in return or what if you loved someone you could not have?"

"That would be painful indeed," Noelle said, "but if I truly loved him, I would find some way to become his."

Guinevere stared at her for a moment. "I believe that you would. I sense a fighter in you. Let us hope that Sir Gavin is all that you long for." Her voice had an infinitely compassionate tone. "I shall go now and let you rest—then you can prepare for the feast. On the morrow, we can ride out and gather greenery. This is one Christmas that I look forward to." She paused at the door and smiled. "Please invite your lovely ladies to join us. My ladies will attend also."

Guinevere had no sooner gotten out the door than Carolyn and Isabelle rushed into the chamber.

"What did she say?" Isabelle asked.

"What do you think of the queen?" Carolyn added before Noelle could respond.

Noelle regarded her companions with amusement. "You know perfectly well what the queen said because you were both listening."

"But did she say anything about Sir Lancelot?"

"Or Sir Osborn?"

These two were hopeless romantics.

"I am certain that King Arthur's knights will be required to have guards around them for protection from you two," Noelle said.

"From us, milady?" Isabelle said as she pointed to herself innocently.

"Do you blame us, milady? We are at court with the boldest and bravest knights in all of England," Carolyn said. "Not to mention something to behold."

Isabelle nudged Carolyn with her elbow. "Aye, and probably just ripe for the picking." The teasing laughter returned to her eyes.

"Isabelle," Noelle said. "Remember, you are a lady."

"A lady I might be . . ." Isabelle paused, and then gave her companions a conspiratorial wink, "but I have lots of healthy blood in me."

In a small room off Noelle's chamber, a large wooden tub had been set up in front of the hearth.

The bathman had filled the tub and sprinkled the water with dried rose petals, as chambermaids waited to assist Noelle. She dismissed them, wanting to be alone as she soaked.

She needed some time to herself. So much had happened and she wanted time to think.

Soon she was engulfed in warm water, resting her head on the back of the tub. She had to figure out how to escape this marriage without hurting her people. There had to be a way. She simply had not thought of it yet.

Shutting her eyes, she let her arms float in the warm water and then she remembered *the kiss.*

His kiss.

The one forbidden kiss that had made her long for more. She sighed. That would be her secret.

"You must be having a pleasant dream by the way you are smiling," Carolyn teased as she swept into the small room to attend to Noelle.

"Aye. 'Tis one I would like to relive again."

"Tell, tell," Isabelle chirped in right behind Carolyn.

Noelle hoped her smile was noncommittal as she looked at them. "Someday I will tell you both, but for now it's my secret. You two go get dressed. Or we will never make it downstairs."

After they left, Noelle knew she hadn't heard the last from Isabelle. Isabelle couldn't bear secrets that she knew nothing about. Therefore, it gave Noelle pleasure in teasing her.

Noelle slipped on the emerald-green cotehardie that Carolyn had placed on the bed. The sleeves were full and tied at intervals so the tighter-fitting sleeves of her kirtle beneath would show and provide a good contrast. The green velvet added some warmth.

Noelle realized that she was cold. She swung around to look at the fire. It had burned down to embers and needed stirring.

Moving over to the hearth, she picked up a few small logs that had been left in a large basket and tossed two onto the grate. Sparks leapt up the chimney, and she stepped quickly back to avoid getting her gown singed.

"Mustn't go ruining your dress when there are servants to do such work," Carolyn said as she and Isabelle returned.

"It's better than freezing while I wait. And you both should know that I am no helpless simpleton." Noelle paused and looked at them. One had dressed in light blue and the other in a darker blue velvet.

They were so excited that they were radiant. "You two are beautiful tonight. King Arthur's knights do not stand a chance."

"I'll wager that someone is nervous." Carolyn laughed. "You have not done your hair."

"I dread this meeting," Noelle admitted. She felt the screams of frustration at the back of her throat. She had to escape this marriage somehow.

"Sit." Isabelle pointed to the chair. "We'll not have you shame us. Let me fix your hair."

Noelle obeyed, wondering how she could have gotten two bold and brazen, not to mention bossy, ladies-in-waiting. Most were meek and mild.

Isabelle brushed Noelle's hair until it glistened like

gold threads. Then she pulled the golden mass up on the sides and wound gold chains through her honeyed curls. "I think we have it," Isabelle proclaimed. "Let us be off . . . our knights await."

They could see the glow of light long before they arrived at the Great Hall. They paused in the doorway to take in the sight before them. It appeared that a hundred rush lights were suspended from the sconces on the walls, providing good light for the room. The air smelled of juniper from the roaring fire.

The Great Hall was full of knights and ladies and their retinues. Two long trestle tables had been set up for the feast, but so far no one had taken their seats. Noelle glanced at the dais where Arthur and Guinevere stood talking to Tristan and two other gentlemen she didn't know.

There was a saltcellar in front of where the king would sit; all the tables had already been set with pewter bowls, awaiting the guests to take their places.

"Have we died? Is this heaven?" Isabelle whispered playfully to Carolyn.

"Aye," Carolyn nodded. "They are better than I imagined. Have you ever seen such brawny men?"

"It's too hard to pick. Maybe we could have several."

Noelle joined in their fun. "You're welcome to mine."

"He is sure to be a fine one," Carolyn admitted. "But look at the one who just entered the hall. Every lady has turned her head, yet he has acknowledged no one."

Isabelle took a deep breath. "I think I will go over. Someone must introduce us."

Noelle's eyes widened. For there in the doorway dressed in crimson and black, was a warrior who certainly stood out in the crowd. Every ounce of him exuded strength and power. The lights made his dark brown hair glisten as his amber eyes searched the crowd like a predator's.

Never in her wildest dreams did she think she would ever see *him* again. So he wasn't a peasant. He was anything but.

He was bold and commanding as he surveyed the room. Would he remember her? Would he embarrass her in front of the king?

She swung around.

Isabelle and Carolyn gaped at Noelle's sudden movement. They both asked, "Do you know him?"

"Who?"

"The knight you were just gawking at," Isabelle said.

"No—no, I don't know him." Noelle gathered up her skirt. "Now if you will excuse me, I am going to meet my future husband," Noelle said, not glancing back at either as she left. They would ask too many questions if she stayed. However, she did hear their parting remarks.

"Since when does she want to meet her future husband?" Isabelle asked.

"Since she doesn't want us to ask any more questions."

"We will find out more later," Isabelle said, and then she nudged Carolyn. "It's time to find an introduction to some of these knights. I wonder which one is Lancelot."

"Let's go find out."

THREE

As Noelle made her way to Guinevere and Tristan, she could hear murmuring all around her. Many different conversations were taking place, but she felt as though every eye was on her. She knew it was her imagination. Then she thought, *Was he looking at her?*

"Here she is now," Guinevere said. The queen was wearing a red overtunic, belted at the waist. The full, open, half-length sleeves ended in long, flowing tippets of white fur. She held out her hand to Noelle as she curtsied. "Sir Gavin, may I present the Lady Noelle."

Sir Gavin bowed low. "Milady, I've looked forward to this moment," he said as he held her hand up so he could kiss the back.

"Sir Gavin," Noelle said. Drat! He was nice, she thought, and looked to her brother for help.

Suddenly, she could think of nothing to say, so Tristan came to her rescue. "I heard your last campaign was successful," he said and the two men struck up a conversation.

Noelle had to admit that Sir Gavin was comely, but his appearance wasn't everything. He had dark brown hair and warm brown eyes, and she wanted desperately not to like something about him. He might be a kind and gentle man, but he was not the man of her choosing. There was no feeling there. It was like meeting her brothers.

Suddenly, Noelle stiffened.

She felt *him* long before he spoke.

"Sir Nicholas," Guinevere said, looking past Noelle. "We have missed your presence in Camelot."

"As I have missed being here, my queen." His deep, rumbling voice sent chills down Noelle's spine. It was a commanding voice . . . one that soldiers used to make their men snap to attention. "What is this good news I hear, Sir Gavin?"

"I plan to be married," Sir Gavin said with a smile. "Milady, our most fierce knight, Sir Nicholas the Dragon. He is well named, for he breathes fire upon his opponents."

Slowly, Noelle turned around, avoiding Nicholas's eyes as she focused on his massive chest.

Would he embarrass her?

She waited for him to say something. Anything.

Everyone was waiting.

He said nothing.

Finally, she had to look up at him. The memory of the burning kiss came flooding back. She would never forget a single detail of his face and that kiss. The silence lingered between them. She must say something. "Milord, it is nice to make your acquaintance."

Nicholas couldn't believe his eyes. He experienced a gamut of perplexing emotions. When he'd first glimpsed the beautiful woman across the hall, he'd assumed his eyes had deceived him. But standing before him, with hair that looked like polished gold and wearing a gown of the finest green velvet, was the woman of the lake. The one he'd thought was a peasant. What gave her away were her emerald eyes. The same ones that had spit fire at him. Oh, but how he'd love to taste that fire.

Sir Nicholas tilted his head to the side. "Have we met before, milady?"

Her brow rose a fraction, and then he saw a determination settle upon her face she wouldn't allow him to embarrass her, no matter what he did. It was almost as if she were daring him. He smiled. So she had fight in her—he liked that.

She stiffened, momentarily abashed. "Not unless you have been a guest at Cranborne Castle, sir."

"Ah, Cranborne. I have traveled near there just recently, but, alas, I have never been a guest."

Tristan cleared his throat. "The next time you travel across our land, please come and visit with us, milord. I have heard many good things about your daring deeds."

Gavin laughed. "Watch that you don't give Nicholas a bigger head than he already has."

Nicholas cut his gaze to Gavin. "Congratulations on your marriage," he said, then added before Gavin could answer, "Have you known your lady long?"

"We have just met for the first time," Gavin told him.

So the lady hadn't known Gavin when she'd kissed him, Nicholas thought. She'd been as free as he was . . . not that it mattered. That was in the past.

"Do you not greet your king?" King Arthur said, speaking for the first time.

Nicholas straightened immediately. However, Noelle noticed he neither blushed nor looked contrite for slighting the king. "Sire, I must confess that the lady's beauty made me forget my manners." Nicholas made a sweeping bow. "I have completed your mission and tamed the heathens as you requested."

"So I have heard." Arthur smiled. "I believe you and I have another matter to discuss, if everyone will excuse us." He motioned for Nicholas to follow him.

"Let's begin to take our places at the table," Guinevere said. "I'm sure you both would like to become better acquainted," she told Gavin and Noelle.

Noelle nodded. She let Sir Gavin take her elbow and guide her to the middle of the long, oak table where they took their seats. He sat on her left. Isabelle was across the table. A large man sat on one side of Isabelle, and Sir Lancelot was on the other side, so Noelle knew that her friend was very well entertained. Isabelle had finally gotten her wish—to meet the man of her dreams.

The chair to Noelle's right was still vacant, but she had no opportunity to ponder who would sit there because Sir Gavin began talking to her.

He was pleasant enough, Noelle thought, but she felt nothing. She tried to carry on a conversation with Sir Gavin, but her gaze kept wandering to the king and Nicholas, who were still talking, their heads bent. She wondered what kind of man Nicholas really was.

* * *

When Arthur had Sir Nicholas off to the side, he said, "I believe you and I had a small wager."

Nicholas gave a slight smile. "Aye, sire. And I will be collecting my horses within the week."

Arthur stroked his gray beard. "I know I have not heard of any unhappy ladies. Are you sure you have been without a fair maiden all this time?"

Nicholas groaned and looked heavenward. "Trust me, sire. I have been true to my word. As I told you before, I never lose a wager."

He was so arrogant, Arthur thought. And playing right into his hands. "It is far too easy a task that I gave you. I should have made it harder." Arthur eyed his opponent, folded his arms across his chest, and said, "A good man can usually go the distance of any challenge, but when pushed beyond his endurance, he usually crumbles."

"You, my king, are throwing out a gauntlet and issuing another challenge." Nicholas's voice, while courteous, was patronizing. "Is it not bad enough you've lost your two best white war-horses?"

"I admit that I will miss my whites, but they are a pair, leaving me with another pair. How would you like to see if you could win Briercliff?"

"Your castle?"

Arthur nodded. "I have been trying to think of the proper reward for all your brave deeds. I have a feeling that this bet might be your biggest hurdle yet."

Briercliff was a small castle on the cliffs of Cornwall. It overlooked the sea and would be a perfect home, Nicholas thought. It wasn't as grand as Camelot nor as well protected, but Briercliff had stood vacant for more than a year.

Nicholas tapped the side of his leg as he looked curiously at the king, wondering what Arthur was really up to. "You will regret this day, for you will have lost both your horses and a castle."

"Then you accept?"

"I am made of iron, sire," Nicholas said with a nod. "State your terms."

Arthur leaned over and whispered, "Can you forgo your manly urges until Christmas Day?"

Nicholas looked at Arthur and smiled. "Even though I had looked forward to finding a wench after the feast tonight, I will wait until Christmas Day. For you see, sire, I can live with or without a woman."

Arthur laughed. "One of these days, cousin, you are going to meet a lady who takes your breath away. She'll seep into your blood and then you'll find that she means as much to you as the air you breathe. You'll not be able to eat, sleep, or work without thinking of her."

Nicholas chuckled and raised his eyebrow. "And you, my king, sound like many of those besotted fools who think they cannot live without a wench. Wenches are like horses. If one lets you down, you can mount another."

Arthur clapped Nicholas on the back. "Let us go take our places at the table so we can begin the feast." Arthur started toward the table. "But I am telling you now that one day those words that so easily spew from your mouth will change. I, for one, cannot wait until that day to remind you that you are as mortal as the rest of us."

Nicholas gave a half-smile. "We will speak of that matter on Christmas Day, sire."

"On Christmas Day it is." King Arthur nodded as he took his chair at the head table and motioned for Nicholas to take the empty chair.

Nicholas was feeling quite pleased with his wager until he saw where Arthur had placed him. At least the beautiful Noelle was taken, Nicholas thought as he sat down beside her. However, he could have a little fun teasing the lovely lady and watching the sparks ignite. Then the whiff of roses seemed to surround him, and he groaned ever so softly as his body responded to the scent of the woman beside him.

God's wounds, he needed to be made of stone. And there was a certain part of his body that felt like stone right this very minute and desperately needed easing. He had boasted to the king that he was made of iron. He just hoped he hadn't lied.

A horn blew, signaling the time for washing of hands. Servants entered with ewers, basins, and towels for each guest.

Trying to ignore Nicholas as much as possible, Noelle washed and dried her hands. There was a tingling in the pit of her stomach . . . she ignored that, too.

She didn't acknowledge that he'd sat down.

A trencher had already been placed before her and would hold the roasted fish that she'd share with Sir Gavin.

King Arthur rose. Silence immediately spread over

the room. Once it was quiet, he said grace. Noelle bowed her head dutifully, but couldn't help peeking at Nicholas. The moment she did, she wished she hadn't because his eyes were open and he was watching her. He smiled broadly at her for being caught.

She snapped her eyelids shut. Drat the man! Must he always have the upper hand?

After grace the servants started filing into the room, one behind the other. Their trays brimmed with roasted mutton sprinkled with fresh herbs and several dishes of peas and beans.

The pantler paused beside her to place bread and butter before her.

Sir Gavin sliced the fish and Noelle realized she was very hungry as she placed the first succulent bite in her mouth with the tip of her knife. She would like some mutton, and decided she'd try that next. She hadn't eaten since early morning, which would explain the butterflies in her stomach, she thought as she reached for another bite of fish.

"I like a lady with an appetite," Sir Gavin said.

"I do like to eat," Noelle admitted.

"Have you met Sir Lancelot?" Isabelle asked Noelle.

"Nay."

"I am Lancelot of the Lake, milady," Lancelot said with a slight nod of his head. "Welcome to Camelot."

"It is nice to meet you," Noelle said. "And Isabelle, this is Sir Gavin." Noelle nodded toward Sir Gavin. "Isabelle is one of my ladies-in-waiting."

"And who—" Isabelle looked directly at Nicholas,

but she couldn't seem to get the rest of the words out.

"I am Nicholas, and on your other side, milady, sits my first in command, Dirk Johnstone."

Isabelle looked at Dirk. "What part of Scotland do you hail from?"

"From the borders, lass. It is God's land," Dirk replied as he stabbed a hunk of white fish with the tip of his knife and offered Isabelle a slice.

"Now that we have made the introductions, I have a question," Noelle said. "Is it true that Meleagant has been ransacking villages again?"

Dirk spoke first. "A gentle lass such as yourself shouldn't be worrying of such matters."

Noelle smiled at his kind words, but before she could reply, Lancelot commented. "Meleagant has burned several villages," Sir Lancelot paused, "but we will rout him out before long."

"He has threatened Cranborne as well," Noelle said.

"He will cease his threats after our marriage," Sir Gavin said with confidence.

So that was the reason she wished to be married, Nicholas thought. "When you marry one knight, fair lady, you get all of us," Nicholas said from beside her.

Noelle felt shivers run all over her, and she found she wanted to turn and talk to Nicholas instead of Sir Gavin. No matter how much she ignored him, she was well aware that he sat next to her. Damn his soul. Why couldn't he have been a peasant as she'd first thought?

Noelle turned to Nicholas. "It is a comfort to know."

He smiled at her and in that moment a connection was made between them. It was as if he climbed into her head and was reading all her thoughts. She felt her cheeks heat, and it took extreme willpower not to touch him.

"Tell us, Nicholas. Have you changed your mind about Lady Clarisse?" Gavin spoke, breaking the magical spell.

Nicholas frowned at the mention of the woman.

Sir Gavin continued, "She has been staring at you all night."

Noelle glanced at Gavin, and he pointed to a woman at the other end of the table who was, indeed, staring at Nicholas. She was pretty with dark hair and eyes, and Noelle wondered what kind of relationship they had had.

Nicholas sighed impatiently. Finally, he turned and looked in the woman's direction and nodded.

She smiled.

Nicholas didn't. He turned back to Gavin. "You have always possessed the knack for bringing up things I care not to discuss. The lady is of no interest to me."

"You see, milady . . ." Sir Gavin leaned over to talk to Noelle, "ladies seem to find Sir Nicholas and Sir Lancelot most irresistible. I, myself, don't see this."

" 'Twould be hard for me to choose," Isabelle admitted.

Noelle laughed. "Isabelle has never been reticent."

"Well, milady," Isabelle placed her hand on Lancelet's arm, "if you were not spoken for, could you resist these fine knights?"

Noelle gave Isabelle a murderous look.

"What do you have to say, milady?" Nicholas prodded from beside her.

Noelle was strangely flattered by his interest. "Even though you are both fine knights, I am afraid I would have little interest. I would leave you for the other maidens," she said sweetly, knowing that wasn't the answer he'd expected.

Nicholas said for her ears only, "Oh, really? I believe I would like to challenge that statement."

"Well said, milady," Sir Gavin complimented. "We have one lady who can resist your charms."

"Miracles still happen." Nicholas smiled at his jest just as the others laughed. "Such as you wanting to wed when you told me several months ago it was the furthest thing from your mind."

"I hadn't met Lady Noelle at that time," Sir Gavin countered. "Could one blame me for changing my mind?"

"Nay," Nicholas conceded just as fresh fruit and almond pudding was served.

Noelle thought Sir Gavin's statement was strange, considering they had just met.

"Is it true that King Arthur was merely a page before he was king?" Isabelle asked, drawing everyone's attention. "I have heard many stories."

Noelle wondered why she couldn't have been more outgoing, like Isabelle. There was never a lull in the conversation when she was in the room. On second thought, no one was like Isabelle.

"I can recite the tale as Merlin told it to me," Sir Lancelot offered.

Noelle took a sip of wine and placed her chalice on the table. "Where is Merlin? I have not seen him," she said.

"He was here two days ago, milady, but has gone to visit the ladies of the lake. I'm sure he will be back soon."

"I am sorry I interrupted," Noelle said. "Please tell us the story—I would love to hear the truth."

Sir Lancelot sat back in his chair and folded his hands across his middle. "When King Uther died, the realm of Britain was without a king. The barons and lords began to quarrel over who their next leader should be. Wars broke out. Neighbor fought against neighbor. All but forgotten were the sowing and harvesting of crops, and soon famine gripped the land. Everyone was hungry.

"The Archbishop of Canterbury summoned Merlin, knowing that Merlin was the wisest man in all of England.

"The archbishop bade Merlin to find England a king, one who was a wise leader and could defend the country from its enemies.

"Merlin simply smiled and said he had such a king who was of Uther Pendragon's own royal blood.

"The archbishop asked how this could be? So Merlin told how he had taken Uther's child when he was first born so that the child might be safe."

"Merlin actually took the king's son?" Isabelle asked.

"More to the point, Merlin can foresee the future, so he took the child to protect him," Lancelot explained.

"But what would make them accept one king?" Noelle asked as she reached for the grapes.

"That is what the archbishop asked. How will the lesser kings, who feel themselves worthy, accept such a leader?

"Merlin said he would use his magic to create a test. The person who passed the test would show all the world that he was the rightful overlord of England."

"What did he do?" Noelle interrupted again and then said, "I'm sorry, go ahead with the story."

"Merlin placed a huge white marble stone at the gates of the greatest church in London. Upon the marble block stood an iron anvil. Thrust into the anvil, almost to its hilt, was a sword. The hilt had precious stones encrusted in the gold. The blade was of Damascus steel. Upon the stone in gold letters were these words: *Whoso draweth out this sword from the anvil is the rightful king of Britain."*

Lancelot paused, taking a sip of wine from his gold goblet. Noelle and Isabelle were captivated by the story.

"Go on. Don't stop there," Isabelle pleaded.

"Aye, I'm enjoying your story," Noelle said.

"Nicholas, would you like to finish the tale?" Lancelot said. "Since your father was there."

Drat, Noelle thought. Now she'd have to look at

Nicholas. But her fascination with the story was greater than her desire to ignore Nicholas. "Please," she finally said.

"Let me see . . ." Nicholas replaced his cup on the table. "It was this time of year. The archbishop called all the nobles together in London so that each could try to remove the sword. It just so happens that there was to be the greatest tournament ever held."

"Just like the one we'll have on Christmas Eve," Noelle said.

"It is so." Nicholas nodded. "Among the noblemen who came for the tournament was a middle-aged knight, highly born, named Sir Ector of Bonnemaison. His fame was great. He never broke his word to peasant or prince, and he never betrayed a confidence, so that is why Merlin trusted him to rear Arthur.

"Arthur was only eighteen. He was page to his brother, Kay, who was going to joust in his first tournament, which means Arthur was busy sharpening swords and making sure all of Kay's equipment was readied.

"On the day of the tournament, Kay fought hard. When Kay rode back to his pavilion, Arthur came running with a goblet of wine for his brother. Sir Kay told Arthur to go and fetch a sword from their father's pavilion with due haste. Arthur ran. But upon entering the tent he could find no sword, and he panicked. He couldn't let his brother down. Kay would look like a coward. Then, Arthur remembered the sword in the stone.

"When Arthur arrived there was no one in the

courtyard, for everyone was at the tournament. All he saw was the marble stone and the shining sword sticking out of the anvil. Without further hesitation, Arthur climbed upon the stone and placed his hand on the hilt of the sword. The fit was perfect as his fingers curled around the gold. He pulled strongly and the sword came smoothly forth from the anvil.

"He ran with all speed and handed Sir Kay the sword. Kay paled upon seeing the gold sword, for he knew what it was and what it meant.

"Sir Kay, knowing how young his brother was, told him not to say anything about the sword. And Arthur agreed."

"It was dishonest," Noelle interjected, realizing that she was so intrigued with the yarn Nicholas was spinning and with the man who was telling the story that if he leaned over and kissed her this very minute, she would have offered very little resistance. She rested her chin upon her hand as she gazed, trancelike, at him.

"Aye, it was dishonest, indeed. However, Kay thought Arthur was too young and Sir Kay was more experienced. So in his mind, he sought to protect his brother."

"I see," Noelle nodded. "So what happened?"

"Sir Hector, upon hearing the tale that Kay told, looked at his son with much doubt. He placed his arm around his elder son and said, 'As you know, the rightful King of England is the only one who can pull the sword from the anvil, so if you have truly drawn the sword out then you should be able to thrust it back again.' "

Noelle giggled. "The rat has been caught in his own trap."

Nicholas gave her a heartwarming smile and then continued. "Kay decided to brazen it out, and still he said nothing. Upon reaching the stone, Sir Kay put the sword-point to the anvil and bore down with all his weight.

"Nothing happened. So Kay turned to his father and complained that the task was impossible. Finally, Arthur spoke up and asked if he could try. When his father asked why, Arthur told him he was the one who had pulled the sword from the stone in the first place. Not only did Arthur shove the sword back into the anvil but he pulled it out again. Arthur was truly the rightful king."

Noelle glanced at the head of the table where Arthur was just rising, the sword by his side. "So is that the sword?" she asked.

Sir Lancelot answered this time. "Nay. The sword from the stone was broken in battle. Merlin took Arthur to get the sword he now carries, which is called Excalibur, but whence it came from I cannot say. Only Merlin and Arthur know. As long as Arthur carries Excalibur no harm can befall him."

"Thank you for the telling of the story," Noelle said softly, then realized she was staring at Nicholas with longing. That would not do. "It made for a pleasurable dinner tale," Noelle said, coming quickly to her feet. "I bid thee good night."

Nicholas and Sir Gavin rose and watched the lady retreat. "You chose wisely, Gavin," Nicholas said, a tightness forming in his throat.

"Truth be told, my friend, I did not choose at all. Arthur chose for me, but he did choose well."

"There will be a hunt after we set up our pavilions tomorrow. With this crisp air the hunt should prove fruitful." Nicholas placed his chalice on the table and refilled it. It was strange. Would Arthur be choosing Nicholas's wife someday? Not bloody likely.

"On the morrow," Sir Gavin said, raising his own goblet.

"Tomorrow." Nicholas hoisted his chalice in salute. There wasn't enough wine in the hall to dull the ache inside him tonight, for the Lady Noelle would prey on his mind.

Damn his wager! Damn it to hell!

FOUR

The next morning Noelle rose early from her feather bed, pulled back the linen hangings, and tied them back to the bedpost. She wouldn't admit to herself or anyone else that her lack of sleep was because of a knight—not the knight she should have been thinking of, but the wrong one.

The one with the golden eyes.

The one who needed no one.

Wrapping a blanket around her, she shuffled over to the fireplace. She sighed and she could actually see her breath in the cold room. Clearly, not enough wood had been stacked in the hearth last night. She reached for an iron poker and stirred up the embers until they were cherry-red. Letting the blanket slip to the floor, she retrieved several logs and threw them into the hearth. She knew she could call a servant, but this was quicker, and since they had always been short-staffed at Cranborne, she had built a fire many times. Besides, if she complained to the steward, someone might be reprimanded for letting the fire go out. She didn't want to cause anyone to be punished for something she considered trivial.

Snatching up the blanket, she went to the window

to see what kind of day it would be. Noelle was excited to be included in putting together the festive decorations. Gathering greenery and tying ribbons would be a welcome change from the everyday routine she'd been accustomed to at Cranborne Castle. She glanced out the window and saw that the sky was gray and overcast, and again she thought of snow, but more than likely it would rain.

Down below, the bailey was coming to life as the merchants returned to their stalls where they sold vegetables, cloth, and whatever was needed. The soldiers' barracks were to the right, the stable to her left. In front of the stable, under a small shed, a smith was hammering on a horseshoe. The clang of the hammer hitting the anvil was much louder than the roosters crowing as they announced daybreak.

A dog started to bark and several others joined in the chorus, barking at the knights walking across the courtyard. The lymas were not making as much of a fuss as the greyhounds, who were jumping all around the men, begging for attention. The lymas, like true bloodhounds, had their noses to the ground, picking up the scents of those who had traveled before them.

The knights were heading for the stables. Evidently they were going to the field to begin the day's training.

Noelle recognized Tristan walking next to Sir Gavin and his page. She was glad that her brother had finally been granted his wish to train with the knights he so admired. It had been his dream since they were children, but when their father had died unexpectedly, John, the oldest, couldn't run the castle without Tristan's help. So Tristan's dreams had been put aside just as he was now asking her to do.

Of course, her dreams were just that . . . dreams. She had no other offers of marriage. And she hated to admit that Sir Gavin was very nice, and pleasant to look upon. Any other woman would be thrilled to have him smile upon her . . . Still . . . She sighed. Something was missing.

Nicholas strolled into Noelle's line of vision, and her gaze followed him. It was hard not to, for his shoulders were massive and broad, his arms bulged with muscle, and he was taller than most of the other knights. He turned her way slightly, and Noelle could see his hard face. It was a warrior's face and showed very little emotion.

Suddenly, he thrust his arm, clad in a special glove that covered his hand and wrist, up over his head. In the blink of an eye, a bird swept down from out of the sky so quickly that Noelle jumped back from the window.

Repositioning herself, she saw that a falcon had come to rest on Nicholas's arm. The bird's wings flapped several times, then Nicholas reached into a small sack and took out some food. He fed the bird something red, which Noelle assumed was some type of meat.

Noelle recalled the day at the lake. A falcon had been near Nicholas then, too, flying above his head. She knew little about the hunting birds except that they were the favorite pastime of the kings.

Nicholas fed the bird pieces of meat, and when he was finished, he stroked its head so gently that Noelle smiled. Who would have thought that a man so big and strong could be gentle with something so small? A deliciously wicked thought ran through her head, and the heat from her thoughts warmed her body much better than any fire could. She really mustn't have such wicked thoughts, Noelle reminded herself. It was indecent. Yet, something about Nicholas the Dragon intrigued her. Would he be gentle with her?

Nicholas tossed the bird up and the falcon soared, making large circles overhead. Suddenly, Nicholas turned around and glanced at the castle as if he realized he was being watched.

Noelle jerked back, embarrassed to be caught spying.

After several minutes, she looked out again, and was relieved that he had turned back to the group of men. Noelle watched as a groom brought out the most spectacular white destrier she'd ever seen. He was at least two hands taller than Thor, and Thor was considered huge.

She shouldn't be surprised that the groom led the horse over to Nicholas. She could see him reaching for the reins. He mounted the animal as the other knights followed suit. Without a backward glance, they rode from the castle's walls. Noelle leaned her head against the stone wall and wondered if she had just experienced the most exciting part of her day.

Deciding she could mope by the window or get dressed and experience the day, Noelle chose the latter. She went over to the washstand and tried to pour water into a basin. Nothing came out. She looked in the pitcher and saw a layer of ice had formed. She punched a hole in the ice and poured the water into the basin.

The chill had finally left the room, so she washed her face, gasping as the cold water took her breath away. She dressed in a light gray, long-sleeved tunic, followed by a dark gray mantle embroidered with light gray and rose. Since they would be outside most of the day, she'd wear her fur-lined cloak, which was dark green to match her eyes.

Moving over to the small mirror mounted in a wooden frame, she combed her hair and began to braid it, tying off the end with gray-and-rose ribbons.

"Good morning, milady," Carolyn called as she swept into Noelle's room. "I would have helped you dress."

"There was no need as I arose early. Where is Isabelle?"

Carolyn chuckled. "It's taking Isabelle longer to move around this morning. Just how much wine did she consume last night? And what kind of conversation were you having with the knights? The few times I glanced your way everyone seemed so intent on whatever Sir Nicholas was saying that no one else seemed to matter."

"Sir Lancelot and Sir Nicholas retold the story of how Arthur was chosen to be king," Noelle explained. "That's why Isabelle's head is hurting." Noelle nodded, thankful that she was not afflicted with the same kind of head pain this morn. "The better the story got, the more Isabelle hoisted her cup."

"But what was said?"

"It was the story of King Arthur."

"Fie. I wish I could have heard the tale."

"Why are you two shouting?" Isabelle grumbled as she stumbled into the room, holding her head and groaning at the same time.

"Will you be able to accompany us this morning?" Noelle asked, trying hard to hide her smile at her friend's comical appearance.

Isabelle laughed and then caught herself. "Aye, as long as the horse doesn't bounce."

"I shall order you a donkey," Carolyn teased.

"Well, my head may hurt," Isabelle admitted as she eased herself down upon a chair, "but I would not trade a minute of the company I kept." She looked at Carolyn. "And did you see that big Scot who sat next to me?"

"Aye. He was a fine one. But I thought you wanted Lancelot," Carolyn reminded Isabelle.

"Methinks I am fickle." Isabelle gave a slow smile. "But lovable."

Noelle gave Isabelle a sisterly hug. "I agree with lovable. Now, let us fetch something to eat before we venture out."

Once downstairs, they found Guinevere already seated at the table, waiting for them. She motioned for everyone to join her. The serving maids immediately produced trays of breads, cheese, and fresh fruit.

"I am having some cloth cut so we can place holly and evergreen upon it. Last year, I did not think I'd get the holly home for the thorns pricking my horse."

"It is a good point," Noelle said. "Last year, I had to have a cart pick up our branches."

"We mustn't forget the mistletoe, for the kissing ball," Isabelle reminded everyone.

"Since when do you need mistletoe?" Carolyn laughed.

Isabelle frowned at Carolyn. "You must not listen to her, milady. I am usually very quiet."

Noelle choked on her mead. When she'd regained her composure, she said, "I have very unusual ladies-in-waiting, milady. As you remember, we grew up together."

"They *are* most unusual," Guinevere agreed. "But I envy you in many ways. These two ladies seem good friends to you, something that I have not had since I came to Camelot," she said as she reached for a hunk of bread. She looked at Carolyn and Isabelle. "When we are alone, please speak freely around me."

Isabelle smiled. "Yes, milady."

"We will gather the holly first and then look for the mistletoe. It was not abundant last year."

After breakfast, Guinevere's two ladies-in-waiting, Lynette and Ettarre, joined them and together they walked to the stables where the palfreys were saddled, along with Thor.

"Such a big horse you have. I do not remember him," Guinevere said as she patted the animal's neck. "I would be afraid of such a beast," she admitted.

Noelle mounted, adjusting her cloak for warmth. "I raised Thor from a foal, so never have I thought of his size. He is a beauty, I will admit. Father gave him to me before he died."

The small party rode from the castle with two guards. On the field outside the castle, the squires and pages had just started pitching the pavilions. The few tents already up were of many different sizes and as diverse as the knights themselves. On the tops of each flew the banners of the knights. Some larger, some smaller, their white silkiness and painted symbols or coat of arms very colorful.

She did not see Nicholas's banner; she wondered what it would be like, and then wanted to scold herself for thinking of him at all. Why did she think of Nicholas? Was it because of the man? No, of course not. She just wondered what his banner looked like, nothing more.

Workmen were preparing the jousting field and the stands where the nobles would sit to watch the tournament. Noelle had actually helped Tristan practice jousting, but when she had unseated him, he refused to joust against her again. She smiled. He probably feared that she'd become better than he.

Noelle turned back and looked toward the forest. She realized she'd been hoping to catch a glimpse of Nic—no, Sir Gavin, she corrected her conscious.

"It's colder than I thought," Carolyn commented from behind them.

"Aye," Noelle said as she looked at the sky. "I think those dark gray clouds are heavy with snow."

"You have been talking about snow for days. You know it's early yet," Isabelle said.

"I can always hope," Noelle told her.

Guinevere pointed. "Look, there are some holly trees."

Since there were several stands of trees, Carolyn, Isabelle, Lynette, and Ettarre went over to one group, and Noelle and Guinevere dismounted and started cutting fresh holly at the cluster of trees closer to them.

"I hope you were able to spend some time with Sir Gavin," Guinevere said as they removed their knives and began to cut the smaller limbs full of dark green leaves with red berries and place them on big, heavy cloths spread on the ground.

"Aye, he sat on one side of me, and Sir Nicholas on the other."

"Then you were the envy of all the ladies," Guinevere commented as she bent over and placed holly boughs on the cloth.

"How so?"

"Many a lady would have liked to have been in your position in between two such fine knights."

"Ouch," Noelle said when a holly leaf pricked her. She slid her finger into her mouth for a moment to stop the stinging. "I'm surprised that neither Nicholas nor Gavin has married."

Guinevere laughed. "Some men resist all the way to the altar."

"Did King Arthur?"

"Nay." Guinevere smiled. "He has always been sweet and loving. I am lucky," she said as she placed a few more branches on the cloth.

"Then you loved him from the very start?"

Guinevere shook her head. "Nay. Not in the way that you mean. I have always cared deeply for Arthur, and I do love him, but not in that way. Perhaps there is no such thing."

"I am beginning to wonder myself," Noelle mumbled.

Guinevere took her filled cloth to the cart, then leaned against the wooden boards. She glanced at the guards and saw that they were not in hearing distance, but were helping the other ladies. "What did you think of Sir Nicholas?"

Noelle placed her bundle in the cart, too. "I think that he is arrogant."

"Aye, that he is. And well he should be. There is not a maiden in court who has not tried to seduce him," Guinevere said with a knowing look. "I see you are surprised."

"Nay. But a Lady Clarisse was mentioned. Is that someone he loves?"

"She wishes that were true, but it's not. Clarisse complained that Nicholas was toying with her affections and making promises that he kept not. That is why he was sent to Ireland."

"Was it true?"

"I think not. He saw Clarisse as just another easy conquest, so you should be careful of him."

"He is of no interest to me. I was just curious," Noelle quickly assured her. She must not have the queen thinking she was excited over a man she'd just met.

Because she wasn't.

She was just curious.

"I see," Guinevere said. "I do hope that Nicholas finds a special lady one day. I have always been fond of him. He is not like the other knights."

"How so?" Noelle asked before she could stop herself. She really wasn't interested . . . she just needed to remind herself more often. She went back to get a few more holly branches that she'd left on the ground.

"Nicholas is of royal blood, but his life has not been easy. His parents died when he was but ten, and Nicholas has had to fend for himself since then. He had no holdings, no money. No family. Arthur is his cousin, but Nicholas was too proud to ask for help. He was fostered out to a family, but he ran away from them."

Noelle couldn't believe what she was hearing. To see Nicholas, one would think that he held himself above the rest because he was wealthier than most. Now she could see his mannerisms were a protection . . . a way to distance himself. And how did Nicholas the boy survive at such a young age without a family's protection? What horrors had he seen? She could only imagine.

"What happened to his parents?" Noelle asked.

"That is something that Nicholas will have to tell you. There have been so many terrible tales. I am not sure which is the truth, but it is something he will not discuss."

"It's none of my concern," Noelle commented stiffly. "And retelling the story must be painful for him."

Guinevere looked at Noelle. "I am not sure. Nicholas speaks naught of himself. But one day he will find a maiden he cannot forget so easily as the unfortunate Lady Clarisse. Someone who can melt the ice from his heart."

"Perhaps." Noelle wrapped another cloth around the bundle of holly and evergreen. She straightened and looked at the queen. A slow smile spread across her lips. "Miracles do happen."

It would take a miracle for a lady to get along with that man, Noelle thought. She sensed he threw women aside and never bothered to look at them twice.

Thank God, she wasn't one of them.

FIVE

Laugher floated through the air as Carolyn, Isabelle, Lynette, and Ettarre came back to the clearing, their arms full of greenery.

"We've gathered plenty, milady," Carolyn said as she dropped her bundle of evergreens, then clutched her cloak tighter around her. "I believe it is getting colder out here. It truly feels like Christmas."

Noelle glanced up at the gray clouds. "It will probably rain soon if those dark clouds are any portent. A roaring fire will feel good upon our return."

Guinevere finished tying up a bundle of limbs. "We can tie ribbons for our wreaths and have hot wassail." She straightened. "But first we need to find some mistletoe."

"It is most important for the kissing ball," Isabelle said with a merry twinkle in her eye.

Noelle knew that Isabelle would surely make use of the mistletoe the first chance she got. It was amazing how different her ladies were compared to Guinevere's. Noelle smiled. She liked her lively ladies best.

"It has been hard to find this year," Guinevere said.

"If we all take different directions, maybe we can locate it faster," Guinevere suggested.

"I remember seeing a clump of mistletoe in some trees that we passed on our way into Camelot." Noelle walked toward her horse. "I'll take Thor and ride over to the path we traveled, and if I can locate the spot, I will come back for some help."

"Take a guard with you," Isabelle insisted.

"Nay, I'm only going a short distance and the guards should stay with the queen. Now, let us make haste so we can warm our bodies by a roaring fire."

Noelle looked up at the tops of the trees as she rode slowly through the woods. The leaf-carpeted forest floor muffled Thor's hooves. A faint tinkling sound caught her attention. She turned her head toward the noise and lowered the hood of her cloak to better hear the sound.

It was a bell. But out here in the middle of nowhere? She pulled on the horse's reins. Strange, indeed, to hear such a sound so deep in the forest.

Following the sound, she wondered where it came from. She must be getting closer, for the tinkling grew louder and more pronounced.

A fierce wind had started to blow and the chimes became more insistent with the strength of the wind. Noelle gathered her cloak around her and buttoned it under her chin. She wondered, for a moment, if she should return to the others, but as she turned the bell seemed to float on the wind towards her. She scanned the tops of the trees, the mistletoe of little concern now.

Finally, she found the source of the noise when she came upon a medium-sized fir tree. It was a falcon perched at the very top of the tree. Every time the wind blew, the bird would spread his wings and try to fly, but he couldn't.

Apparently he was caught on something. Noelle gasped in dismay. She could not leave the unfortunate bird. He wouldn't be able to help himself, and she couldn't bear to see animals in trouble, even those as fierce as this falcon.

Dismounting, Noelle slipped off her cloak and threw it across the saddle. The frigid air immediately made its presence known, and she shivered. Pulling the back of her cotehardie between her legs, she tucked the tail end beneath her belt and tightened it, forming a makeshift pair of trousers.

That took care of one problem. She didn't want to tumble from the tree because her clothing caught on something, and it would be easier to climb dressed thusly.

Moving over to the tree, Noelle reached for the first branch. Thank God, she'd played as a boy when she was growing up and had climbed many trees. Hopefully, she had not forgotten the skills of her childhood.

Noelle knew she couldn't climb the tree where the bird was because there were no lower branches. However, she could climb the beech tree, whose boughs swept the fir tree, in hopes of reaching the falcon and setting him free. Carefully, she clambered up the tree, trying not to tear her cotehardie.

Soon, she was a hundred feet straight up. Noelle decided it was best that she not look down just in case she wasn't as brave as she used to be. Her fingers were cold as were her nose and cheeks, but she was not going to let a little discomfort stop her. This magnificent bird needed her help.

Finally, Noelle reached the falcon. She scooted out to the end of a slim branch, feeling as if she were a copper-colored beech leaf that might at any moment fall to the ground at the mercy of the wind.

Of course, a leaf would float, but she would not, so Noelle whispered a small prayer to please help fools such as she.

Be brave, she told herself.

When she opened her eyes, she noticed that the falcon's beady black eyes were focused on her, and he opened his mouth. If he could speak, he would likely be calling her a fool, as well.

"Easy, my brave poppet. I won't hurt you," she soothed.

A gust of wind swept through the beech and fir trees, sending limbs and branches soaring up into the air and back down again. When the branch settled, Noelle clung to it for dear life.

After several moments, she convinced herself that she had to open her eyes. When she did, she saw that the falcon was caught on a notch of the tree by the silver varvel which was attached to his jesses.

On the leather thong was stamped the figure of a

dragon. Noelle sighed impatiently. She should have realized that this bird belonged to Nicholas.

Again the boughs of the beech tree surged toward the pine, and Noelle reached to grasp the bird's yellow legs, but the falcon opened her bill and hissed with fear, anger, and warning.

"I'm not going to hurt you," Noelle whispered soothingly before the wind divided them again. While Noelle waited for the next gust, she got a good look at the bird. It was beautiful to behold with its blue-gray feathers across the top of its head, back, and wings. It had a dark stripe down its face, and its underbelly was light-colored.

The wind again brought her precarious perch close to the bird. Every time she came near, she came face-to-face with the cold black eyes of an untamed creature who looked none too friendly.

Several stronger gusts of wind whipped at the trees, sweeping Noelle up and down until she felt nauseous. She squeezed her eyes shut and realized how stupid she'd been to climb the tree in the first place.

With the next gust the needles scratched her face and brought her, once again, near the falcon. Noelle opened her eyes. The bird's eyelids were half-closed, its head turned away from the wind, feathered flanks protecting it from the blast of wind. This was her chance. Noelle located the notch where the varvel was trapped and grabbed at the limb to break the flimsy branch and free the bird.

It was a big mistake.

The moment she snapped the twig, a new gust whipped through the forest, ripped at her precarious perch, and Noelle lost her balance as the limb gave way.

In desperation she clasped the bird to her chest, screaming as she fell through the air. Her screams were lost in the wind as she tumbled from one wide-spreading bough to another, the speed of her fall lessening each time she hit a limb.

Somewhere on the way down, she let the bird go, and he flew away, not giving her a second thought.

Ungrateful beast, Noelle thought as she hit the ground with a thud, knocking the breath out of her.

She lay there wondering if anything was broken and gasped for air.

She could not breathe.

My God, she was dead and her body just didn't know it yet.

How long she lay there, Noelle did not know. Finally, she managed to move her hands to her throat. She needed air, but she could not make herself breathe.

Suddenly, she was being pulled to her feet. Someone pounded her on the back, and she breathed blessedly cool, fresh air. She gasped and then took several deep breaths until her lungs were filled again.

She could finally speak again. The guard would surely kill her if he kept pounding her on the back with such force.

"You little fool," the gruff voice said. "What, pray tell, were you doing climbing in yon tree like a squirrel?"

Noelle turned to protest such impertinence—and found not a guard, but a knight. Her knight.

No, not Gavin.

Nicholas stared at her as if he was not sure whether to wring her neck or clasp her to him. He appeared to be leaning toward the first option, Noelle decided as she gaped at him and wondered how he'd found her.

Finally, her senses returned. She felt battered and bruised, as though someone had beaten her, but luckily she didn't think she had any broken bones. Grateful as she was to be rescued, she was in no mood to have someone shouting at her for some paltry reason.

"I was trying to save your bird, you simpleton," she blustered. "He was caught yonder on one of those branches," she explained. She pointed upward and noticed that the bird was soaring overhead.

"You could have broken your neck."

"But I didn't," she countered.

His eyes blazed amber fire. "But you could have," he argued, his gaze moving down to her bodice.

Noelle followed his gaze and saw that her bodice had been torn. Quickly, she straightened her cotehardie to cover herself, and counted three additional tears as she moved away from him. She found her cloak on the ground, but Thor was gone.

The wind cut through her with the sharpness of a new knife in spite of the way Nicholas's gaze made her burn. It was as if he could see beneath her clothes . . . beneath her skin . . . and into her soul.

Noelle turned away from his penetrating gaze. She needed to keep some distance between them, so she remained with her back to him to mask her emotions. Her body ached all over.

And Nicholas's attitude wasn't helping. He infuriated her. How could he be so condescending when she had just saved his thankless bird? "A thank-you would suffice."

Nicholas stiffened as though she had struck him. However, he said nothing in response. Instead, he held up his arm, and the falcon swooped down and landed.

"This is the problem," he said as he undid the silver ring. "I let her fly free, but I forgot to remove the ring this morning."

He examined the bird's wings, then he threw his arm up and she took flight.

Noelle watched the bird soar against the wind. "What is her name?" Noelle asked.

"Athena," Nicholas said as he watched his falcon wing away. "She is a peregrine, the fastest animal alive."

"I see you named her after a god, as I did my horse."

Nicholas nodded. "Aye. And what did you name your mount?"

"Thor. He is a war-horse."

"You ride a destrier instead of a palfrey?"

"Aye."

He studied her intently. "Why does that not surprise me?" He paused, then posed another question. "How did you happen to wander so far away from the others?"

"I was searching for mistletoe when I heard your bird's tiny bell. But it was hard to tell which direction the noise came from, so I kept following the sound and soon found I was lost. I have no idea where I am or where my horse has gone. Have you seen my companions?"

"Your ladies are safe. I met them on the road while I searched for Athena. They told me you were out here lost. Since a storm was approaching, I sent them back to Camelot." He'd no more than gotten the words out than the first icy pellets began to fall. "We must return."

"Nay. Not without my horse."

Nicholas nodded, then mounted his destrier. He well understood the value of a faithful mount. He held his arm down to her. She grasped his forearm, and he swung her up behind him. Noelle wrapped her arms around his waist, then they rode off in search of Thor.

"You have a beautiful destrier," Noelle complimented.

"He was a present from Arthur."

"It was most generous," she said.

Nicholas chuckled. "I thought so."

"You have a nice laugh," she said, but figured he didn't hear her because he failed to comment. She wondered if he laughed very much. She had a feeling it was something he rarely did.

The sleet grew heavier, and Noelle pulled up her hood to protect her hair. She laid her face upon Nicholas's strong back to protect herself from the biting wind.

Twenty minutes later they paused, and Noelle called to Thor and heard his whinny. A moment passed, then he came trotting out of the trees toward them.

Nicholas turned and helped her slide to the ground, but she landed wrong on her foot and tumbled to the ground with the cry of a wounded animal. "My ankle!"

Quickly, Nicholas was on the ground beside her. "Is it painful?"

"Aye," she said, wanting to cry, but willing herself not to. She felt stupid enough as it was.

Nicholas shook his head. "How can you fall from a tree, escaping with mere scratches, and then dismount a horse and twist your ankle?"

She looked at him and gave him a half-smile. "Perhaps my luck finally ran out."

He almost smiled. "Will you be able to ride?"

She nodded. "If you'll help me mount."

He scooped her up into his arms and lifted her up to her horse who was dancing around from the bad weather. "Easy, Thor," she soothed her skittish mount.

"Cease." Nicholas's booming voice made her jump. However, Thor obeyed.

She looked at Nicholas. "Do you always get such cooperation from animals?"

"Aye. And men, as well."

Arrogant, she thought. She'd make sure she didn't jump to do his will.

They faced the horse, and Nicholas placed her on Thor's back with hardly any effort whatsoever. Her heart hammered foolishly at his nearness.

Seated, she looked down at him. "You will catch your death if we do not get out of this weather soon."

"We have wandered so far away from the castle in search of Thor that it is too dark to return. There is a sutter's hut that will give us some protection from the storm until the soldiers are sent for us with torches to light our way." Nicholas mounted. "Follow me."

She nudged Thor and noticed that ice was forming on the horse's mane. "Poor boy," she murmured as she patted him on the side of the neck, feeling very guilty about leaving him out in the cold for so long. By wandering off, Thor had had to put up with this frightful weather when he could have been in a nice warm stable.

The wind whipped the icy sleet across her face, stinging her cheeks, punishing her for her mischief. At the moment, a nice warm stable sounded very inviting even to her.

Quickly she ducked her head and yanked her hood up further as she followed Nicholas in the fading light. It would be dark soon and she didn't know how they would be able to see to make their way through the woods.

Finally, they reached a rundown hut. The roof was intact and so were the walls, but there was a large, gaping hole where a door had once stood. They rode the horses into the building.

She brushed the ice from her cloak. It felt good to be out of the icy weather. Safely inside, she didn't have to worry that Thor would slip on the ice and injure a foreleg. She dismounted and was immediately reminded her ankle was still tender.

Nicholas helped her up. "You could have waited for help."

"I'm used to doing things myself," she said, then

admitted, "I also forgot about my foot." She shifted her weight to the other leg.

"Stand here while I move the horses over to the side. I have been here before. They keep fresh hay for the animals and if we are lucky there will be a few blankets."

When Nicholas returned, he carried a couple of old blankets that had been in a corner. He shook the dust out of them and spread them out on the far side of the room on top of some hay.

Returning, he scooped her up into his arms, causing a gasp to escape her lips.

"Did I hurt you?"

"Noooo," Noelle said. She'd expected to lean on him and make her way over to the blankets. But to be held firmly in his arms had caused a dizzy sensation to race through her.

"I wish we could build a fire, but I don't have any dry kindling. We will have to huddle together under these blankets."

"You should take off your surcoat," Noelle suggested. "It is wet. We can spread my cloak across us. It is fur-lined and should keep us from freezing."

Nicholas did remove his garment and tossed it to the side. Then he slid onto the blankets next to her, spreading the fur-lined cloak over them. He propped against the wall and moved her so her head rested on his chest.

"Someone should be coming soon," Nicholas said. "They will have torches. However, the ground is getting slippery so they may wait until morn."

"We will freeze," Noelle said.

"Nay. With the heat from our bodies and the fur, we will survive through the night. You need not fear, milady."

His voice had such a husky tone that Noelle felt wrapped in an invisible cloak of warmth. "I have no fear," she confessed.

"Good."

Noelle wished she could see his eyes and see what he was thinking. He was probably bored at having to spend an uncomfortable night with her. So maybe it was better she didn't know what he thought.

She stared out at the sleet, which was turning to snow. The fluffy flakes floated softly to the ground. It was as beautiful as it was cold. Noelle hated to admit she was quite comfortable snuggled next to Nicholas's body, his muscular leg pressed next to hers. But she mustn't think of him. She must concentrate on something else. For when she thought of Nicholas, her musings seemed to wander off in the wrong direction. So she stared out at the only thing she could see . . . the beautiful white flakes.

The horses stamped their feet as they shuffled in the corner. It was a comfort to know she wasn't completely alone with the knight. But it was much too quiet. "It isn't often we get to see snow," Noelle said, breaking the silence when she could bear it no longer.

"It is a nuisance." Nicholas sounded bored.

But Noelle wanted to talk. When she was talking, she wasn't thinking. "It is beautiful," Noelle insisted.

"Are you always so stubborn?"

"Aye."

He grunted. "I thought as much."

Evidently he thought the conversation was over, but he didn't know her very well. "Where is your falcon?" Noelle asked.

"She is never very far. She's taken refuge in the cover of some thick trees or she could be perched in here and we cannot see her."

"How long have you had her?"

"I've had Boots—"

"I thought you named her Athena," Noelle said.

"Aye, but her nickname is Boots, which is what I call her most often."

"Odd name."

"If you look close, you will see brown feathers on both her legs that resemble boots," he explained.

"Now that you mention it, I do recall seeing her brown legs when we were in the tree," she said.

"That was foolish."

"But necessary," Noelle retorted with a smile.

"I can see one of your flaws."

"It's dark. You can see nothing."

Nicholas laughed.

"What is so amusing?" she asked, her voice taking on a sharper tone. He was laughing at her, something she did not like.

"Milady, it would seem that you must have the last word. It's a flaw."

"I have no flaws, thank you."

"I have my doubts." He was laughing again.

"Are you trying to make me angry?"

"Nay. I need your heat to stay warm," Nicholas said, but she could hear the smile in his voice.

This time she laughed, too. "Since it is my body, my cloak . . . you should be very nice to me."

He laughed as if sincerely amused. "I shall remember that."

Noelle had to admit she enjoyed this easy banter between them. Nicholas seemed so relaxed now, nothing like the man she'd seen before. Still, she wasn't ready for the silences. "You never answered me. How long have you had Boots?"

"Near seven years. Boots has warned me of danger more times than I care to admit. She is loyal, but one day she will find a mate, and then I will have a family of falcons."

"She does seem loyal. Have you always had falcons?"

"Nay. Truth tell, I never had a pet as a lad," he said matter-of-factly. "Boots actually chose me. One day while I was riding alone in the forest, she followed me all day, and she has never left my side since."

Noelle laughed with sheer joy. "Love at first sight?"

Nicholas chuckled. What a delightful creature, he thought. He couldn't remember when he'd laughed so much. The lass was good company, but he couldn't let her know that. "Sounds like some silly maiden's thoughts."

"I've never experienced love myself, but I've been told it's a possibility." She punched his arm. "So do not laugh at me. I do know one thing about falcons."

All right, he would ask, though he probably shouldn't. "And that being?"

"Falcons mate for life. That could explain why Athena has never chosen another," Noelle said softly, her breath fanning his ear.

Nicholas turned his head towards her. He could smell roses. His body reacted immediately.

God's wounds. He clenched his fist—he didn't need to react to her. His body felt as if it was half ice and half flame. "I think Boots stays more out of loyalty. What would she see in me to love?"

The sound of his voice held sadness, and the many unspoken words tugged at Noelle's heart. Who wouldn't love this man? But she could never tell him such. She felt a strange heat seep through her body and wondered why it seemed to happen every time she was near Nicholas. She didn't love him.

All right, she'd concede that she could possibly be drawn to Nicholas.

But that was all.

Finally, Nicholas asked, "Have you gone to sleep?"

"Nay. I was thinking of your question."

"You can't think of one thing, can you?" His voice held a slight raspy tone.

"It is a silly question. There are many things about you to love." She tried to keep her voice light and positive. "Let me see, you are brave, and a loyal knight to the king."

"As are others. You are saying that I should be loved by what I do, and not who I am," Nicholas said as he shifted his weight.

Her body tingled from the contact. "You must be loved for who you are."

"There are those who love for what one owns. I

should say, they want what one owns. There is no love, only greed."

Was she the only one who believed in love? "Have you ever loved anyone?" Noelle whispered.

"Nay." He shifted again, and suddenly she was closer to him. And then he surprised her by asking, "Have you?"

Was it her imagination or had his voice changed . . . become tender? "Nay, I have not loved, but I know he is out there somewhere." She sighed and then added, "We are a pathetic pair, you and I."

Nicholas let out a long, audible breath. "Perhaps we are both just alike."

Noelle shivered and then yawned. It had been a tiring day.

"You are cold, milady?"

"A little."

"You need to be closer," he said, and her blood began to race. He placed his arm around her and pulled her closer. She fitted perfectly next to him. "We should share our heat until help arrives."

"What if they do not come?" Noelle asked.

"When first light breaks we will ride to Camelot. It will be safer with a blanket of snow over the ice. If we tried tonight, it would be treacherous for the animals."

"I agree." She yawned again.

"It has been a long day," he said, absently rubbing her arm. His touch was oddly soft and caressing. "It will be a long night. Why don't you put your head on my shoulder and I'll keep watch."

"It isn't proper," she said sleepily but shc had to

admit that her head felt very heavy. She needed to rest against something. Yet an undeniable magnetism was building between them, and she didn't know how to handle it.

"Noelle," he said her name, and it sounded like a caress. "There is no one around but you and me. Lay your head down and try to sleep. You are safe with me."

She settled back and enjoyed the feel of his arms around her, and the softness of his chest made a good pillow. She placed her hand across his chest. His hand was there, too.

"Do you really not think that the white snow is beautiful?"

"Aye." Nicholas sighed. "But the snow reminds me of a dream several years ago."

"You dreamed you rescued a fair maiden hung in a tree?"

Nicholas laughed. "Nay. I dreamed I lay upon a field dying and I could see the white, fluffy flakes falling. They fell upon my face, but I could not lift my hand to remove them. It was a helpless feeling," he said in a somber voice.

Noelle wanted to say something to lift his spirits, for he sounded so sad. "At least it was a dream, nothing more."

"Aye, yet I cannot forget the dream. But you are right—it was just a dream. If I did not tell you before, thank you for saving Boots," Nicholas whispered.

Noelle reached for his hand, placing hers upon it. "You're welcome. And thank you for rescuing me." Slowly she started to relax. Nicholas's warmth surrounded her like a goose down quilt. He was gently rubbing his thumb back and forth across her hand. So tender, she thought. He was so big, so strong, but there was more to Nicholas than he let people see.

"Nicholas," she said, "do you know I have never talked to anyone as I have to you this night?"

"Nor have I." Nicholas leaned down and kissed the top of her head.

She sighed and squeezed his hand as her eyelids gently closed. Contentment eased her into a deep sleep; he could tell by the sound of her breathing.

Sir Nicholas the Dragon was in trouble. A trouble he didn't know how to handle.

SIX

The sun peeked over the trees, making the needles and leaves glisten like crystals. The ground was covered in fluffy, white snow and would provide safe footing for their horses.

Nicholas really hadn't wanted the sun to come up this morning, because he'd felt something he had never felt before . . . contentment. And that wasn't something he liked admitting. For once, he was going to allow himself the pleasure of feeling completely relaxed.

He glanced at the woman sleeping in his arms. The light of the rising sun bathed her face. With her head resting on his chest and her glorious blond hair spread out across his arms, she looked like an angel in sleep. Her long, sooty lashes rested on her creamy skin, and her breathing was smooth and slow. She seemed contented to be in his arms, the arms of a stranger. Nicholas lifted a lock of Noelle's hair and caressed it with his fingers. It felt of silk and, of course, she had to smell of roses.

Nicholas smiled. She always smelled of roses, a fragrance he found much too alluring.

She was so small, he thought, and his desire to protect her was strong.

He grinned. First, he'd have to protect her from himself. "Oh, how I ache to make love to you," he whispered, knowing that she could not hear him. "It would be so easy to take you here and make you mine. I know you do not love Sir Gavin, nor does he love you, but it was an arranged marriage. That being said, it doesn't make me desire you any less."

Nicholas twisted the golden threads around his finger. "Somehow, I feel different where you are concerned." He frowned at the admission. "It is a problem, you see. I feel . . . when I have never felt before. And I do not need such paltry emotions. It is far too dangerous for a warrior such as I." He rubbed a finger across her cheek. "This I promise you, I shall never act upon these feelings unless they are returned tenfold." He gazed at her with a longing that made his heart ache.

Finally, he could bear no more. He lowered his head and ever so lightly, so he wouldn't wake her, he brushed his lips across her cheek. Then he sighed for what could never be. "You are very special, Noelle, and I have enjoyed this night like none before."

He brushed his knuckle over her soft skin. Sad that the night had come to an end, he stopped the urge to touch her.

If the king could only see him now, he'd smile that all-knowing smile, that perhaps he'd been right. Nicholas had found something he could not have. But he would spite Arthur and prove how much of a man he truly was. He would win Briercliff and claim the cold castle as his own, and then some wench would easily satisfy these lusty needs of his.

Maybe that was the problem . . . he'd been too long without a woman.

Noelle knew she'd found heaven. She was so comfortable and contented that she never wanted to leave this place . . . only she didn't know where she was.

She knew she must be dreaming. But the dream was too good to end. Strong arms held her and a man whispered how much he loved her. She knew then it was right. She'd found what she had been looking for. Merlin had been right . . . her knight was truly wonderful.

Reluctantly, she opened her eyes and blinked several times as she looked up at a very fine-looking man. He paid her no heed, but stared out the open door. Noelle wanted to reach up and touch his face, but she was afraid to move lest the moment of happiness pass.

Finally, he glanced down at her, and their gazes locked. For just a moment, there was something other than cold disinterest in Nicholas's eyes . . . there was hope of something Noelle didn't recognize. Finally, she asked, "Did you say something?"

Nicholas looked surprised but his voice seemed normal as he answered, "Nay, you must have been dreaming. Did you sleep well?"

Fully awake, Noelle realized that she was sprawled across Nicholas in a very intimate manner. "I—I did not mean to take so much room from you. You must have truly been uncomfortable last night." She sat up, already regretting losing the warmth from his body.

Nicholas smiled—a smile as intimate as a kiss. "I was not uncomfortable. You kept me quite warm."

Noelle's cheeks heated. "I-I guess we should be going. Is it safe?"

"Aye." Nicholas nodded. "It appears that a blanket of snow has covered the ice. The horses should be fine. At least by the light of day, we can see where we are going." Nicholas rose to his feet, then went over to retrieve his surcoat, slipping it on his arms.

"It is still damp," Noelle said with a frown. She could imagine how uncomfortable the garment must be, the wet and cold material clinging to his body.

"Aye, but it is all I have. I will be fine until we reach the castle."

"You will be sick," she insisted as she got to her feet, brushing off her gown. Feeling the pain of her still-tender ankle, she placed most of her weight on the other foot.

Nicholas stood in front of her. "Noelle, I have been in weather much worse and with less on. I am a knight of King Arthur's Round Table. I need no comforts."

He stared at her in a manner that completely robbed her of all breath, and she longed to kiss him so much that she knew he was truly a temptation for her. Such an attraction could be perilous. Yet, was this not exactly what she'd longed for?

"So you need nothing," she said in a whisper.

Nicholas placed his hands on her arms.

Her pulse beat rapidly in her throat.

She wasn't exactly sure what was happening to her. It wasn't love that she felt. She hadn't known Nicholas long enough to feel love for him, but there was no denying that she felt something.

And by the saints above, she liked these feelings. It was as if an invisible web of attraction was building between them, sending shivers of anticipation down her spine.

Would Nicholas kiss her?

Would she let him?

"Noelle, I learned long ago not to need anything or anyone. I must live by my own wits and depend on no one," Nicholas said in a tone that sounded as if he were trying to convince himself.

"That sounds so lonely," Noelle said. "One day you'll change your mind."

"Maybe. But I think not," Nicholas said as he scooped her up and placed her in the saddle. "It's probably better to be careful of your ankle for another day or so," he said as if to explain why he had taken her in his arms.

"Thank you." Noelle nodded as she gathered Thor's reins. For some reason, she felt sad when she'd felt so wonderful only a few moments ago. She knew that Nicholas was a very lonely and cold man, but she wanted to wrap her arms around him and tell him that everything would be all right.

But she couldn't reassure Nicholas any more than she could reassure herself.

"Thank you for coming to my rescue yesterday," Noelle said. "I would not have survived the night in this weather without my horse."

"Brave knights are supposed to rescue damsels in distress. However, I must admit it's the first time I have found a lady in a tree." Nicholas chuckled. "I simply followed the bell. Did you know that when I hear bells, I think of angels?" He grinned at her.

Noelle nudged Thor to move beside Nicholas's horse. "And did you find your angel?"

"I'm not sure. She looks like an angel, but I cannot be sure."

Noelle smiled and brazenly said, "Perhaps one day you should find out." With that statement she walked Thor out into the snow. "It's a beautiful day, is it not?"

Nicholas was still in the hut staring at the beautiful woman who, he thought, had just issued him an interesting invitation. But Noelle had completely changed the subject and now spoke of the weather. Was she trying to drive him mad?

He had a throbbing in his loins that would not go away. Uncomfortable, he adjusted himself in the saddle.

Finally, he urged his horse out into the fresh, clean snow. "It's most beautiful," he agreed. "It is as if the snow has washed the earth of all its problems and sorrow, leaving cleanness in its path."

"What a lovely way to look at things. You do not speak like a brave and fierce knight at all," Noelle said, teasing him. "Which way?" she asked.

Nicholas pointed and they rode through the wood until they came to the open road where they could ride side by side, each quiet in their own thoughts.

Suddenly, Noelle pointed and said, "Look."

Nicholas reined in his mount. "What's wrong?"

She pointed to a snow-covered tree in front of them to their left. "It's mistletoe. That was one of the reasons I had wandered away from the others. You see, I remembered that I had seen mistletoe when we rode in the other day, and I tried to find it."

"Maybe the others found some by now," Nicholas suggested.

"Guinevere said herself that mistletoe has been hard to find this winter," Noelle countered. "I must get some. You hold my horse. I shall climb the tree and cut some sprigs to take back to the castle."

"Nay. I have seen the way you get out of a tree. It's not good."

"That was an accident." Noelle laughed. "Please."

"Here, hold my mount's reins. Against my better judgment, I shall fetch your weed."

Noelle took the leather straps, her fingers brushing Nicholas's cold hands. She longed to warm his hands, but that would never do, so she did nothing as she watched Nicholas climb the tree. One of the branches snapped from his weight, sending the fluffy snow floating through the air. Nicholas would have fallen had he not had a good grip on the limb above him.

"Do be careful," Noelle called to him and she saw him frown.

He removed his dagger and cut down a huge batch of greenery with white berries. "Is this enough?" he asked, holding the clump of mistletoe up to her.

"Aye. Thank you," Noelle replied as Nicholas made his way down from the tree. "Do you participate in the kissing ball?"

"Not if I can help it."

Noelle grinned at his quick answer. "Are you shy?"

Nicholas looked at her, tilted his head, then asked, "Would you care to find out?"

"It is a challenge that you offer . . . and I usually do not back down from such." Noelle leaned over to kiss him from her position on her horse, and the next thing she knew, she was being pulled from her mount. Her back rested against the animal.

Nicholas placed his hands on Noelle's shoulders, causing her flesh to tingle in anticipation. She wondered if she should feel some guilt instead of this excitement that held her spellbound.

His lips brushed the fullness of her lips.

Her heart jolted. Her pulse beat rapidly.

And then Nicholas pulled back, and Noelle almost fell to the ground. He steadied her. Disappointment filled Noelle as she looked up at him with the unanswered question in her eyes.

"Someone approaches," Nicholas said as he shoved her back up on the sidesaddle. He handed her the mistletoe.

Noelle pulled on Thor's reins, and her horse circled to stand beside Nicholas's mount.

Nicholas settled himself in the saddle and they started riding forward. Once around the bend, they came upon a group of knights who had evidently been sent to find them.

Sir Gavin was among the knights. "Thank goodness you both are safe," he said. "We could not ride last night for fear of damaging our horses. I have never seen such ice."

"I figured that is what had transpired. As it was, I found Lady Noelle, who was attempting to rescue a falcon from a tree."

"You actually climbed a tree?" Sir Gavin asked with a look of surprise.

"Aye." Noelle nodded. Did they all think that women were completely helpless? "Boots was tethered to the tree and needed to be freed." She didn't want to go through the entire story right now. She was more concerned about Nicholas. His coat was still very damp. "It is cold out here and Sir Nicholas's clothes are damp. We should ride for the castle and speak later," Noelle suggested.

"Aye." They all agreed.

On the way back, she heard Gavin ask Nicholas, who was riding beside him, "Where did you find refuge from the storm?"

"In the thatcher's cottage. There was no dry wood to build a fire, but with some old blankets we managed to stay out of the ice till morn."

Gavin nodded. "I am glad you found milady. She would likely have frozen if you had not done so."

Noelle started to inform Sir Gavin that she wasn't invisible and thus could speak for herself, but she thought better of it. She didn't want to answer any questions. Plus, she still felt a soft, warm glow inside from the night before, and such contentment that she wanted to savor the feeling. For when she returned to the castle, everything would change back to the way it had been.

Looking up at the sky, she saw that Boots flew

guard overhead, and Noelle realized that the bird was very loyal to her master.

But how did she feel about Nicholas?

Confused? Certainly.

Intrigued? Definitely.

Several hours later, Noelle had to admit that the countryside was beautiful covered in snow. She could hear the children laughing, singing, and playing in the small village that lay just outside of Camelot's walls.

All of the knights' tents had now been pitched, and each knight had his own banners flying in his compound. Of course, the first one Noelle noticed was Nicholas's. The red dragon snarled on the pristine white banner, and was quite impressive as it fluttered in the wind.

They didn't stop there, but rode into the bailey where the stableman and grooms ran out to get the horses. Noelle slid to the ground. Remembering her ankle, she clung to the saddle so as not to land in a heap on the ground.

Immediately, Nicholas and Sir Gavin were by her side. However, Nicholas was two steps ahead of Sir Gavin, and he scooped Noelle up into his arms.

Sir Gavin gave Nicholas a quizzical look. "What is the meaning of this?"

Nicholas looked at him. "I neglected to mention that Noelle injured her ankle falling from the tree, and since she did it trying to save my falcon, I feel that I owe her the courtesy of seeing her safely inside." Nicholas took two steps and twisted around to face Gavin. "Unless you object?"

"Nay." Sir Gavin waved a hand. "Carry on—you seem to have things well in hand."

Noelle was very much embarrassed, fearful that the entire castle would soon be gossiping about her. "If I but had a crutch, I could walk myself."

Nicholas glanced down at her. "First, I shall get you inside, and then we will see about a crutch of some type," he said as if he didn't expect her to argue.

And to Noelle's surprise, she didn't. Truth be told, she liked being carried in his arms. She liked it a great deal.

Guinevere and her ladies were in the Great Hall with the greenery and the red ribbons spread across the table. As soon as Nicholas entered with Noelle in his arms, Isabelle and Carolyn stopped what they were doing and scurried over.

"What's wrong?" Carolyn asked.

"Why is he carrying you?" Isabelle inquired at the same time.

"It is a long story," Noelle said as Nicholas set her on her feet. "Thank you for coming to my rescue, good sir."

Nicholas's brow raised a fraction as he looked at her just for a moment . . . a moment that seemed to linger in time and warm her. Then the moment passed. "My pleasure," Nicholas replied as formally as Noelle had. He turned and left the room.

"Why was he carrying you?" Isabelle asked again.

"I have twisted my ankle."

Guinevere moved over to her. "We were all quite worried about you. Tell us what happened while we tie the bows on the greenery. That is, if you feel like helping."

"Of course I do. It is only my ankle. I really do not feel bad," Noelle said as she made her way to the table with Isabelle's help.

Isabelle whispered, "And when we are alone, we want to hear the real story. You come waltzing in here in the arms of the most delicious man at court and you want me and Carolyn to believe that nothing happened?"

Noelle looked at both of her ladies and smiled that kind of smile that suggested she might tell them later. Or not.

"I am not that naive," Isabelle whispered. "Something happened. I can see it on your face."

As Noelle helped tie the bows on the greenery, she retold her story of hearing the bell and finding the bird.

"You fell out of the tree?" Isabelle said.

"Aye."

"Well, thank goodness Sir Nicholas found you," Guinevere said with a look of relief.

"Shall we start placing the greenery?" Carolyn asked.

"I know just the spot for the kissing ball," Isabelle said with a smile.

"I will hand you the greenery since I cannot climb."

"Nay." Isabelle shook her head. "Stay and help Lady Guinevere tie bows. That way you will not have to be on your feet at all. Carolyn will be helping me along with a couple of knights, if we are lucky." Isabelle winked at Noelle and then she left the room.

As Noelle and Guinevere finished tying the bows, Guinevere said, "You know," she paused as she straightened the streamers on the bow, "it has been a long time since I have seen Sir Nicholas smile, yet he was smiling when he swept through the door with you in his arms. Perhaps you have been good for him."

"Nay. I think not. He is simply easy to talk to."

"Most do not see it that way," Guinevere countered. "Sir Nicholas is a solitary man and avoids company."

"What makes him that way?"

"It is a sad story that Nicholas should tell you, but I will tell you that Nicholas has known no love in his life. Not even from his mother or father." Guinevere shrugged. "So I am afraid he doesn't believe that love exists."

Noelle didn't comment. All she could think of was what she'd said to Nicholas—that love was all that mattered. He must have thought her the fool.

Guinevere took the bow Noelle held up. "I hope that one day Nicholas will find someone who can show him love and make him believe that there is such a thing."

"I was told at dinner that he used to keep company with Lady Clarisse."

"Keep company? That was what he was doing, indeed." Guinevere chuckled. "He was simply using a warm body. And when she demanded marriage, he did as he usually does and walked away. I can tell you five such women who have had their hearts broken by our Sir Nicholas. Yet they knew what he was like when they allowed him to dally with them."

Noelle sighed. "The heart is such a complicated beast."

"Aye. It's a shame we can do nothing to control it."

Noelle looked at her, puzzled. "What do you mean?"

"That there are times when you cannot control who you love," Guinevere said in a dreamy kind of voice. "Love just happens. And it is the most magical feeling of all."

"You sound like someone who has experienced such feelings."

Guinevere looked at Noelle and smiled. "Aye. And I hope one day you will feel the same thing. Or perhaps, you already do with Sir Gavin."

"Nay. He is not the one."

Guinevere stopped straightening a ribbon she'd just tied and looked at Noelle. "What are you going to do?"

Noelle shook her head. "I know not," she said with a sigh. "A Christmas miracle would be nice."

Guinevere smiled. "There have been many miracles this time of year. We shall see what the future will bring." She stood up. "You will be all right in here by the fire while we go and decorate the doors with greenery. I would ask for your help, but I fear you should rest your ankle for a couple of days more."

"I will be fine. It is my own fault."

Just then, the door of the Great Hall opened and Lancelot and Dirk, Nicholas's commander, entered.

"You wish some assistance outside, milady?" Lancelot said as he bowed.

"Aye. I think we could use some help with the higher places." Guinevere moved towards the door, her hands full of red ribbons.

Isabelle had come back to pick up an armful of greenery, and Carolyn retrieved the holly. Isabelle turned to look at Noelle and gave her a mischievous wink.

"It is so nice of you to help us," Isabelle said with a smile that made Noelle smile, too, as she watched her friend move directly over to stand beside Lancelot.

As the group went to the door, it opened and a man with long black robes swept through.

Guinevere turned and looked over her shoulder at Noelle. "I think we have just found the very person to keep you company."

SEVEN

He stood in the Great Hall.

His white hair flowed down his back and mixed with his long white beard. Dressed all in black except for the silver trim about the edges of his full-length robes, he carried a scepter, which he leaned upon as if he were weary and needed a rest.

Guinevere stepped to the side, and Noelle could see that it was Merlin, the fabled wizard, who had finally made an appearance. Excitement bubbled in Noelle. She wished she could run to him, but she knew it was wiser to favor her ankle for now. Perhaps, he would keep her company in front of the fireplace while the others were outside.

Merlin's wisdom and power were greatly appreciated by King Arthur, in spite of the sorcerer's strange beginnings. The wizard was the son of a Cornish princess and an angel who had fallen out of favor with the gods. He had been reared by the Druids, and from them he learned astrology, spell-making, and how to change his shape when the need arose. But the most important gift Merlin received from his unknown father was the gift of second sight, and this was the gift that Noelle most admired. Though it would be wonderful to be able to change shapes at will, as well.

Merlin greeted Guinevere, then allowed his gaze to sweep the room as if he were looking for someone. Then he saw Noelle and smiled. "Excuse me, your majesty," Merlin bowed his head to the queen, "I see an old friend whom I have not seen in a long time." He started across the Great Hall toward the hearth.

"Is this the child whom I once dandled upon my knee that I now see before me?" Merlin smiled broadly in a grandfatherly sort of way. "You have grown into a lovely young woman as I knew you would," Merlin said as he kissed her hand. He took a seat on a blue tapestry chair across from her and folded his hands across his middle before saying, "Tell me about yourself since I last saw you."

Noelle smiled. "There is not much to tell. Cranborne was never the same after you left. I do see, however, that you have not changed at all. You are just as I remember, except your beard is a little longer." She laughed, then added, "I have missed you."

"As I have you, my dear. I still remember how you loved to sit and listen to my stories."

"I was but a child, and your stories fascinated me. Especially the one where you told me I would find true love."

Instead of commenting, Merlin changed the subject. "I heard you became lost yesterday. Have you partaken of any food today?"

"Nay." Noelle shook her head. "So much has happened that I forgot about food," she admitted, hoping that Merlin would probably have a servant bring something to eat.

Merlin reached into his pocket and pulled out three stones. He selected one and held his arm up in the air. He made a swirling movement with his other hand, and the stone turned into a loaf of newly baked bread, which he handed her. Then he waved his hand over the two other stones and they turned into two ripe peaches, one for her and one for him. Merlin handed her a peach and said, "This will hold you over until tonight."

That was the most marvelous thing about Merlin—one never knew what he was going to do next, Noelle thought. "How do you make your magic?" she asked. Then she took a bite of the delicious, ripe peach and realized she was much hungrier than she'd thought as the juice dribbled down her chin. It was strange—she hadn't thought of food at all when she'd been with Nicholas. She wiped the juice off her chin with her hand.

"It is something that I do," Merlin said, shrugging. "Tell me, what do you think of Camelot?"

"Its beauty is far greater than anything I could ever have imagined," Noelle said. She tore off a piece of warm bread and inhaled the aroma, then offered the rest to Merlin, who shook his head. "How did Arthur come to design something so grand?"

"It came to him in a dream . . . a castle like no other with thick stone walls and many towers . . . a fortress fit for a king. When you have had a chance to explore the castle, you will find that it has many rooms, instead of one large room with many fingers."

"This I have noticed, although I have not had the privilege of seeing the entire castle. I have heard many stories of the Round Table, yet I have not seen it in the Great Hall."

"It is another thing that Arthur has done differently. Upon seeing the beauty of the table, he decided that no food should ever touch the surface and mar the wood. Since he had not finished the castle, he had another Great Hall built, which he calls the Small Hall, on the back side of the fortress to house the Round Table. When Arthur holds council, no one enters the room except for the serving maid, Matilda."

Noelle nodded as she took her last bite of peach. Arthur was a wise man in many ways, she realized. He saw beyond his years. After setting the peach pit on the small table beside her, she knew she shouldn't put off asking Merlin any longer. She was frightfully curious, and needed answers to so many questions. "You once had a vision that I would find a man who I would love with all my heart."

She took a deep breath. "I have held onto these dreams for many years. I have waited. I have hoped. But nothing has happened. No man has come to me." Hoping to find an answer, Noelle searched Merlin's black, sparkling eyes.

He sat silent for a moment, his brow wrinkled with thought. "So you doubt my words?" he asked as he arched a bushy white eyebrow. His gaze was sharp and assessing. "How do you know that you haven't already met the man?"

Noelle tapped her chest lightly with her hand. "Because I would feel it in here," she declared. "And I feel nothing for Sir Gavin."

"Yet, I have heard that you are to marry him."

She laughed bitterly. "That was not my doing."

Merlin leaned forward in his chair and stared at the fire. "Sometimes the roads we travel are not clearly defined. We start the journey and think we see the destination for which we seek. Sometimes the harder we try to reach the end, the longer the road becomes. Then, suddenly the road turns and takes us in an entirely different direction." He looked at her and asked, "Do you understand?"

Noelle thought for a moment. "I'm not sure," she replied. "Do you mean that sometimes we travel a different road than we started out to take?"

Merlin nodded.

"But will I find the man that I can love and who loves me?" Noelle asked, completely confused. "Will I marry for love?"

Merlin chuckled. "I see you would like to have everything in order first so that you know that it is safe to proceed?"

"It would make it much easier." Noelle smiled and then added in a serious tone, "I only want to do the right thing. I don't know that Sir Gavin is the one for me, but if you say he is the one, then I will not fight the marriage."

"Fate leads us in many different directions and sometimes in the wrong direction, so it is up to you to choose your fate wisely," Merlin said, steepling his fingers and propping his chin upon them. "I will tell you this. You have already met your destiny, and it will be up to you to figure your course. Choose wisely, my child. Remember, the greatest satisfaction in life is won and not handed to you."

"If I have met my destiny, then I shall wait."

"I know it is not the answer that you wish," Merlin said with a slight smile. "But if you are fortunate and wise, all that you seek will be within your grasp. Now tell me, why are you in here talking to an old man when you could be making merry with the other ladies?"

"My ankle turned and it's tender."

Merlin sat on the edge of his chair and brushed his long sleeves back. "Let me see."

Noelle turned her leg to show him. He reached down and touched the tender and swollen flesh, closing his long fingers around her ankle; heat shot up her leg while a swirl of sparkles swept around her ankle. Then Merlin let go.

"You can stand now," he said with a nod.

Fearing the inevitable pain, Noelle hesitated. Finally, she pushed herself up to a standing position and tested her leg, slowly putting the weight on it. So far there was no pain. She smiled, then walked over to the hearth and back to her chair. "It is much better. I can walk normally again. Thank you."

Slowly, Merlin pushed himself to his feet. "I made your ankle well, yet my own bones are stiff." He shook his head. "Such an irony. Now, I must seek Arthur."

"Will you stay in Camelot, so that we may visit again?"

"Aye. I will be here for Christmastide. We will

speak again. I am most anxious to discover what you have learned."

Nicholas realized he was very tired now that he was back in Camelot. The back of his neck felt as though a sword had been rammed down his back.

He made his way to the stable to make sure his horse had been properly rubbed down. There, sitting on a perch at the far end of the stable sat Boots, looking at Nicholas as if to say, *What took you so long?*

"You, my fine feathered friend, led me on a wild goose chase." Nicholas shook his head. "Of course, I did like your choice of prey this time," he added as the falcon flapped its wings as if he understood. Nicholas yanked out a brown bag. He pulled open the drawstrings, retrieved a small slice of meat, and gave Boots his treat. "Get some rest, my friend, as I shall do. Something tells me we are going to need it."

Walking to his pavilion, Nicholas thought it probably would have been faster to ride since the tent was located several hundred yards outside of the castle walls, but the walk wouldn't hurt him.

He had sat in a cramped position all night—not that it was unpleasant holding a beautiful woman—but still, his muscles reminded him with every step that he had slept in uncomfortable accommodations.

The snow crunched under his boots as the wind whispered around him. Nicholas realized that he still wore his damp coat. No wonder he was so damned cold. He needed some good ale and a place by the fire. Aye, that was what he needed: a fire to warm his arse.

Glancing across the field, he noticed that the men were clearing the snow so they could continue to practice in case it remained on the ground several days.

That was good. This was one jousting match he meant to win. Then, he intended to win his wager with Arthur. It would be one fine Christmas.

Nicholas stopped to warm his hands when he reached the fire that had been built in front of his tent. He greeted his men as they gathered around and patiently answered their questions on what he wanted them to do today.

Nicholas put his hands on the small of his back and stretched back. He really couldn't remember ever being so tired. After all, he'd spent many a night awake in the past.

Someone tapped him on the shoulder, so Nicholas turned to see who it was.

"Did ye have a good time chasing Boots, or did I hear that ye had other things to accomplish?" Dirk said with a wicked smile. "Something about a fair maiden who was lost?"

"Since when do I have to report to you?" Nicholas said in a grumpy tone. He blamed the lack of sleep for his disposition.

"Methinks somebody needs to look after yer arse. Look at ye," Dirk raised his voice. He flung his hand towards Nicholas. "Are ye shaking, lad? You need to take yer coat off and get into some dry clothes, and I'll bring back some hot food to the tent," Dirk said as he held the flap aside.

"You sound like a shrew."

"Do I now?" Dirk grinned. "Were ye kept warmer than ye're letting on?"

"Nothing happened," Nicholas snapped. "Do not stand there like a grinning simpleton. Get me something to eat. I'm going to sleep—I have had enough of your harassing. I take it you are through with your questions."

"Yer disposition stinks," Dirk grumbled as he marched off.

Nicholas couldn't remember when he'd been so cold. His toes felt like chunks of ice, and he knew they would burn like fire when he began to warm up. That is, if he ever warmed up again. He stripped off his clothes and slipped into some dry ones, then climbed into his cot and pulled the fur up to his chin. If he just closed his eyes for a moment, the rest would relieve some of his aches.

Yes, even now he could feel a little warmth seeping into his bones. Now, if he could but sleep, he'd feel like a new man. Or, at least, the one he was before his misadventure of the night before.

Upon Dirk's return, he found Nicholas fast asleep, so he decided not to wake him. He placed a few hot stones in the middle of the tent to keep some warmth inside. After Dirk placed the last stone in the pit, he again glanced at Nicholas. "By the saints, he's smiling," Dirk said to himself. Maybe Nicholas had finally found something that would make him happy. And Dirk couldn't help wondering if it was the lovely lady of Cranborne. He smiled, shook his head, then returned to the other men to continue training. Snow or no snow, training was a must.

Noelle saw no one when she walked out into the bailey. Everyone must still be at the church putting up greenery, she reasoned. However, she was still exhausted from her adventure last night, so she decided not to seek them out. Thinking that this would be a perfect time to look around the castle, she turned to go back into the Great Hall.

She walked across the hall and down a long corridor that led into a passage. She knew she was headed towards the kitchen by the smell of the roasting chicken that drew her. At Cranborne, their kitchen was in a separate building, but here it had been joined to the main castle by a passageway. She passed a bakehouse and a buttery; just as she walked past the pantry, an elderly woman came out. Her black hair had streaks of gray running through the long braids. Her shoulders were bent, probably from years of hard work, but her face was pleasant even though she was mumbling to herself about some oaf. When she saw Noelle, the woman came to a complete stop.

She placed a bowl of potatoes she'd been carrying on a table just outside the door, then looked at Noelle. "Is something amiss, milady?"

Noelle shook her head. "Nay. What is your name, good woman?"

"Matilda, milady. I assist the steward with the household staff. Can I get you something?"

"I would like to see the Round Table, if you could point me in the right direction."

"I was told that you are not to be walking, milady," Matilda said firmly.

"That was true. But Merlin was just here, and he has taken the pain away. I'm fine now, as you can see." Noelle turned around. "I do not wish to bother anyone, but I would like to see this grand table that I have heard so much about. If you could just tell me which way to go."

"It is no bother, milady." Matilda smiled, then took Noelle's hand and tugged her forward. "Guess I know this castle better than almost anyone. I can show you if you do not mind an old lady showing you 'round."

"I would like nothing better. How long have you worked here?"

"Since shortly after Camelot was built. You see, Merlin chose me to keep an eye on our king when he was but a small lad. So I have watched him grow into the man that he has become. And a fine one he is."

"King Arthur must trust you a great deal."

"Aye."

They arrived at a set of doors with a single gold ring in the center of each. Matilda pushed open the door and gestured for Noelle to enter a large chamber. The walls were brightly painted, the floor a smooth marble stone. In the very center was a beautiful table wrought in precious woods, huge in size, with fifty chairs surrounding it. On the back of each chair was a knight's name printed in letters of gold. All but one chair, which had nothing on it.

"It is impressive," Noelle said, "but why does the one chair lack a name?"

"That seat is the Siege Perilous. Only the purest knight can have that seat."

"May I sit there?"

"Nay." Matilda caught Noelle's arm. "I am sorry, milady, but no man shall sit there but the one who we have yet to see. If any man sits in the chair other than the pure knight, he shall either suffer death or sudden and terrible misfortune for his temerity."

"I see," Noelle nodded. "I will remember that in the future," she said as she ran her hand over the back of a chair. Then she noticed Sir Nicholas's chair. "I wonder who the knight will be?"

"We will know when his name is placed on the back of the chair as on the others. The names just appear on the chairs. It is magic. So far no one has taken a chance to see if he is the chosen one."

"I imagine that you have heard many things going on in this room," Noelle said more to herself than to anyone. Then she asked, "Has King Arthur held council of late?"

"Nay. Usually they gather every fortnight, or if King Arthur has an issue with one of them, it could be sooner. But not your knight, milady. He has never been called to task by the king."

Noelle looked at Matilda, not understanding what

she meant. "I beg your pardon?" Surely, Nicholas was always being taken to task, she thought.

"Sir Gavin. He is a fine knight."

How could she have misunderstood? "So everyone tells me," Noelle said as she tried not to frown at her mistake. But she couldn't control the heat that rushed to her face. The minute Matilda had said, *Your knight,* Noelle had immediately thought of Nicholas, which was silly because he wasn't hers or anyone's. Thank goodness no one could read her thoughts.

"Now, Sir Nicholas—" Matilda stopped and nodded toward the chair that Noelle had her hand on. "—I really shouldn't say more."

"Please do," Noelle said a little too quickly. She saw Matilda's eyebrows go up. "He came to my rescue yesterday when I lost my way, so I am a little curious about him."

"I don't want you to think that I gossip, milady," Matilda said as she started around the table and adjusted each chair.

"I will not think such. Remember, I asked the question of you. You did not volunteer."

"Sir Nicholas is the bravest of all the knights because he has so little to lose. When one has nothing to lose, he takes dangerous chances." Matilda had made the complete circle and now stood beside Noelle again. "Guard your heart from that knave, milady."

"That is not the reason I was asking," Noelle rushed to assure Matilda. "He was very noble when he rescued me." Noelle saw Matilda staring at her with knowing eyes, so Noelle stopped explaining. The more she protested, the more Matilda would read into it. The old woman was like Merlin—she knew more than she should.

Noelle knew she shouldn't ask any more questions, yet she found herself wanting to hear more. "Why have you warned me about Sir Nicholas?"

Matilda gave a sly smile. "I am an old woman who speaks too freely."

"I think you are a wise woman who sees and knows things others do not. Please tell me about Nic—Sir Nicholas," Noelle quickly corrected.

"As you have probably noticed, Sir Nicholas is pleasant to look upon. Is he not?"

Noelle nodded. Why not admit what the woman already knew. "Aye."

"He has charmed every maiden he has ever known. The problem is that while they lose their hearts to him, he remains aloof, keeping his own heart well protected. In the end, it is always the same—he leaves them for the next one. I believe he looks at his dalliances as conquests."

"I heard Sir Gavin speak of one such lady just last evening."

"That would be the Lady Clarisse. She thought she could trap Sir Nicholas by getting herself with child."

"Oh—" Noelle eyes widened. Would he walk away from a woman carrying his child? If so, he wasn't very noble at all.

"It is nothing to be embarrassed about, my child. It's a natural thing between men and women, as you will find out for yourself."

Noelle blushed. "I know little of such matters, as my mother died when I was small."

"I see." Matilda took Noelle's hand. "I felt the same as you when I was your age, but you will learn."

"Did Nicholas leave her with child?"

"Nay. He takes certain precautions so that no woman can claim a child that is not his."

"What does he do?"

Matilda leaned over and whispered in Noelle's ear.

"Oh," Noelle said, knowing her face had to be completely scarlet. "Why does he do thus?"

"If he wanted an heir, he would marry. But it will never happen. He's afraid of—" Matilda trailed off, not completing her sentence.

"How do you know so much about Nicholas?"

"Arthur and Nicholas are cousins. I worked at Thornberry Castle and cared for Nicholas when he was a babe."

"Matilda," a serving maid called from the hallway, since she wasn't allowed to enter the room.

"I'm coming," Matilda said as she started for the door. "Come, my child, we will finish our talk another day."

Noelle followed respectfully, but she didn't want to wait for another day. She wanted to hear the rest now. And then Noelle realized she was becoming too much like Isabelle. The thought made her smile.

She could wait, Noelle decided. Besides, she was only curious. It wasn't as if she had fallen in love with Sir Nicholas the Dragon. She'd have to be a fool to give her heart to a man who so obviously didn't have one.

As Noelle made her way back to the Great Hall, she admitted to herself that she liked Nicholas.

But that was all.

She'd never be as foolish as the others. . . .

Her heart was safe . . . She would just have to keep reminding herself every so often of what Matilda had told her.

She was merely curious about the man who had rescued her from the cold.

That was all. . . .

EIGHT

Snow crunched under Tristan's boots as he walked between the pavilions after a visit with Sir Gavin, who had told him about Noelle's adventure. The foolish girl would one day get herself killed if she was not careful.

Tristan looked up to see Dirk coming from a different direction with a small black pot in his hand. "What have you there?" Tristan asked.

"Something hot, lad. Have you eaten?" Dirk asked as Tristan fell in beside him.

"Aye. A while ago," Tristan answered with a nod. "I was informed that Sir Nicholas had rescued my sister from yet another foolish stunt and has brought her safely back to Camelot. I haven't seen Nicholas anywhere, so I thought to look for him in his tent."

"Come with me. It is where I am headed. The fool dragged his sorry arse in this morning, and in a wet coat, at that. He hadn't bothered to tell any of us he was heading out or we would have gone with him," Dirk grumbled, sounding more like a wife than first in command.

"All I knew was that Sir Nicholas's falcon, Boots, hadn't returned, and that he had gone looking for her.

He told me later, when he found yer sister, that she was in a tree with Boots, trying to rescue him."

Tristan laughed. "It is my sister, all right. I fear she is a bit wild for her own good. When she was a small child, we were forever pulling her out of trees. And, do not make the mistake of challenging her with a bow and arrow. Believe me, you'll not win."

Dumfounded, Dirk looked at Tristan. "Really? Yer sister is an archer?" Dirk asked as they passed several tents.

"Aye. A damned good one, too."

"That's most unusual."

"It is Noelle. She is a most unusual woman."

The red dragon on Sir Nicholas's tent waved in the cold wind, making it look as though the creature was snapping and charging, as though the cloth monster had challenged their right to enter. Tristan was so intrigued he hadn't noticed that Dirk had stopped, and Tristan ran into the big Scot. "Sorry."

"Yer sister appeared to be a gentle lady last night at dinner," Dirk said as he reached for the tent flap that served as a door.

Tristan chuckled. "Looks can be deceiving. There is not anything gentle about my sister."

"I'll remember that in the future," Dirk said with a smile as he held the flap open so Tristan could proceed before him.

"Ye have company, old man," Dirk announced once he was inside. He looked down at the sleeping man and shook his head. "I can remember when ye could go days without sleep. Now look at ye." Dirk set the pot of hot soup on the warm stones piled in the middle of the pavilion. Since he'd gotten no response, Dirk looked back toward Nicholas. "Are ye going to get up or sleep all day?"

Nicholas didn't move. Dirk frowned. "It is not like him," he mumbled as he went over to the far side of the tent where Nicholas lay wrapped in blankets. "Ye must get up and eat, mon."

Tristan bent down on one knee and placed his hand on Nicholas's forehead. "He burns with fever."

Dirk shook his head. "Never seen him like this. We must get someone from the castle to tend him."

Tristan straightened. "I think we should move him inside the castle. This cold and damp ground cannot be good for him. Noelle is good with fever. She has the gift of healing." Tristan, who had been staring at Nicholas, got to his feet and looked at Dirk. "If we're going to get him to the castle, we are going to need a few more men to help carry him."

Dirk half laughed. "He isn't a wee one, I'll say that much. I'll go fetch a couple of men."

Six men struggled as they carried Nicholas into the Great Hall to a gaping Matilda. "What have you done to Sir Nicholas?" she cried, hurrying over to them.

Dirk looked at Matilda and frowned. "We have done nothing, woman. Nicholas is sorely sick and needs tending to. What room can we put him in?"

"Take him to the solar in the tower. It has the largest bed. Then I'll summon a leech for him. Follow me," she said, and turned to leave.

"Nay," Tristan said as they followed the old woman.

"My sister, Noelle, has the gift of healing. I shall fetch her to attend to Sir Nicholas after we get him to bed." Tristan grunted while carrying the knight, who weighed as much as a large rock . . . a very large rock.

Finally, they entered the sparsely furnished solar; Matilda had been right—the bed was larger than most. They placed their burden on the bed.

"I'll show you to Lady Noelle's chambers, milord," Matilda said and then pointed to Nicholas. "These clothes are still damp. You need to strip him and place him under the rugs to warm him."

Tristan followed Matilda down several winding passageways and up the stairs, until he found his sister's chamber. Matilda left him so she could get more quilts. Tristan knocked on the oak door and waitcd.

Noelle opened the door. Her surprise at seeing her brother was evident on her face. "Tristan, I have not seen you since we arrived. Where have you been?" she said and backed away from the door so he could enter. "You look troubled. Is there a problem?"

"I heard of your adventure yesterday," Tristan said. His gaze swept to her feet. "I thought you had hurt your ankle."

"Aye, I did," she replied, then did a very unladylike thing and lifted her skirt to show him her ankle. "I saw Merlin earlier today, and he relieved me of my pain with his magic."

Tristan nodded. "Aye. It is amazing what that man can do. I had forgotten that Merlin was here. But I did not come to chat. Did you pack your herbs and medicines and bring them with you?"

"Are you sick?"

"Nay, I am fine. Did you bring them?" Tristan snapped.

"You are in a fine mood. Are you the one who is feeling poorly? It is your stomach making you grumpy, isn't it?" she asked as she started for her chest to get the herbs.

"Nay." Tristan shook his head and chuckled. "It is not for me, but for Sir Nicholas."

Noelle swung around and gaped at her brother, but said nothing. She felt lightheaded, as if all the blood had drained from her brain. She hurried the rest of the way to her chest. "Something has happened, hasn't it?" She snatched out a small, brown bag from deep within the confines of the trunk and turned back to Tristan. "But Sir Nicholas was fine this morning. What has happened? Is he all right?"

Tristan looked at her with the oddest expression.

"Oh no!" she gasped. "It's bad, is it not?"

"By the saints. I don't believe it," Tristan finally said as he opened the door.

"Believe what?"

"You have finally found the one you've been searching for. You care for Nicholas," Tristan declared.

"Of course I care for him. He is a kind man, and he came to my rescue yesterday. Had he not, I might have frozen to death alone in the forest. Now, let us be off." Noelle tried to brush past her brother.

Tristan grabbed both her arms and turned her towards him. "You love him, do you not?"

"You speak nonsense, Tristan. I have just met Sir Nicholas," Noelle said. She tried to jerk out of his grip. She wasn't ready to answer questions about Nicholas.

"I am your brother, Noelle. I can see something in your eyes that I've not seen before. You are not good at hiding your feelings, my dear sister."

She completely ignored him. "I thought you were in a hurry. If he dies . . ."

"He has nothing but a fever," Tristan said, and then added, "I shall not take another step until you answer me."

Noelle sighed and folded her arms. Her brother was as stubborn as she was, and she could see that they were not getting anywhere, and they were losing time. Fevers could be serious, so she needed to go to Nicholas. "All right. I don't know how I feel about Sir Nicholas other than I find his company pleasant. There," she said and squared her shoulders. "Are you satisfied?"

"Aye." Tristan gave her a wicked grin. "We will talk more later."

Noelle successfully brushed past Tristan this time and into the corridor. "Not if I can help it." She heard Tristan chuckle and his good humor at her expense didn't help her disposition one bit. The man knew her too well.

She followed Tristan's lead and was surprised when they started to climb the tower's stairs. "When did the fever start?"

"I'm not sure. Dirk was grumbling about Nicholas's wet clothing. With the weather so frigid, he has probably caught the grippe."

"It was the damp jacket," Noelle said as she followed her brother. "I tried to warn him, but he had nothing else to wear."

Tristan turned and waited for her. "It seems, then, that you're the reason Sir Nicholas is unwell."

Noelle slanted a glance at her brother. "Thank you for making me feel so much better."

Noelle left her brother and climbed the remaining circular stone staircase to the tower. As in most castles, the stairs turned in a clockwise direction so men could fight with their right hands and still climb if they so needed. Noelle and her brothers had played on the stairway at Cranborne when they were children, and this one was no different.

The door to Nicholas's chamber stood ajar, but Noelle couldn't see inside. She took a deep breath, pushed the door open, and entered the room.

Matilda, an expression of concern on her face, was placing quilts over Nicholas. The old woman seemed to have a soft spot in her heart where he was concerned and Noelle thought that was sweet. After all, she had raised him when he was a boy.

Dirk was down on one knee beside the hearth, building a fire. The room was sparely furnished and quite cold. One very large bed, a small brown table, and a straight-backed chair were the only pieces of furniture in the small chamber.

Dirk had just placed a final log on the fire when he turned her way. "Milady, yer brother tells me ye have the gift of healing."

"Aye." Noelle nodded at Dirk, but then her gaze went right back to Nicholas, who wasn't moving at all. Noelle bustled over to him. Placing her hand on his forehead, she found he burned with fever. She opened the drawstring on her brown leather bag, dug around in the pouch, and pulled out a small cloth sack. "Matilda, will you take this bit of barley and bring it to a boil? Drain it, then bring the barley to a boil a second time. After you have finished, bring the mixture to me with some honey and a chalice." Noelle thought a moment, trying to remember if there was anything else. Her eyes never left the old woman, who looked as worried as Noelle felt. "Do you understand, or must I repeat it for you?"

"Nay, milady. You seem to know what you are about. Therefore, I shall leave Sir Nicholas in your capable hands," Matilda paused. "He is a fine man, milady. Let nothing happen to him," Matilda said, then went to get the things that Noelle needed.

Noelle smiled. Matilda seemed to display a motherly attitude for the brave knight. At least Nicholas had someone.

After the servant had left, Dirk moved over to the bed. "I removed his damp clothing, milady. I have sent for dry clothes." Dirk slowly shook his head as he looked at Nicholas. "I have never seen him so sick before. It is usually the other men feeling poorly."

"I tried to warn him not to put on that damp garment, but he is a stubborn man, and had nothing else. I feel guilty that he has gotten sick because of me," Noelle admitted.

"Nicholas is an honorable man, milady. He would never leave ye unprotected no matter how uncomfortable he might be. It was this damnable unexpected weather that made him ill, not ye."

Noelle couldn't help reaching and touching Nicholas's forehead again. Was it out of duty that he had been so gentle with her?

"His fever might last a couple of days," she said, realizing her voice sounded choked. "But I'll stay with him until he is well and back on his feet again."

Dirk bowed to Noelle. "Then I will be in yer debt, milady."

Noelle smiled at Dirk. He was a huge man, even bigger than Nicholas, and she felt very small next to him. But to be so commanding in size, she sensed that Dirk had a gentle side that he kept hidden. "You must think a great deal of Sir Nicholas."

"I have been with him nigh on four years, now. We've fought side by side in many battles. He has my loyalty," Dirk said, and then gave her a peculiar look.

"What?" Noelle asked.

Dirk smiled before saying, "Ye don't look as contrary as Tristan said."

Noelle laughed. "You don't know me very well."

"It is the same thing Tristan said." Dirk chuckled. "If ye don't need me, I'll check on the men."

Matilda entered the room as Dirk left, followed by Noelle's ladies-in-waiting. Of course, Isabelle stopped and smiled at Dirk. "I might need your help as we finish our decorating," she said, fluttering her eyelashes at him. "Those big, strong arms can help with our Yule log, I have no doubt."

"I would be most happy to help ye at any time, fair lady," Dirk said with a slight bow. He lifted Isabelle's hand to his lips. "Ye have but to name the time and place."

"Tomorrow, then," Isabelle said in a breathy whisper. Then she turned and swept into the room with a smile that seemed brighter than the sun.

As Noelle was draining the barley, with Matilda's help, Carolyn looked at Isabelle. "I see you have given up on Sir Lancelot."

"Aye. His loyalty lies with the queen, and he pays attention to none other. But you must agree that Dirk is a fine and brawny man, and I think he might like me just a little."

"Greetings, ladies." Noelle smiled at them as she mixed the barley and honey together until it was a smooth consistency. "I take it you have not missed me today."

"On the contrary," Carolyn said. "At least, *I* missed you. Isabelle had a hard time not gawking at the knights and their squires."

"I did not," Isabelle said quickly. Then she added, "Well, mayhap one or two."

"Ladies," Noelle said, gaining their attention. "I need your assistance. If you both will take Nicholas by the shoulders and tilt him up, I must get this potion into him. It will do him no good in the bowl."

Both women took a place on either side of Nicholas. After much tugging, they managed to get him to a sitting position.

Isabelle grunted. "He weighs many stones."

Matilda handed Noelle the chalice, which she held to Nicholas's lips. He tried to turn away from the lip of the cup.

"Do not," Noelle murmured and soothed him until she managed to get some of the mixture into his mouth. And just in time too, for Nicholas began to thrash, sending both ladies away from him and onto the floor. Carolyn landed on her backside.

"He is no weakling, even in his sleep," Carolyn said, rubbing her bottom as she got up.

Noelle sighed. "Matilda, I'll need fresh water later."

Matilda nodded. "I will go fetch some and will come back to check on you later, milady."

Noelle nodded. "Thank you."

Once Matilda had gone, Carolyn said, "We heard that your ankle is much better."

"What is the matter with Sir Nicholas?" Isabelle asked at the same time.

"My ankle is much better," Noelle said to Carolyn, then she looked at Isabelle. "Sir Nicholas has caught fever," Noelle answered. "Did you finish decorating the Great Hall?"

"All but the church," Isabelle said. "We ran out of greenery."

"I can help with the greenery."

Isabelle grinned. "You seem to get lost when we let you out of our sight."

Carolyn giggled, too. "And look who she came home with! Only the finest knight in the kingdom." Carolyn nudged Isabelle. "Not only that, but she spends the night with him, and we haven't had the chance to ask her one question about her adventure."

"Tell . . . tell," Isabelle said.

"I was lost. Sir Nicholas was searching for his falcon, and he found both of us."

"And . . ." Isabelle prompted.

"There is nothing else. The weather was so icy that it was too dangerous to return, so we found a small hut and stayed there out of the sleet and snow until morning."

"It must have been horribly frightening," Carolyn said.

"And cold," Isabelle added. "How did you stay warm?"

Noelle felt herself blush as her inquisitive friends continued to ask their pointed questions. "We shared my cloak," she answered simply. It was the truth. As far as it went.

Nicholas moaned, drawing Noelle's attention. "No more questions, ladies. Nicholas is very sick, and needs my full attention."

"You are going to let us wonder and imagine all kinds of things?" Carolyn asked.

"No, ladies. We did nothing but sleep. Now, go away if you are not going to help. I have more important things to do at the moment. Now be off." Noelle waved them away. "Go and pray that our own Nicholas recovers soon."

"We will, milady," Carolyn assured her.

"Our Nicholas?" Isabelle's eyebrows shot up. "Should we tell Sir Gavin anything?"

Noelle frowned at the reminder. "Nay. You two can keep him company. Now go."

When they reached the door, Isabelle turned back and looked at Noelle. "Have you found the one?"

Noelle looked at her all-knowing friend. "I do not know," she said simply. "I honestly do not know."

NINE

Noelle watched Nicholas. His breathing seemed normal, and that was good, but his fever was still high.

He didn't seem to be responding to any of her herbal medicines. She'd given him twice as much as she would a normal man, but then Nicholas was more man than most. She was impatient for him to recover, and this waiting made her feel like she was falling apart inside.

His fever still raged; she kept bathing him down with cool, damp cloths, but he just lay as still as death. She didn't like that.

He was much too still.

Nicholas needed to fight the fever because she'd done all she knew how to do. She was going to try the barley once more, but it was really too soon.

Noelle's head felt so heavy she could hardly hold it up. Her eyes burned and she felt like weeping, which would do no good. It would only show her weakness. Perhaps if she could lay her head on the bed for just a minute, she'd feel better. She placed her hand on Nicholas's arm so she would know if he moved or needed her, and then she laid her head on her arm.

In no time, much-needed sleep overtook her.

Somewhere in the wee hours of morning, Nicholas jerked and shouted, bringing Noelle out of a hard sleep. He was thrashing back and forth so much that she was afraid he'd hurt himself.

Nicholas's arm caught Noelle across the chest and sent her tumbling to the floor. Quickly, she scrambled to her feet. If he got much wilder, she'd have to tie him to the bed or knock him over the head.

Going over to the small table, she wet the cloth and wrung it out before moving back to the bed. She tried to place the cloth on Nicholas's feverish forehead, but he was fighting everything she did. She looked around frantically. Maybe a good whack over the head would help. But Nicholas's voice stopped her.

"Mother, why are you so mean to Father?" Nicholas muttered in a childlike voice. Noelle went completely still at the sound.

"But we love you," he pleaded.

Noelle watched the strong knight, now reduced to a helpless child as he tossed and turned. Not only was he fighting fever, he was fighting his dreams. Just what secret hell was Nicholas reliving? She realized he must be remembering something from his childhood, some demon that had haunted him for a very long time. Noelle wanted to help him, but she didn't know what to do. Would Nicholas start talking again so she could find out what plagued him?

Her question was answered as he once again began

his incoherent speech. Noelle held his hand as she listened, struggling to make sense of the words.

* * *

Nicholas knew he must be in Hell because nothing less could produce this insufferable heat. Something cool brushed his forehead from time to time, but it wasn't enough.

He needed relief!

The next thing Nicholas knew he was falling, and he couldn't stop as the black hole jumped up to swallow him.

And then there were the flames.

Flames everywhere.

Once again, Nicholas was a small boy running through the castle in search of his mother. He was afraid of the fire, and he wanted to leave. But not without her.

Not without his mother.

"Mother," he called frantically. Not receiving an answer, he raced down the corridor away from the fire, but something stopped him. He turned back. His mother stood at the end of the long corridor, a torch in her hand, while flames shot all around her.

Nicholas started toward her. "Come with me, Mother. I shall save you."

"No, Nicholas, it is too late. Everything was wonderful until you came here. Then everything changed. You are the cause of all this, Nicholas. You do not deserve to be loved."

"I'm sorry, Mother," he cried. "What did I do? I

will do anything you say. I will make it better. I promise."

But the flames caught the hem of her dress and engulfed her. Her screams were so shrill that Nicholas had to put his hands over his ears to shut out the sound. The jest was on him, for he still heard the screams every night in his dreams. Tears streamed down his face. "I'm sorry," he cried out again and fled the burning castle.

Many of the servants had made it safely outside and stood in small clumps, staring at the blazing flames. Nicholas recognized one of the serfs as Rogers.

"Where is Father?" Nicholas asked.

"He never came out, lad," Rogers said and placed an arm around Nicholas who, by now, was sobbing.

"I couldn't get Mother to come out. It is all my fault," he wailed.

"Nay, child. Sorry as I am to say it, your mother is daft and evil. She has brought misery to this household. I just pray that you have inherited your father's blood instead of the tainted blood of your mother."

Nicholas straightened and stared at what used to be his home. Why had his mother not loved him? Had she always been sick?

Had he been the cause of her illness as she had said? No, that could not be. Still, the pain inside was hard to bear. But he would show her. He would show them all.

When the pain inside Nicholas hurt so bad that he wanted to scream and fall to his knees, he stood tall. He never wanted to feel such pain again. To love someone was much too painful; therefore he would avoid love in the future. After all, his blood could be tainted; Rogers had said so.

Wiping the tears from his cheeks, Nicholas vowed he would never cry again. He was but ten years old and all alone.

It was time he was a man.

Nicholas squeezed Noelle's hand so tight that she feared he'd break her bones. He tossed his head back and forth on the pillow, trying to flee the demons that plagued him.

Noelle studied his face as he frowned, and she thought she saw the boy he spoke of. Nicholas's lashes and cheeks were damp from tears. Her cheeks were streaked from her own tears as they had tumbled down her face. Noelle didn't want to let go of Nicholas's hand long enough to wipe them away.

She sensed that he desperately needed comfort though he said otherwise.

Through Nicholas's delirious mumbling, Noelle had been able to piece the story together. What pain Nicholas had gone through! She'd give anything to take his pain away.

Finally, she pried her fingers loose so she could get a damp cloth. His lips looked parched. She sat on the edge of the bed so she could reach him more easily. After she had wiped his face, she reached up and touched his cheek, running her hand down the side of his jaw.

He was magnificent. Even when ill and wracked with fever.

He bore a couple of scars, probably from the battles he'd been in, but they only added character to his features.

Gently, Noelle wiped the tears from his cheeks. She shut her eyes and prayed that his fever would ease soon.

"Milady." Nicholas's voice, weak and tired, came out of nowhere, and Noelle looked at him. He stared back at her. "You are so good, and I am evil. You should stay away from me for I will only bring you pain."

"Nicholas, you know not of what you speak."

Slowly, he smiled. "Since you are in my dreams, are you not going to kiss me?"

Noelle smiled. First he warned her to stay away from him, and now he wanted to kiss her. The man was not only delirious, he was very fickle.

Noelle knew that Nicholas was still out of his head and knew nothing of what he said, but it was a tempting invitation. She looked at the door. It was shut, so who would know? Besides, Nicholas would never remember when he was well once again. And it would be an easy way to satisfy her curiosity.

So Noelle leaned over and placed a light kiss on Nicholas's lips. His mouth was warm but dry beneath her lips, and she was a bit surprised when his arms came up around her and pulled her on top of him. Evidently, he still possessed some measure of strength, even in his weakened condition.

Noelle knew she should get out of this sinful position, but curiosity bade her stay put as she opened her mouth to taste him.

The kiss was passionate and just as wonderful as she remembered from the lake. His mouth moved in slow hunger. It was a kiss that made her moan with all the desire she felt for him.

Nicholas stroked her back as his tongue did lustful things with her mouth. She wanted more of his hot, searing kisses. She wasn't sure if she burned from his fever or one of her own.

It was sinful to be taking advantage of someone who was sick, and Noelle liked having his arms around her far too much. She liked the taste of Nicholas. Pulling back, she gazed down at him for a long moment. His eyes were glazed with fever as he stared at her.

Suddenly she was overcome not only with exhaustion but also with the emotion she felt for this man. She wished she knew what he was thinking. She should never have teased him with a kiss. Her lack of discipline left her wondering why she acted as she did around him.

"I enjoy kissing you, my sweet," Nicholas murmured, then he went completely still and back into his deep sleep.

It was for the best, Noelle thought with a longing sigh. Before she could slide off him, the door opened.

"Do you need—" Isabelle began. Her mouth dropped open, then she regained control and arched her brow disapprovingly. "I see that you do not need my help. Is it a new method for curing a fever?"

Noelle had never been so embarrassed in her life. Her body burned as if she, too, had a fever. "Get in here," she hissed at Isabelle, who still stood in the doorway. Then Noelle slid off Nicholas and back to her feet. "I–I—"

"You need not explain, milady," Isabelle said. "It is none of my concern. I could well see what you were doing."

"Nay." Noelle shook her head. "It was not how it appeared."

Isabelle gave her mistress a saucy look. "Was it not?"

"Nay. Yes." Noelle stumbled over her words, then finally threw up her hands. "I do not know. I just wanted—"

Isabelle placed a hand on Noelle's arm. "I know what you wanted. It is only natural."

"But I am promised to someone else."

"Aye. Someone you didn't choose. Perhaps Sir Nicholas is the one. I have not seen any man that you have wanted to take advantage of before," Isabelle teased. "And now you pick one who is sick and has no idea of what is going on."

Noelle finally smiled. "It is sinful, I must admit. But I was simply curious and got carried away."

"I can see why," Isabelle said as she watched Nicholas. "Perhaps I could satisfy my curiosity as well."

"Nay," Noelle said much too quickly.

"Aha," Isabelle said. "You *are* jealous. I believe Nicholas is the one."

"Nicholas is not the one." Noelle shook her head. "He would only break my heart as he has others."

"How do you know?" Isabelle asked.

"I have been listening to him in his delirium, and I'm not sure Nicholas is capable of love."

"Such a shame," Isabelle shook her head, "for he is a fine one. Perhaps he hasn't found the right person to love. How is his fever?"

"I am going to mix up another potion and give to him. I must break his fever. It has gone on much too long." Noelle went over to the table and pulled open her leather pouch. "Here, take this barley and bring it to a boil, strain it, and bring it back to me. And don't forget a touch of honey. Nicholas must have strength to fight and conquer this fever," Noelle said.

"If anyone can nurse him though this illness, you can," Isabelle said. Then she touched Noelle's arm. "What if he dies?"

"I will not allow him to die. If there is a breath left in me, I will make him well."

"Just as I thought." Isabelle nodded.

"What?"

"Methinks that you are in love with Nicholas. You might as well admit the fact," Isabelle told her firmly.

"I-I don't know. I do feel something for my brave knight." A cold knot formed in Noelle's stomach. She couldn't deny the evidence any longer. "Enough of this nonsense. I must get some water into him. Help me lift his head before you leave."

Isabelle moved to the other side of the bed and pulled Nicholas up so Noelle could get the liquid down him. Nicholas coughed and twisted, but finally the task was accomplished.

"Why don't you go and try to sleep. It has been

two days now, and you must rest yourself," Isabelle said.

"I cannot. Nicholas could get worse. Perhaps the night will bring the end to his fever. Now go and prepare the barley, and daydream of your own knight. You have picked one out?"

"Aye. I like Dirk," Isabelle admitted. "There is just something about that Scotsman that draws me to him and makes me smile. I get a funny feeling whenever he is near me. Do you know what I mean?"

Noelle smiled. "Aye. I do know such a feeling. Your Scotsman *is* a fine one. Now, be off with you."

Isabelle returned, and they managed to get the brew into Nicholas. Then Isabelle left Noelle alone with Nicholas. Now the long task of waiting lay before her.

Noelle bathed Nicholas down when his fever seemed to reach a high as the sunset brought about the end of the day. Sometime in the wee hours of morning, when she couldn't hold her head up any longer, she pulled the chair as close to the bed as she could and again placed her hand on Nicholas's arms and went to sleep.

Sometime in the early morning, Noelle jerked awake. The skin beneath her hand was damp and clammy. She glanced at Nicholas and saw that he stared at her, his eyes still weak and glassy from the fever.

"Why are you in my bed?" Nicholas asked in a raspy voice, then added, "water."

Noelle rose slowly. She was still stiff from sleep and chilled to the bone. The fire had gone out during the night and no one had been there to toss on another log. "I'm not in your bed. You are in Arthur's castle," Noelle explained. She poured some fresh water into the basin and then into a cup. Her back and legs protested from being in a cramped position for so long, but she forced herself to move. She brought the cup back to Nicholas. He managed to prop up on one elbow and take a few sips of water.

"How do you feel this morning?" Noelle asked.

Nicholas blinked several times. His eyes felt as though they had sand in them. Where was he? He could remember coming back to Camelot, but nothing more. And why was Noelle at his bedside? If he'd propositioned her, be could remember nothing. He looked at her again. She looked very tired and there were dark circles under her eyes.

"Where am I? And why do I feel so ragged?"

"I just told you. You are in the castle's north tower." She took the cup from him. "Dirk brought you here because you were burning with fever. Remember that wet surcoat?"

"Aye. I remember now," Nicholas said as he sagged back against the pillows. "How long have I been here?"

"It is the third day."

Nicholas looked puzzled. "And why are you here?"

"I have always had the gift of healing, so I was called to attend you. I am glad to see that I have not lost my touch." Noelle smiled as she looked down at him.

Nicholas frowned. "I am sorry that you were burdened with me," he said.

He was taking this all wrong, Noelle thought, so she rushed to tell him. "I chose to take care of you."

"Why?"

Noelle stared at him long and hard. She didn't know how to put her feeling into words . . . words he probably wouldn't believe, anyway. "I honestly do not know," she finally said.

"Have you been here the whole time?"

"Aye."

"Then I am grateful."

"It was probably my fault that you are sick. It's the least I could do," she said.

"Then you watched me out of duty?"

"Do not twist my words, sir." That wasn't what Noelle wanted Nicholas to think. But what could she say? "I stayed because I cared about what happened to you," she said almost in a whisper.

Nicholas felt as if his breath had been sucked from him. He reached over and took Noelle's hand and held it. As he stared at her, he wasn't sure what he wanted to say, but he did know that her words pleased him a great deal. He wanted to pull her closer and just be near her for a moment, but before he could react to his thoughts, the door opened.

"How is my cousin?" King Arthur asked.

Noelle jerked her hand from Nicholas's and curtsied to the king. "His fever must have broken during the night, sire," Noelle said.

"Good." Arthur nodded. "We cannot have him getting lazy by staying in bed so much. And I admire you, milady. You have stayed the entire time with him when you could have had a servant relieve you. But now I think that you need your rest, too."

"But sire, Nicholas might need something," Noelle protested, not wanting to leave just yet.

"The king is right," Nicholas said. "You need your rest. Maltida can fetch me something to eat and drink. Besides which, I have lingered in this bed much too long as it is."

Arthur looked at Nicholas. "You should rest for at least another day. You will need your strength. Meleagant is acting up again, attacking villages down south."

Nicholas attempted to rise. "I will go, sire." However, the words didn't match his strength—he collapsed back onto the bed.

"I think not," Arthur said. "Rest now, and I will have Matilda come to look in on you."

Arthur took Noelle by the elbow so she didn't get a chance to protest again. Once they were out in the hall, Arthur said, "Thank you for attending Nicholas. I am sure he received better care than he could have from our leech. I have heard how good you are with your herbs. I now see for myself that the rumors are true."

"It was the least I could do after Sir Nicholas came to my rescue yestereve."

"I wanted to tell you that I have sent Sir Gavin to deal with Meleagant. Your banns have been posted for your forthcoming marriage so you can marry during the Christmas season, but I cannot tell you which day."

Now was the time to tell the king, Noelle thought. She should tell him that she wished to marry no one. But he'd argue that it was time to marry, and how could you argue with a king? Noelle opened her mouth to protest, but the words were not forthcoming. So she merely nodded as they walked down the corridors.

Upon entering the Great Hall, she saw a small table had been sent up near the throne with a small chair on the other side.

"Have you enjoyed your time at Camelot?" Arthur asked.

"Aye, sire. It is truly beautiful here." Noelle glanced around. "I see the hall has not been completely decorated."

"Guinevere and your ladies have gone to fetch more greenery," Arthur said. "After you have rested, you can join in the festivities. Come, sit with me. I have had some food prepared."

Noelle could smell the barley bread as she took her seat. There was a mound of honey butter on a small trencher, and the main dish was fruit and salmon pie topped with almonds and saffron.

Arthur adjusted his sword so he could sit down. The gold hilt that glittered with encrusted rubies and emeralds caught Noelle's attention.

"It is truly a magnificent sword," Noelle said as she sliced the loaf of bread. "Sir Lancelot told us the story of how you pulled the sword from the stone. But he said this sword is not one and the same. I would have thought that a sword which could pierce stone would last forever."

Arthur picked up a slice of cheese. "One would think so," he chuckled. "But my first sword was shattered when I fought King Pellinore."

Noelle placed the knife on the table, then picked up her chalice. "Where did you get this one?"

"Should I bore you with such a story, milady?"

"Please do. For it interests me."

"I was given this sword by the Lady of the Lake." He paused to drink his mead. "When I destroyed my other sword, I asked Merlin where to find another, and he said, *Cease to trouble. I know of only one good sword; it is in a lake inhabited by fairies. Thus if you are able to gain this sword, it will last you through to the end.*

"So we rode close by the sea, then turned left towards a mountain, and thus came to a lake where Merlin asked me how the lake looked. I told him that it looked extremely deep." Arthur chuckled and placed his chalice back on the table.

"What did he say?" Noelle prompted.

"Merlin told me that no man had ever entered the lake without the permission of the fairies and not died as a consequence. However, the sword of which Merlin just spoke was in the lake. I merely looked at him, wondering how I could obtain that sword. It seemed to be a daunting task. Then I happened to glance back at the lake, and I saw a sword appear from beneath the waters, held aloft by a hand and arm clad in white samite. It was so beautiful. It took one's breath.

"I gaped at Merlin and he nodded. *The sword of which I told you.*

"I was about to ask him how I was supposed to retrieve the sword when a damsel came towards us, gliding over the surface of the lake as if she were on the wings of a dove. She was so beautiful, clothed in a sea-green garment with long, flowing red hair."

"Who was she?" Noelle asked as she nibbled on some cheese.

Arthur leaned over and said, "Merlin told me, *This is the Lady of the Lake. Within the lake is a rock, and inside the rock is the fairest place on earth. This is where the Lady lives. She is the only one who can give you the sword.*

"Finally, the damsel was standing in front of me, and I asked her what sword was that yonder and that I wished it were mine, for I had no sword." Arthur shifted on his throne. "She said the sword was mine, and called Excalibur, which means cut-steel. It is a sword of destiny which can be wielded only by a king.

"I asked her what I had to do to obtain this sword, and she told me, *I will give you the sword if you will give me a gift when I ask it of you.*" Arthur chuckled as he reached for a piece of cheese. "I told her I'd give her whatever gift she asked for.

"So I boarded the barge and rowed to the place where the sword came out of the water. Taking a deep breath, I gripped it by the hilt, and the hand and arm sank back beneath the water. When we reached the shore, the damsel had gone. So I received the most beautiful sword in all the land with the condition that before I die I must return the sword to the Lady of the Lake."

"I hope that will be a long time coming, sire," Noelle said with a smile. "What a beautiful story. Will the sword always keep you safe?"

The king wiped his mouth, then leaned forward with a very serious expression. "Which do you think is the better, the sword or the scabbard?" Arthur finally asked.

Noelle looked at him, puzzled. "The sword."

"Nay." Arthur shook his head. "Exactly the same thing I said. But Merlin advised me that the scabbard is worth ten of the sword, for while I wear the scabbard I shall never lose a drop of blood, however sorely wounded I am. Therefore, I always keep the scabbard on me."

"The Lady of the Lake was correct . . . Excalibur is a sword worthy of a king," Noelle said as she stood. "Merlin has been a good friend and has stood by your side. I believe he has great wisdom as well as the sight."

"It is true—Merlin can foresee many things that we cannot."

"By your leave, sire," Noelle said with a curtsey, "I will go and rest now."

Arthur nodded his approval. "Milady, you deserve a long rest."

Noelle's legs felt as though they were forged of lead as she made her way to her chamber. She should undress, but she was much too tired. Instead, she stretched out on the bed and pulled a rug over her. Sleep soon claimed her.

It had been one of the longest days of her life.

TEN

When Noelle finally awoke she wasn't sure how long she'd slept. Isabelle and Carolyn were standing at the end of the bed saying something she couldn't quite hear in her sleep-drugged state. Slowly, she blinked several times to clear eyes that felt as if they were filled with sand. Then she sat up.

"We came to see if you want to help us decorate the Great Hall," Carolyn said.

Noelle yawned and stretched. "How long have I slept?" she murmured sleepily.

"Since yestereve," Isabelle told her as she held up a bedrobe for Noelle to slip into. "We didn't wake you for dinner last night for you were sleeping so soundly and appeared very contented."

"How is Nicholas this morn?" Noelle said as she tossed the quilts off her. "I should look in on him."

"He is gone," Isabelle said.

"Gone?" Noelle felt all the blood leave her head. "You mean he died?" Noelle asked, her eyes welling with tears; a feeling of deep sadness filled her heart. "I knew I should not have left him. But he was doing so well and King Arthur insisted that I sleep—"

"Wait," Isabelle said to stop her. "Nicholas is well. Matilda told me he left at the break of morn."

Noelle closed her eyes, relief swelling her heart, yet feeling utterly miserable that she wouldn't see the handsome knight again. It was a feeling she hadn't expected. She should feel rested and glad that Nicholas was well enough to return to his men. And she was, but she had to remember that she couldn't keep Nicholas; he wasn't her pet.

"Are you feeling ill, milady?" Carolyn asked.

"It's nothing. I am still full of sleep. Perhaps some cold water on my face will help. Help me dress, and then we shall be off to decorate the hall."

They spent the morning in the Great Hall tying bright red bows on evergreen and holly branches. After today, the main table would be left up and decorated in the hall until after the Christmas feasting.

Isabelle and Carolyn placed evergreen branches and holly on the walls and windows.

Noelle and Guinevere placed the greenery down the center of the table, then tied red bows on the twelve candelabras, which held twelve candles. It was the season for twelve. There would be twelve holiday foods, twelve wassailing, and tables would be set in twelves.

Noelle hummed a Christmas tune she remembered from her childhood. All seemed fine and well, in spite of her impending and unwanted marriage to Sir Gavin. It was funny how fast she could shove the marriage to the back of her mind. She knew deep down she kept expecting something to save her.

"I have seen little of you since I lost you in the woods," Guinevere said as she tied a bow. "I hope you are not ill."

"I am sorry if I caused you worry, but as I searched for the mistletoe, I found a falcon trapped in a tree and couldn't leave him caught as he was." Noelle chuckled. "Though I am not sure the foolish bird appreciated my efforts."

"I heard of your adventure," Guinevere remarked as she tied yet another red bow. "I still cannot believe that you climbed the tree to save that bird." Guinevere shook her head. "Those falcons are very unpredictable. I just thank God that Nicholas stumbled across you when he did. You could have frozen to your death out there."

"Aye, I am thankful, too." Noelle paused. "I fear that I caused Nicholas to become ill from his efforts. I have spent the past few nights nursing him. I am glad to say that he is now well recovered." And she *was* glad, though she still regretted that she would see him no more.

"So how did you find our Nicholas now that you have spent time with him?"

Noelle felt her cheeks heat. "I know not what you mean."

Guinevere chuckled. "I have been a woman longer than I have been your friend, and I know the ways of women and men. You need not be ashamed to tell me how thrilling it was to spend the night with the most sought-after knight in all the kingdom."

Noelle smiled. "He was noble and protective and kind. My virtue is still safe, yet I felt something about him . . ." Noelle paused, then admitted, "I find myself liking him when I do not want to. After all, I am betrothed to Sir Gavin. It's not something I should admit, I suppose, but since we are friends. . . ."

"You are not the first to be taken in by Sir Nicholas. He has broken many a heart, yet he chooses none." Guinevere nodded toward Lady Clarisse, who was also working in the hall. "She is a perfect example. She is beautiful and charming, yet Nicholas tarried with her, but made no offer. I could introduce you to her, if you would like."

"Another time," Noelle said.

"I think no one will trap Nicholas into a marriage. Perhaps he was not meant to marry," Guinevere said, then added, "Do you know that he and Arthur have made a bargain?"

Noelle shook her head. "Nay. What manner of bargain?"

"I probably shouldn't say."

"You have my curiosity up. Pray, do not stop now. I will not say anything of what we speak," Noelle told Guinevere.

"Arthur wagered that Nicholas couldn't abstain from the ladies, and Nicholas accepted the wager. The prize is a castle that Nicholas has longed for, so much is at stake for him."

"For how long must Nicholas abstain?"

"Until Christmas Day." Guinevere chuckled. "It's a long time for a strong, handsome man like Nicholas."

Noelle didn't say much. Was Nicholas really so notorious that he would make wagers with the king? Everyone said thus, but she sensed a different side of Nicholas, a sweeter, more vulnerable side. It was foolish, she knew.

"Such a shame," Noelle said, realizing her thoughts had slipped out into words. "I speak too freely. Nicholas is none of my concern. I believe my heart is safe."

Noelle turned around and saw that Isabelle was having the kissing ball hung on one of the wooden cross beams overhead. "Isabelle will be the first to use the kissing ball. I do not believe there is a shy bone in her body."

"She is a joy to me and all she meets," Guinevere said.

"Where are the men this morning?" Noelle asked as she selected another length of ribbon.

"The men have gone out hunting. Then they will practice for the joust in the field this afternoon, now that the snow has melted away."

"It was quite a treat to have such a lovely snowfall at this time of year. It seems to add something to the season, but it didn't last long enough," Noelle said with a sigh. "Do you know that I have always dreamed of being married with snow on the ground? And I would wear a very special gown."

"You almost had your dream, then," Guinevere said.

"Almost," Noelle said, but somehow the dream seemed far away from the marriage she was preparing for.

"It is so early in winter to have snow. But I agree it was lovely to see those big, fluffy flakes falling from the sky," Guinevere said as she glanced around the hall. "I think everything looks quite beautiful, do you not agree?" She looked back to Noelle. "It's so nice to have you here this Christmastide. I hope it will be one of your most memorable Christmases."

"It is always nice to be with old friends. Have the church decorations been finished?"

"Aye. Everything is prepared for Saint Nicholas Day service. The men will join us tonight in church when we celebrate the feast of Saint Nicholas."

The December air was crisp, but had warmed some since the men had ridden out earlier that morning. Arthur rode his great white destrier up next to Nicholas's matching one and Arthur reined his mount in as he came to a halt. "I see that Boots is in rare form today. She has now brought back her fourth fowl." The horse stamped impatiently, blowing out great clouds of white breath as he waited.

Nicholas chuckled. "You know how bloodthirsty wenches are, sire."

"Aye." Arthur nodded. "It's good to see the color back in your face. You looked close to death when they took you to the tower. Lady Noelle took excellent care of you."

"She is well-gifted with healing."

"She is also a very lovely woman. I was told that she never left your side the entire time you were sick. I'd say that Noelle is most devoted to the things that she cares about," Arthur said as he nudged his horse forward again.

"Devoted as in her cures and medicines?" Nicholas said as he urged his own horse into step beside the king. Nicholas wondered exactly what the king was trying to tell him.

"Aye. I think she will make Sir Gavin a good wife."

Nicholas tensed. He didn't like the notion that Noelle was promised to another, and he did not understand why. "Aye, she will," he said, but his voice lacked the enthusiasm it should have had. Nicholas could not feel joyful at his friend's good fortune.

"I heard that Meleagant attacked Wayfair, and that you sent Gavin to meet him."

"Aye. Meleagant has been much too quiet of late. I fear he is up to no good. Meleagant's judgment is poor. He figures if he can capture enough of the smaller holdings, he can use those men to overcome Camelot."

"It will never happen, sire. Not while I breathe."

"Nor I. Meleagant has had his sights set on Cranborne Castle for a very long time, and now that Cranborne is vulnerable, I fear he will strike."

"The castle was once well defended. What happened?" Nicholas asked.

"King John, when he was alive, had many men and Cranborne prospered. However, after he died, his eldest son John made poor decisions and squandered the money away. Tristan wasn't old enough, nor was he next in line, so he could do little to prevent John from doing his will. I think Tristan will one day be a strong baron, but John needs more guidance." Arthur glanced over at Nicholas. "How does he fit in with the other knights?"

"I like Tristan and see no reason why he hasn't been knighted before now. He is a good man."

"He has been too long under his brother's control, and Tristan did not want to leave his sister unprotected for the quest, so he has put everything aside until Noelle weds."

"Is that why you have promised her to Gavin?"

King Arthur arched a brow. "It's one of the reasons. I was good friends with her father. I think of her as a daughter, and I would have only the best for Noelle," Arthur said as he watched a black scowl cross Nicholas's face. "She is quite a remarkable young woman."

"Aye," Nicholas agreed and then grew quiet as they rode back to Camelot. He was hard-pressed to put his feelings into words . . . aye, Noelle was exceptional . . . and spoken for. And that was the rub.

The sunny afternoon was spent in sword practice. Nicholas took great pleasure in besting his opponents one by one. It kept his mind off that which he wished not to think of.

When the day was finally over, Nicholas made his way wearily back to his tent. Dirk sat just outside on a stump, having finished practicing long before Nicholas. Dirk was bent over a stone, sharpening his knife.

"For someone who has been on his backside for two days, ye fought like the devil himself was after ye this day," he said without looking up. "Or was there something ye wished not to think about?"

"Do you have something you wish to say, Dirk?" Nicholas snapped.

"Nay. Just making a comment."

Nicholas frowned. "I was practicing, nothing more."

"Ye know, the Lady Noelle is a fine lass," Dirk said, completely ignoring Nicholas's short answers. "If she were not promised to Sir Gavin, I might see if she had eyes for a Scotsman," Dirk said as he held the knife up to test the blade's edge.

"She isn't the right woman for you," Nicholas snapped again as he ducked inside the tent.

"And who is she right for?" Dirk called after him, smiling. He was enjoying needling Nicholas. It was not often that Nicholas discovered something he didn't know what to do about.

"She is fine and fragile." Nicholas stuck his head back through the opening. "You need an outspoken woman who can give you hell when you need it, which is often."

Dirk laughed loud and deep as he held his blade up and examined the edges. "Then she is probably more like someone you would fancy?"

"Dirk," Nicholas said impatiently, "Lady Noelle is promised. I can lay no claims to her even if I wanted to. I will never marry. You know that. Now, find something else to do. You have spent too much time in foolish thought."

* * *

Noelle chose a dark blue velvet cotehardie to wear to church. Her long, flowing sleeves let her light blue kirtle show from beneath the darker blue and flattered Noelle's creamy complexion. Isabelle wove blue ribbons into her hair in a complicated arrangement that Noelle would never have thought of wearing. She paused to look at her lady's handiwork. Yes, she liked it. It suited her. Surely it would suit her lord as well.

However, Noelle wondered which lord she truly wished to please.

Noelle and her ladies started across the bailey to the brown-and-gray flagstone church. The archway of the chapel was carved with animals and mythical beasts. Just above the arch were the Magi awakened by an angel.

As they approached the front of the church, Noelle saw the knights standing in two lines on either side of the steps, waiting for them to enter.

Sir Lancelot turned, and with a sweep of his hand said, "Miladies, please go before us."

"Thank you," Noelle said with a nod, then proceeded through the avenue made up of handsome men before starting up the church steps. The knights all nodded a silent greeting as Noelle and her ladies passed.

Noelle noticed that Nicholas was not with the knights and she wondered why. After all, he likely had been named for Saint Nicholas. He would surely be there on his namesake's day.

Isabelle nudged Noelle and whispered into her ear, "I would rather stay out here with Sir Lancelot."

"Shh," Carolyn hushed Isabelle as they stood in

the church vestibule. The church was bathed in warm candlelight, and the pews were almost full. An usher walked back to get them.

"Follow me," he said. He escorted them to the pew where they were to sit. Noelle curtsied to the cross and then entered the pew, followed by Isabelle and Carolyn. When Noelle moved down the row she realized that the pew was already half full, but until she reached her seat she couldn't see who she'd be sitting beside.

She knelt down next to a gentleman who had his head bent in prayer. Noelle said her prayers, and when she had finished, she eased back to her seat.

"Milady," the gentleman next to her said softly.

Noelle glanced to her left and was pleasantly surprised to see Nicholas. He looked healthy and much too good. The candlelight bathed his dark skin and highlighted the lighter places in his hair. His golden eyes glowed like those of an animal. Yes, Sir Nicholas looked very well indeed. Noelle realized her thoughts were wandering, so she stopped herself from thinking and asked, "How do you feel this eve? Are you well?"

"Much better, thanks to you, milady," he whispered. His boldly handsome face smiled warmly down at her.

Every time Nicholas's gaze met Noelle's, her heart turned over. The priest entered the church and began to chant. The music started and saved her from having to say anything else. They both stood to sing. Nicholas had a beautiful voice, she noted.

When they were seated again, Isabelle leaned over

to Noelle and whispered, "Would you like to change places?"

"Shh," Noelle replied.

Father John stood behind the pulpit and began his sermon. "Saint Nicholas day is a blessed day," he intoned as he raised his arms to the heavens and the large, white sleeves of his alb flowed down to his waist. The garment was embroidered with green and red down the center, front and back. When Father John lowered his arms, he started again. "When Saint Nicholas was born, he was given the name of Nicholas, which means conqueror of nations. After his birth, his mother, Nonna, was immediately free of pain, and from that time until her death, she remained barren.

"Saint Nicholas showed himself to be perfect in every aspect of his life. He avoided vain friends, idle conversations, shunned conversation with ladies, and seldom looked at them. Saint Nicholas preserved a true chastity."

Isabelle nudged Noelle. "He does not sound like our Nicholas," she whispered.

Noelle frowned at Isabelle. "You are incorrigible. We are in church. Behave."

A knight on Nicholas's other side cleared his throat, and Noelle finally had to smile, having heard of Nicholas's reputation.

Father John continued. "Saint Nicholas's marvelous wonders were performed on land and sea. He helped those in distress, he saved those who were drowning in the deepest sea, he gave healings to many, sight to the blind, power to walk to the cripple, and he was the champion of children," the priest said. Then he added with a nod, "He was truly a saint."

This was the first time Noelle had heard the full story of the saint. Now she knew that Saint Nicholas was a very exceptional man. Was his namesake just as special? Perhaps Nicholas kept his goodness hidden.

Noelle felt Nicholas's thigh press next to hers, and she found she was very aware of the man next to her. Being close to him wasn't displeasing.

Her hand rested on the pew next to her skirts. Without any indication of what he was about, Nicholas reached over and placed his hand on hers. His fingers were warm and strong.

Noelle didn't jerk her hand back even though she knew she should. Instead, she curled her fingers around his hand. His warm skin felt wonderful next to hers. She could feel strength in his hand and her skin tingled at his touch. She realized Nicholas hadn't intended to hold her hand. His action had been spontaneous. She liked the tender gesture.

Did he care for her just a little? Or was she just another one of his potential conquests?

Noelle began to think that Father John could talk forever, but much too soon he ended his sermon and bade them to sing.

Nicholas let go of her hand as they rose, and disappointment immediately replaced the warm feeling Noelle had felt but a moment ago. She tried to glance at Nicholas without him noticing, but she could read nothing on his face.

As they sang "Nowell, Nowell: In Bethlehem,"

Noelle wondered how she was going to manage to get more time with Nicholas. She needed to sort out all these strange feelings. She wanted to talk to him. Aye, she wanted to know more about him. Perhaps if she prayed for a Christmas miracle, she could have some time with him.

Father John introduced the two boy bishops that had been chosen to preside over the services on the Feast of the Holy Innocents on December twenty-eighth. The two lads then followed the priest from the church.

When the service was over, Noelle and the congregation began moving toward the back of the chapel. Once outside, Isabelle turned to Dirk. "I was hoping you would sit with me as we sup tonight."

"I would like nothing more, lass," Dirk said, and held up his arm to Isabelle.

Isabelle punched Noelle discreetly in the side, trying to get her to do something.

Noelle stood looking at Nicholas, but she didn't know what to say.

Nicholas finally smiled and asked, "May I escort you and Lady Carolyn to dinner, milady?"

Sir Alex walked up behind the ladies. "Nay," Sir Alex said. "It's not fair that you have both fair ladies." Alex looked at Carolyn. "Milady?" He held up his arm and Carolyn accepted with a smile.

"That leaves the two of us," Nicholas whispered softly.

Noelle's breath caught in her throat. When she glanced around she saw that all the others were across the bailey heading for the Great Hall. When she looked back at Nicholas, she became captivated by his gaze. "Shall we join the others?"

He held up his arm to her, and she placed her hand on his and they started toward the hall. "Are you enjoying your stay at Camelot?"

"Aye. It's beautiful. I look forward to seeing my first real jousting match," Noelle said.

"Do you know anything about jousting?"

"I do," Noelle said as they reached the bottom of the steps where a torch has been mounted onto the wall. "I have competed before and won."

Nicholas chuckled. "Who would compete with a woman?"

She pulled her hand from his arm. "Just because I am a woman does not mean I'm helpless."

"Women are weak."

"It is not always strength that matters. Sometimes a good mind can make one strong."

"You do not need to be competing with men."

Nicholas was arrogant, just as her brothers and every other man she had met were, she thought. Noelle would just have to show Nicholas that he could be outwitted, but before she could say anything . . .

Nicholas glanced over her head at the torch. A slow smile formed on his mouth.

Noelle turned to see what Nicholas was staring at. And then she saw the red bow and the sprig of mistletoe dangling from it. She turned back and looked at Nicholas with a smile. What would he do? she wondered.

"It would seem that your ladies have done a good

job of decorating, and you, milady, have been caught," Nicholas said in a husky voice. He lowered his head.

The intensity of his gaze made Noelle tremble. She should do something. It was the custom to kiss whoever you caught under the mistletoe, but she was promised to another. But this kiss really wasn't important, just a tradition, she thought to herself, as Nicholas's lips met hers.

All thought of resisting fled her mind.

After all, it was Christmas.

Nicholas's mouth brushed gently over hers. He gave her time to pull away.

She did not.

Good, he thought.

Nicholas's arms went around her. He was going to end this attraction he felt for her once he gave her a thorough kiss. Her arms slid around his neck, and he shook with a raw need that shot through him like a spear.

When he pressed his mouth against her lips, she parted them slightly and let him delve into her sweetness. God, she was pleasing. She responded to his touch, and when she molded her body to his, he thought that what little reason he held on to had surely deserted him.

Her passionate response became a burning need, and he wanted to taste all of her.

Where was the strong discipline that Nicholas prided himself in?

Evidently, he'd left it on the battlefield.

Good thing she wasn't the enemy. Or was she?

The door at the top of the steps opened, and Nicholas forced himself away from Noelle. Reluctantly, he glanced up.

"I came to see if something had befallen ye," Dirk said with a grin. "But I see that ye have things well in hand."

"It was the mistletoe," Nicholas said, his voice raspy.

"Aye. I plan on finding some mistletoe myself," Dirk said, then added, "Ye do realize that the tradition calls for everything to be done in twelves. Lady Noelle now has eleven more times to pass under the mistletoe in keeping with the season." Dirk's grin stretched from ear to ear.

"I had forgotten," Nicholas said, but his gaze was on Noelle. "Thanks for the reminder," he told Dirk, who had already gone back inside.

"I think we should go inside, too," Noelle finally said as she lowered her arms from around Nicholas's neck.

Nicholas looked down at her flushed face. Her lips were slightly swollen and wet. "You are still standing under the mistletoe," he finally said with a smile. "Should we try for the other eleven times?"

She gave him a devilish look. "I will not deny that I enjoy kissing you, Nicholas, but we must—" She stopped, reaching up to touch the side of his face.

He caught her hand and kissed her palm, then bent down and kissed her once more. "It is probably foolish to admit," he whispered, "because one day we will not stop with a kiss. Someday, we will discover just what happens when a spark of fire ignites."

Desire, something Noelle had never experienced, left her frightened, but also curious. She had never dreamed she could feel passionate toward someone . . . but Nicholas was the wrong someone. Yet, she couldn't stop these feelings. Nicholas stared at her as if his statement should frighten her, but he had to learn that she was not the weak female he thought she was.

Noelle liked a good challenge.

"Until that day, milord," she finally said, then turned and started up the stairs.

ELEVEN

Once inside the Great Hall, Noelle could see that everyone was ready to celebrate the feast. They stood in several groups, talking excitedly. Their work this day had made everything festive.

Carolyn and Isabelle met Noelle as soon as she entered the gaily decorated room.

"It is almost time. We must take our seats at the table," Carolyn said.

"It took you a long time to walk that short distance from the chapel," Isabelle commented.

"I was talking," Noelle replied vaguely. She couldn't help looking back toward the door to see if Nicholas had entered the hall and was coming her way.

He was not.

He didn't so much as glance her way as he strode to the other end of the long table.

Finally, the hall grew quiet as they waited for First Foot. Before the feast could begin, the season had to be ushered in.

Suddenly, the King's Surveyor shouted, "Wassail!" to everyone in the room. Then he stepped over to the high table where the king and queen sat.

"May the feast begin, sire?" the surveyor shouted so that everyone in the hall could hear him.

King Arthur shook his head, and then he stood and said, "No. First Foot must first cross the Christmas threshold!"

From the rear of the hall, a voice sounded. "I am here, sire!" A tall and lanky dark-haired jester smiled. First Foot began to dance and half-skip toward the front of the room. His ankle bells jingled and jangled merrily as he danced around the high table.

Finally First Foot danced his way over to a green line that had been marked on the floor to represent a threshold. On one side was Christmas joy, which must be invited inside. "Should I jump?" he asked them as he danced toward the crowd and then back to the line again.

"Aye!" everyone shouted.

With a great flourish, First Foot jumped across the green line, and then danced back to the head table, where he removed his cap and bowed. Everyone at the table tossed coins into his hat.

"Now everyone will have both pleasure and good luck in the coming year," Carolyn said.

"I will take pleasure any day," Isabelle chuckled.

"Let the feast begin," King Arthur announced.

The servants brought in pork in spicy sauce, and game pies. Noelle ate but her mind kept wandering to Nicholas. How did he feel about their kiss? Apparently, he hadn't given it much thought, for he was in deep conversation with Sir Lancelot and Sir Pellias.

Once the feast was over, someone suggested they play

Blind Man's Bluff. A group of twelve, including Noelle, Isabelle, Elizabeth, and Clarisse, formed a circle.

One of the ladies said, "Who will pick the Blind Man?"

"I will choose the Blind Man as well as play," King Arthur said as he joined them. He looked around and saw that Nicholas was away in a corner, talking with men and not enjoying the activities. "Sir Nicholas, you have been chosen to play," Arthur shouted over the music being played by the minstrels.

Nicholas came, but he was still frowning when he reached Arthur.

"You do know how to play this game?" Arthur asked as he tied the blindfold around Nicholas's eyes. When the blindfold was snug, he turned Nicholas around several times and then darted back out of his reach to play the game. Each of the players took turns running up and tapping Nicholas, then darting out of the way so he couldn't catch them—that is, all but one.

Clarisse ran up and tapped Nicholas's arm but he was quick and caught her. "You are it," Nicholas said.

"But who am I?"

"Lady Clarisse," Nicholas said as he drew off his mask.

"I see that you have Lady Clarisse under the mistletoe," King Arthur said.

"Yes, you must kiss her," several of the others chimed in.

Nicholas looked at the king, sending a hidden message that made Arthur smile. Nicholas leaned down to kiss Clarisse, meaning it to be a light kiss, but

Clarisse wrapped her arms around his neck, drew him close, and kissed him long and hard.

"I'm going to see the queen," Noelle said, disgusted by Clarisse's display.

"You don't want to play anymore?" Carolyn asked.

"Nay." She had no desire to watch Clarisse fawn all over Nicholas.

Noelle made her way to Guinevere and the two of them participated in several other games. But Noelle wasn't enjoying the feast as she once had. She didn't like the fact that Nicholas had kissed someone else. She knew her response to the kiss was stupid. After all, it was just a game. But Clarisse had made sure she was near Nicholas for the rest of the night.

He hadn't come over and talked to Noelle once. As a matter of fact, it seemed that he had spoken to everyone in the room but her.

Was Nicholas avoiding her?

When the festivities were over and everyone had started for their sleeping chambers, Noelle wasn't the happiest person as she made her way down the corridor. She knew she was making herself miserable, but she also didn't know how to stop her feelings. This was all so strange and new.

Noelle had been having a pleasant dream of the kiss shared with Nicholas when someone shook her shoulder. Her eyes flew open, and she gasped as a hand clamped over her mouth.

"Shhh," a man said.

Noelle struggled to sit up and freed herself from

the man's grip. "Tristan!" she whispered impatiently. "What are you doing in my chamber?"

"Keep your voice down. I am not supposed to be here so this will have to be quick . . . I need your help."

Noelle got up and went to the fireplace to retrieve a brand, then lit a small candle. "What?"

"My squire, Gareth, is sick and William is too young," Tristan hesitated. "I need—I need you to be my squire today," Tristan said. Then he added, "You have been my squire before."

"But that was play. What is wrong with Gareth?"

"His stomach. He's retching all over the place," Tristan answered. "Please."

"You know the knights would not welcome a lady in their midst."

"They will never know. I have brought Gareth's clothes for you. You are both the same size. You can tuck your hair under this hat. No one will ever know."

Noelle looked doubtful, but admitted, "This could be enjoyable, but none of the lord knights will like it if they discover me," she said as she slipped the braies on under her gown.

"Then do not let them discover that you are a woman. No one will ever know. It's just for today. I'm sure that Gareth will be better by tomorrow," Tristan said. Then, with a smile, he asked, "Did you know that King Arthur is going to knight me today?"

Noelle's head snapped up. She smiled. "I had not heard thus. At least now I can be there." She went over and hugged her brother. "I am proud of you."

"It is about time I made a name for myself. Cranborne belongs to John. I need to find my own holding."

Noelle nodded. It was really unfair that Tristan hadn't inherited Cranborne since he was better suited to run the castle, but she had no control of the rules which had been established long before her birth. "You are up early. Have you not slept?"

"Nay, I have been in the chapel, purifying my soul." He grinned. "According to you, I have had need of purifying for a long time. Now I must go back to the chapel. I only left when William came to tell me about Gareth," Tristan said and started to leave, but stopped. "I will not be the wealthiest knight, but after a few quests, perhaps I will bring riches to Cranborne."

"Then I will not have to marry?"

A look of tired sadness passed over Tristan's features. "Do you not care for Sir Gavin?"

At least she knew this brother cared for her feelings. "Turn your back so I can finish dressing."

Tristan did so, but said, "You did not answer my question."

"Sir Gavin is a good man and a good knight, I judge, but . . ."

"But?"

Noelle sighed. "I do not have feelings of love for him. Nor he for me, I wager."

"Aye," Tristan said with a knowing nod and then added in a low, composed voice, "you love another."

"Nay," Noelle said, not certain she was telling the truth. "You may turn around again. What makes you say such?"

"I have seen the way you look at Sir Nicholas."

How could her brother think such a thing? Had she done something that led him to believe she had feeling for Nicholas? Did anyone else at court think such as well?

Just how had she looked at Nicholas?

Noelle felt her face turning hot. "I-I have made friends with him."

"And I've known *you* all your life . . . you don't look at Sir Nicholas as a woman does a friend. I think you have found the one you have sought all these years."

Noelle sank to the only chair in her chamber and sighed. "You're correct. I have tried not to think of Nicholas at all, but he creeps into my thoughts when I know I should be thinking of Sir Gavin. If that is the way of a woman in love, then it's so." Noelle sighed again. "But he doesn't love me, so it's hopeless," she said. Then she pulled on her shoes.

"Nicholas is the hardest and bravest of all the knights. I know you have heard of his reputation with women."

"Aye, I have heard. So you do not care for him?"

"On the contrary, I admire Sir Nicholas greatly, and I wish I could be brave and fierce like him. He has that strength and coldness of feeling that makes him invincible," Tristan said. "That same coldness allows him to dally with women and leave them without a backward glance. You must be careful that he does not use you in the same manner and break your heart."

"There is nothing I can do. I cannot make Nicholas

love me if he does not. And then there is also Sir Gavin . . ." Noelle shook her head and placed her hands over her ears. "I don't want to talk of this now." She rose abruptly.

"What is all the noise?" Isabelle called as she stumbled into the chamber, followed by Carolyn, who was yawning.

"Tristan. We are not dressed!" Carolyn shrieked. She crossed her arms over the front of her shift. "What are you doing in Noelle's room?"

"That is why I am leaving," Tristan said with a smile. "I will see you later, Noelle."

"Noelle, why are you dressed as a lad?" Isabelle asked.

"I am going to be Tristan's squire for today," Noelle said as she tucked the last stray tendril up under her cap. "Will you both pretend that I am sick or in bed so that I won't be expected at breakfast or on the viewing stand today?"

"You get to have all the fun," Isabelle complained.

Noelle gave her a devilish smile. "It is necessary."

Once outside, the crisp air completely wiped the cobwebs from Noelle's sleepy brain. She liked the freedom her braies gave her. It was nice not having skirts swirling around her legs with each step she took.

She knew what she needed to do when she reached Tristan's pavilion. She had to prepare his armor. Tristan would have to take the cleansing bath after he left the chapel.

Noelle went into the empty tent where she retrieved Tristan's armor and moved it to a small stool outside of the tent. She also picked up a small tub of bear grease. Taking a seat on the small stool, she propped the shield up against her leg and started rubbing the metal with a cloth.

A half-hour later Tristan came strolling by. "How are you doing?" he asked as he ducked into the tent.

"Fine."

"I will be back soon," Tristan said as he came out of the pavilion. "William went with Gareth to the castle. Matilda said she had something that would stop his retching. Will you be all right until I return? As in staying out of trouble?"

"Yes, sir." She gave him a wink.

"Good. Now be a good squire and have that armor polished and ready by the time I return," Tristan instructed. Then he smiled as she frowned and threw the rag at him.

Noelle grabbed another cloth and started polishing in small circles. She knew she could do the duties of a squire, but holding her tongue against her brother's teasing would be another matter. She knew it was customary to treat squires as though they were unimportant. But she was still Tristan's sister, and he'd best not forget the fact.

She took sand and sprinkled it on the cloth and then rubbed it into the metal until it was very smooth and shone brightly in the sun. Next she took a glob of bear grease and smeared it on the armor and shield so the lances would slide off.

Now, she needed to sharpen Tristan's sword, but

she could not find the sandstone. She saw another squire two tents down, and decided to see if she could borrow his sandstone.

Noelle realized as she neared the lad that he was Nicholas's page. Not knowing his name, she bluffed, "Cannot find my sandstone. Mind if I use yours?"

"Morning, Gareth. Sure, it's on the table by Sir Nicholas's bed," the lad said, then pointed. "Drag up another stool and ye can sharpen the sword here."

Noelle nodded, then ducked into the tent only to come up short. "S-Sir Nicholas," she said, disguising her voice. "I did not know you were in here. I-I came to get the sandstone." Noelle kept her head tilted so he couldn't see her face, but she could definitely see him from beneath her lashes. He was moving around in his braies and had yet to put on his tunic. His wide chest was sprinkled with crisp, dark hair. She could plainly see the muscles she'd only felt beneath the fabric of his clothing the night they had spent together in the forest hut. The strength in his upper arms was very evident now that she was this close, and his broad shoulders carried the scars of battle. There was one long mark on his right shoulder that looked as if it must have been very painful. She longed to reach out and touch it.

"Have you grown deaf this morning?" Nicholas asked.

Noelle realized she'd been staring at him, forgetting that she was a lad. He was holding the stone out to her, and she had yet to take it from him. Worse, she couldn't tear her gaze away from his body. He was something fine to look upon.

"I beg your pardon, sir," she said, bowing to keep him from seeing her face. Noelle quickly covered the distance between them and took the stone, still keeping her chin down. She thought she'd managed to escape safely, but as she turned to leave, Nicholas swatted her on the backside. She gasped.

"Thou needs to be alert today, Gareth, for it is Tristan's big day. Are you all right? You seem different."

"I will try to be more alert, sir," Noelle said as she ducked back out of the tent before he could ask any questions. Quickly, she perched on the stool and finished sharpening the sword.

"You did not tell me Sir Nicholas was in there," she hissed in a very low voice that Nicholas would not hear.

"Should it matter, Gareth? I thought ye and Sir Nicholas fared well?"

Drat. She'd forgotten who she was pretending to be. It shouldn't matter that she'd seen the man half-dressed. It shouldn't matter that her blood ran through her body at twice the speed it normally did, just from looking at Sir Nicholas. "He just surprised me, that is all," she said lamely.

The squire nodded, and Noelle was grateful that he had apparently accepted her explanation.

The sword was easy enough to sharpen, but the spear-point would be a little more difficult. As Noelle picked up the spear, Nicholas emerged from the tent.

"Ector, I am going to check on the preparation for the knighting ceremony. Do you have everything ready for practice? I need to make up for the time I lost when I was ill."

"Aye," Ector said. "Ye missed several days with the fever. Dirk said yer sickness was not all that unpleasant, though, with the Lady Noelle tending to ye." Ector grinned.

"Dirk has been mouthy of late. What did he say?"

"Well—" Ector hesitated.

"Ector!" Nicholas sent him a look that brooked no argument.

"Dirk said the beautiful lady took care of ye, so if ye had died, at least ye'd have gone happy." Ector chuckled.

Nicholas frowned. "I think Dirk must need more to do if he has time to gossip like a woman. I will see what I can arrange to keep him busy," Nicholas said and turned to Noelle. "That spear-point is tricky. You must hold it correctly. Here, let me show you," Nicholas said as he moved behind Noelle and placed his arms around her shoulders. He showed her the right angle to hold the spear-point. "Like this."

Unable to speak for the trembling she felt within, Noelle nodded.

When Nicholas straightened, he gave her a curious look and Noelle held her breath.

"Have you been to the castle to see Lady Noelle today? You smell like her roses."

Now what was she going to say? "Aye. I went with Tristan this morning. She is ill."

"What is wrong with her?"

Did he sound worried? Nay, his concern was just her hopeful imagination. Why had Dirk teased Nicholas about her? It was evident he didn't like it. Then she remembered the kiss. Nicholas didn't seem to have a problem with kissing her.

"Gareth, are you daft today?" Nicholas asked, the impatience evident in his voice.

"I do not know, sir," Noelle rushed to say. "She just feels poorly and wishes to rest in bed. That is all that Tristan said. Perhaps it is one of those womanly maladies."

"I see," Nicholas said. He frowned, then turned and started for the berfrois—the spectator stands.

"Do not mind him," Ector said as he watched Nicholas stride away. "He has been grumpier than usual this day."

"Do you know why?"

"Dirk said it was because of the fever." Ector laughed as if he remembered something Dirk had said. "Dirk was angry yesterday. He said Sir Nicholas must have been touched by the fever. I said, 'Why don't ye tell him?' " Ector chuckled again. "No one would make the mistake of telling such a thing to Sir Nicholas. Not if he wished to see another day."

This time Noelle laughed. "Dirk is brawny enough to speak his mind to Nicholas."

"Aye, and well enough he does," Ector said. "But he is also wise enough to know when not to test Nicholas's temper. That could be worse than tangling with a live, fire-breathing dragon."

Noelle looked at the spear's edges, then tested it with her finger. "I think I have finished." When she glanced up, three ladies were walking their way.

"Ector," Lady Clarisse said in a silky voice. "Where is Sir Nicholas? I must talk to him."

This was the first time Noelle had a chance to really look at Clarisse. They had been in the same room several times, but had never officially been introduced. Clarisse was very pretty with long, brown hair braided down her back and held loosely with ribbons. She appeared so feminine and ladylike and perfect that Noelle could not understand why Nicholas did not desire the lady.

"Sir Nicholas has gone over to the jousting field, milady," Ector said.

"Then I shall go and see him," Lady Clarisse said as she walked off.

Noelle had the strangest desire to scratch the woman's eyes out. It was an odd feeling, one she'd never experienced before, but in her position as Tristan's squire she could do nothing but let her go.

Noelle got to her feet, thanked Ector, and then went back to Tristan's tent. But as she walked away her gaze was on Lady Clarisse, who stood speaking to Nicholas.

He nodded several times, then took Clarisse's elbow and led her back toward the castle.

A knot formed in Noelle's throat as she watched Nicholas walk off with another woman. It was silly, she knew. Guinevere had said that he cared nothing for Clarisse, but for some reason Noelle was ignoring any logical thoughts. All she could think was that Nicholas was touching Clarisse and not her. Why did he have to walk back with her? Had he changed his mind about the lady? After kissing Noelle last night, had he found her lacking so much that he now wanted Clarisse?

This feeling . . . it was not one Noelle cared for. Her stomach felt as if it were twisted in a knot.

When she reached the tent, Tristan stepped out. He was dressed in garments of pure white made especially for the occasion, making her forget about her anger for the moment.

"Tristan. You are beautiful," Noelle said as she stared at her brother.

He frowned. "Noelle, men are bold. They are brave, but they are not beautiful."

Noelle laughed, releasing some of her tension. "If you say so. Shall I walk with you?"

"Aye. Just remember, you are my squire and not my sister."

"I will be dutiful and will walk at least one step behind you at all times, dear brother."

They marched in between the pavilions to the jousting fields. A platform had been set up next to the berfrois. As they approached, trumpets blared and the king stepped up on the platform. The priest stood beside him. Father John held Tristan's sword, which had been blessed the night before in the chapel.

The other knights cheered Tristan as he stepped in front of the king. Noelle stood back with the other squires and pages and watched the other knights, who seemed truly happy for her brother. And she couldn't be prouder. Tears sprang to her eyes as Tristan knelt before the king. Noelle blinked several times, trying to keep back the tears. A squire would never weep like a girl.

The king raised the hilt of his sword with its tip pointed toward heaven. Arthur extended his arms, and Tristan kissed the hilt of his own sword. Next Arthur lowered the blade and set it on Tristan's right shoulder. "Do you swear to be gentle to the weak and courageous before the strong?"

"I swear, sire."

"Do you swear to be terrible to the wicked and the evildoer?"

"I swear, sire."

Arthur placed the blade on Tristan's other shoulder. "Do you swear to defend the helpless and hold all women as sacred?"

"I swear, sire."

"And lastly, do you swear to be gentle in deed, pure in friendship, and faithful in love?"

Noelle sighed. Faithful in love? If Nicholas loved her, would he be faithful? Through all that she'd heard, the prospect of such a thing didn't sound likely. But Nicholas was a knight of the Round Table, and he'd taken the same oath. Her brother's voice interrupted her thoughts. "I swear, sire."

"I hereby dub you Tristan of Cranborne. Rise, Sir Tristan."

Noelle kept her head bent so no one could see her tears as she made her way to retrieve Tristan's horse.

When she returned, she held the horse's bridle and waited as the king gave the *colée*—an open-handed whack—knocking Tristan completely off his feet. The *colée* was given to each knight so he wouldn't forget the oath just administered.

She kept the horse steady as Tristan mounted and

reached down for the reins. Noelle gave him a small smile, then handed him his lance and shield. He nodded, turned, and galloped toward the end of the field to the cheers of the other knights.

As Noelle stood watching her brother, Dirk came up behind her. He slapped her on the back, nearly knocking the breath from her. The man didn't know his own strength.

"He'll make a fine one," Dirk said.

Noelle took a deep breath. "Aye," she said in a low voice.

"I am surprised his sister is not present."

"Heard she was feeling poorly," Noelle said.

"It is probably best. At least Nicholas will keep his mind on his training."

Noelle wanted to smile. Did she really have such an effect on Nicholas? She would like to ask Dirk more, but couldn't without him figuring out she was no lad. "I like Lady Noelle."

"What happened to yer voice, lad? Is yer voice changing? Yer starting to sound like a lass."

"Sick," Noelle mumbled. "I must leave," she said as she slipped away from Dirk. She did glance at Tristan, who was attacking the quintain, a dummy fashioned of chain mail covered with a shield and set on a post for the knight to practice with. The other knights were mounting their destriers, too, so they could join in the practicing.

Noelle hadn't been paying attention to where she was going, and ran into Nicholas. "Sorry, sir," she said, quickly averting her head.

Nicholas swatted her backside as he passed by her.

"Good job, lad. Keep up the good work, and mayhap you will be a knight one day." He didn't wait for her reply, but kept moving toward the field.

Noelle watched his back. Such a strong back, she thought. Then she smiled. What would Nicholas say if she pulled off her hat and challenged him at his own game?

It was a shame that she lacked the nerve to find out.

TWELVE

The feast had been long tonight, celebrating Tristan's knighthood. Now, back in her room, she could relax.

It was a good thing that Noelle had learned to be self-sufficient because Isabelle had drunk a little too much wine and probably couldn't help Noelle undress if her life depended on it.

Noelle had dismissed them so Carolyn could help Isabelle. She smiled at the thought of her ladies-in-waiting, and she could still see that silly grin on Isabelle's face.

Noelle was preparing to undress by herself when someone rapped at her chamber door. Quickly, she retied her belt and went to the door to find a servant who looked most agitated.

"Mi-milady," the maid stammered, then paused. "I am sorry to disturb you, but a man named David bears news for you from Cranborne."

"Lead the way," Noelle said as she pulled the door closed and followed the maid back to the Great Hall.

She spotted David, pacing the floor, and an apprehensive shiver went up her spine. The moment David saw her, he quit his pacing and turned to her, his expression grim.

"Sir Meleagant's army is approaching Cranborne!" David blurted out.

King Arthur had just entered the Great Hall. "Sire." David bowed before the king. "Meleagant is preparing to attack Cranborne. I asked for Sir Tristan, but they said he was not here. Sir John said I had to find Sir Tristan and Lady Noelle."

"It cannot be," Noelle interrupted David's rambling. "We were told he had attacked the south."

"All I can tell you, milady, is that there were many soldiers, and they carried Meleagant's banner. Sir John sent me for help. Tristan must return and bring anyone else we can find."

"I have sent a messenger for Tristan," the king said. "He has already returned to his pavilion."

"I must go, too," Noelle said.

King Arthur crossed his arms and rubbed his bearded chin thoughtfully. "This is the third such attack," he said. "Sir Gavin has yet to return from the south, so I have no report of what has transpired. Evidently, Meleagant sent some of his men to one location while he attacked elsewhere. I wonder what game he is about."

Just then, Tristan and Nicholas swept into the Great Hall, answering the king's summons. Neither had changed the clothes they had worn to the feast and both were still a little in their cups.

Arthur motioned for both to join them.

"Sire," Tristan said as he greeted the king with an unsteady bow.

"You wish to see us, sire?" Sir Nicholas asked.

"Cranborne is under attack!" Noelle blurted out.

"Is this true, David?" Tristan asked. "Who?"

"I just told you it was," Noelle snapped but her brother ignored her as all men ignored women.

"It was Meleagant! I saw his Golden Stag banner," David said.

"Then we shall ride," Tristan said, pulling himself together.

"You lack sufficient soldiers," Arthur said. "Nicholas and his men shall ride with you. If you find that you need more men, dispatch a messenger."

"By your leave," Nicholas said as he bowed, preparing to go. He, too, had sobered quickly.

"I shall go with you," Noelle said in a loud voice aimed to gain their attention.

"Nay," Nicholas said, looking sharply at her. "It is too dangerous for a woman."

"But they are my people," Noelle insisted.

"Lady Noelle is right," King Arthur interjected. "She should go, but kept safely away from the fighting. Again, send word if you need reinforcements, but I know from your past battles that you always get the job done. I am going to make certain that Camelot is well protected. If I know Meleagant, he could be planning yet another surprise attack. He has always wanted Camelot."

Nicholas said nothing as he leveled his gaze on Noelle. She shivered. He showed absolutely no emotion as a coldness settled in his eyes. Noelle realized that he was very angry at her boldness, but she was just as determined as he. He would have to learn that he couldn't always have his way.

Tristan bowed. "I will watch after my sister, sire."

"Let me get my cloak and I will meet you in the bailey," Noelle said, then hurried to her chamber.

Back in her room, Noelle fetched her cloak and slipped it on. "Isabelle. Carolyn," she called, wishing she didn't have to wake them, but they would be worried if she didn't.

Her ladies-in-waiting came stumbling sleepily into the room.

"A-are we going somewhere, milady?" Isabelle asked as she smothered a yawn.

"Nay. I merely needed to tell you I am riding to Cranborne. It is under attack. I will be back as soon as possible, or I will send for you."

"Be careful, milady," Carolyn said.

"Is Sir Gavin back?" Isabelle asked as she placed her hand on the wall to steady herself. "Is he going with you?"

"Nay," Noelle said as she walked through the door.

"Then what is the use of going?" Isabelle yelled at Noelle's back. "Our army is not large."

"Sir Nicholas is going with us."

"Oooo," Isabelle said.

Noelle didn't bother to stop, but hurried down the hall. She could well imagine the smirk on Isabelle's face, but it was nothing like Isabelle imagined.

Ever since Noelle had kissed Nicholas, he didn't seem to know that she lived.

* * *

Prince Meleagant sat upon his horse on a small hill facing Cranborne Castle. The Prince of Death frowned. "This could have been easy. Now Sir John will pay the price for going against me."

"What did he do?" Meleagant's first-in-command asked. "I thought you wanted the castle."

"Aye. But I thought to take it without a fight," Meleagant growled. Then he added, "John once promised his sister to me, and then Cranborne would fall under my protection. Instead, he found Arthur's offer more appealing." Meleagant blew out his breath in disgust. "John is such a weakling. Look how he has let the castle run down since his father's death. He does not deserve to live. Now that he has betrayed me, his life will be short.

"It is a shame. I think I would have liked to have had the tender Noelle." Meleagant turned in his saddle and raised his hand. "Attack! Burn everything to the ground!"

Nicholas's small army had ridden all night. Now the sun began to streak the earth with bright orange, adding some measure of warmth, but it was still cold enough to see one's breath in the morning air.

Noelle could smell the smoke before they actually rode to the top of the hill. A dark, hazy cloud surrounded Cranborne and made her breath catch in her throat as she rode up beside her brother. "This does not look good."

"We are too late," Tristan said. "Meleagant has won."

"Aye," Nicholas agreed. "We will have to retake the castle." Nicholas turned and motioned for Dirk to join them at the crest of the hill.

"Take half the men and attack from the back side. We will have the archers shoot first in hopes of clearing a path for us to scale the walls."

"Wait! There is a secret entrance on the back wall of the castle," Noelle said. "If we can go in with a few men and surprise the gatesmen, we can gain entrance through the main gate and save lives."

Nicholas looked at her. "We?"

"I can be of help," Noelle insisted.

"What entrance do you speak of, my dear sister?" Tristan asked.

"The queen's entrance."

Tristan frowned. "That entrance has been barred for years."

"Partially. I have gone through there many times. I can show you."

"Nay," Nicholas said firmly. "You will stay here at the edge of the trees. Tristan can show us the way."

"But I can shoot a bow and arrow as well as any man," Noelle protested.

Nicholas twisted and looked at her. His expression was one of pained tolerance. "I said you would remain behind. And you will. If I have to tie you to a tree to keep you safe, that can be arranged."

Noelle looked at her brother. "Are you going to let him talk to me thus?"

"Only if I agree with him," Tristan said with a smile.

Noelle clamped her mouth shut as the men planned

on how best to attack the castle, completely ignoring her.

Shortly, Tristan and Nicholas rode away, taking several men with them.

As soon as they were on their way, Noelle would do as she pleased. They could issue all the orders they wanted, but she would not obey any of them.

Half the men remained on the hilltop where they waited for the others to circle the castle and hope to gain entrance.

The time dragged by as Noelle waited. It pained her not to be in the middle of the action. She could hear the cries of the soldiers as they appeared behind the allures, the catwalks behind the high walls; she could smell the smoke and taste the fire while the bowsmen prepared to fire their arrows.

There had to be fighting in the castle. Would Nicholas and Tristan be safe? Noelle worried. They had taken only a handful of men. The frustration of not knowing allowed her to imagine all kinds of horrible things. What if Nicholas were mortally wounded?

Tears sprang to Noelle's eyes. No. She wouldn't think that way. She had just found him. He couldn't be taken away from her so soon.

She turned. The second wave of men were preparing to leave.

"Quick, give me your longbow and arrows," Noelle asked one of the horsemen.

He protested, but the expression on Noelle's face brooked no argument. "I will be using a sword and my shield," he finally said. He jerked the bow over his head and tossed it to her. "I must be off." He rode hard to catch the other men, who were now advancing on the castle.

A hail of arrows rattled down from the walls of the castle. Nicholas's soldiers also shot their arrows over the wall, hoping to catch some of the men on the catwalks.

The drawbridge crashed to the ground. Now men could advance and join the melee, but first they'd have to fight their way to the bridge, and into the castle. The advantage was still with Meleagant's men. They were well protected behind the walls.

Three hundred horsemen surged forward. Fireballs rained down upon them, mingled with arrows, as the knights advanced, holding up their shields for protection.

For two and a half hours, the grim battle waged on. Then finally, Nicholas's men were able to scale the walls as the other half surged through the gate.

Noelle could stand the wait no longer; she nudged her horse forward. She wouldn't stand by and do nothing when she knew she could be of assistance.

When the ballistas started firing the five-foot-long wooden darts that could penetrate armor, Noelle decided to try the back side of the castle where she was reasonably certain she would be safe. She'd leave Thor in a protected area of the woods, then enter the castle.

Traveling along the edge of the woods, she remained at a safe distance. Soon she reached the trees and tied her horse. As she turned, she heard a noise and looked up. Boots was perched high in a tree, staring down at her. Noelle smiled. Strange that she hadn't noticed the falcon before. Evidently, Boots had been following them the entire time. But why wasn't the bird keeping an eye out for Nicholas instead of being here with her?

"I hope you are not stuck in yonder tree," Noelle said and then hurried to the old brown door.

The tunnel was dark. She hadn't thought about that. Usually she came from the other way and had the light from a torch. Well, no matter—she would have to make do.

Noelle slung the longbow and pouch over her shoulder and carefully started down the long, dark corridor. She ran her hand along the damp wall to keep her bearings. Halfway in, she was completely surrounded by darkness and had to take several deep breaths not to panic and turn back. She must keep moving.

Finally, she bumped into the door at the end, and she knew she had made it to safety. But how to remain as such, she thought to herself. She darted across the solar and out onto a balcony so she could see what was happening.

There in the bailey, fighting was everywhere. She could hear the sound of broadswords clanging as they struck the upraised shields. Then she saw Nicholas. He was in the very middle of the melee, fighting two men at once. Blood slung through the air every time he slashed his sword. But he didn't see the man approaching him from behind.

Noelle gasped as she realized the danger. Thank God she had brought the bow and arrow.

She dropped her pouch and quickly selected an arrow and positioned it in the bow. Pulling the bowstring back, she said a quick prayer that her aim would be true. If she missed the other man, she'd hit Nicholas.

Her hands trembled.

She took a deep breath.

She could do this, she told herself sternly. She had to.

Pulling the bowstring back taut, she released the string and sent the arrow whistling though the air.

She held her breath.

Nicholas swung his sword mightily through the air, downing the two men in front of him, then turned to see one of Meleagant's men fall at his feet with an arrow protruding from his back. Nicholas glanced up and saw Noelle standing on the balcony, bow in hand. She had killed for him, he thought in disbelief.

She had also disobeyed, he realized with a frown.

Before he could do anything about Noelle's disobedience, Nicholas was assaulted from his left and he was forced to fight once again. Where was Meleagant? Nicholas had been fighting for hours and had yet to see the cur.

But he'd find him before this day was through.

Noelle felt a surge of satisfaction as she watched Nicholas return to battle. He might not like what she'd done, but she had undoubtedly saved his life.

The ungrateful fool!

She was getting ready to fire another arrow when

suddenly a hand clamped around Noelle's neck. She screamed with alarm as she fought off the attacker. Spinning around, she came face-to-face with Meleagant.

"I see the little bird has returned to the nest," he said with a vicious smile as he tightened his hold painfully on her arms.

"You filthy pig. You will be defeated this day," Noelle gasped defiantly and tried to twist from his hands.

Meleagant shrugged. "If so, it will be a small defeat. I have other men," he simply said. "Do you know that your brother once promised you to me?"

Horror ran through her. "It is not true," she screamed, protesting the horrid thought.

"I would but let you ask him. However, Sir John can no longer speak."

She didn't know what Meleagant had done to her brother. Probably tied and gagged him and threw him in the dungeon. She was sure he'd hurt John. "You filthy pig," Noelle spat at Meleagant.

He slapped her hard across the face.

Noelle screamed. She beat on Meleagant's chest with her balled fists, but it had little effect as he dragged her into the solar.

Nicholas had just finished his opponent when he heard Noelle's screams. He glanced up at the solar just in time to see Meleagant dragging her back inside.

God's tooth, if she had only stayed in the woods as he'd told her.

Nicholas ran and grabbed his sword from the man he'd just struck down, then fought his way across the bailey toward the castle.

Just before entering the doorway of the Great Hall, he glanced back and noticed that his men now had the upper hand. Good, he thought, and darted into the hall, taking the stairs two at a time to the solar. He could hear Noelle's screams and that not only fueled his anger, but something odd as well. The muscles of his forearms hardened, and his chest felt as if it would explode before he could get to her.

Nicholas burst into the room to find Meleagant on top of Noelle, his hand up her skirt. "Get off her or die as you are," Nicholas grated out angrily as he swung at Meleagant.

Meleagant rolled to his feet and withdrew his sword. "At last The Dragon and The Death Prince meet," Meleagant sneered as he lunged at Nicholas.

Nicholas was quick and barred Meleagant's sword, forcing the blow down to the ground. The two knights came at each other with the fearlessness of falcons. Noelle held her breath, praying that Nicholas would be the victor.

Steel rang against steel.

Sword sought flesh.

They fought eagerly, giving and taking great blows. Nicholas would land several hard blows and it looked like he was gaining the upper hand, but Meleagant fought back.

The fighting was fierce and endless. Finally Nicholas knocked the sword from Meleagant's hand and held the tip of his sword to the cur's throat.

Noelle shut her eyes. She couldn't bear to see Nicholas take the life of another man. She didn't realize she had squealed, but the next thing she knew, an arm went around her neck and she was hauled up against Meleagant, a sharp dagger point at her throat.

How had Meleagant gained the upper hand?

"Now, great knight, I suggest you stand back before I spill forth this fair damsel's blood."

Immediately, Nicholas moved back and lowered his sword. "Leave her out of this. Your fight is with me."

"I think not," Meleagant said and pressed the tip of the knife against Noelle's skin, drawing blood.

Noelle whimpered from the pain. Now she was truly scared for she knew that Meleagant wouldn't hesitate to kill her, and probably take great pleasure in doing so. She tried to remain still so she wouldn't be cut again.

And she didn't want Nicholas to do anything stupid. Every time she whimpered, she could see the flash of anger in his eyes before he disguised it again with a cold glare that reminded her of death.

"I shall take her with me and if you're lucky, she will live. However, I just might take her for my wife and then this land will be mine legally."

"You forget her brothers," Nicholas said. Noelle could see his jaw clenched. Other than that, he showed little emotion. "Noelle is promised to another."

"Her brother promised her to me first," Meleagant said.

Noelle gasped. This could not be true. Was there no one her brother had not tried to marry her to? She was so angry that she forgot about the knife as she spat, "I would die before I would marry you."

"And you just may," Meleagant said as he dragged her to the door, the knife still pressed against her throat. He swung around and glared at Nicholas. "We will meet again, sir knight, and next time I will take the time to defeat you."

Nicholas took a step forward. "Why not stay and finish it now?"

"I fear I might be outnumbered in a few moments," Meleagant stated and then, with a curt nod, he slammed the door.

THIRTEEN

Noelle tried to keep up with Meleagant as he raced down the corridor that had once been so beautiful. Now tapestries either lay on the floor or hung by a single nail. She didn't fight Meleagant or try to pull away because he'd threatened to slit her throat if she gave him any trouble.

When she stumbled, Meleagant dragged her, jerking on her arm. She had no doubt that if she fell flat on her face, he would drag her by the hair. She meant nothing to him except a means of escape.

Once outside, they ran along the catwalk on the stone wall to a spot where Meleagant didn't bother to stop. He jumped over the wall, taking Noelle with him.

She screamed as they tumbled through the air, hoping death would soon claim her. But she was not that lucky, for they landed in a wagon full of hay that had been placed conveniently ahead of time for Meleagant's getaway.

Noelle didn't have time to think of escaping, for Meleagant was pulling her off the wagon, scattering hay all around them. A horse that had been readied for the escape stamped impatiently nearby.

Meleagant mounted and yanked Noelle up onto the horse in front of him. She had barely gained her seating when he spurred the horse. Not a moment too soon, as a shower of arrows rained down upon them.

Red-hot pain struck Noelle. She screamed and clutched at the spot. Looking down, she saw that one of the arrows had caught her in the thigh.

She moaned at the pain. It did no good.

Meleagant didn't stop. Apparently, he didn't care that she'd been hurt, for he kept heading for the woods and safety.

Once they had made it safely into the shelter of the forest, Meleagant reached down and jerked the arrow from her leg. "It is just a flesh wound," he grumbled. "Do not make a fuss."

Noelle wanted to strike out at the beast, but blessedly, she fainted and knew no more.

Nicholas stared at the closed door. He had never been so frightened. He had actually stopped breathing, and for a moment everything seemed to stand still.

There had only been one other time in his life when he had felt thus, and that had been when he was a boy in a burning castle. He thought he'd lost the ability to feel after that awful day.

He had been dead inside for years . . . until today.

To stand helplessly by and watch Meleagant drag Noelle from the room was not a feeling he liked. Unbearable guilt stabbed at Nicholas. Noelle's whimper had distracted him, giving Meleagant the upper hand. Could he have thrown himself down on Meleagant?

What Nicholas really wanted to do was pick up his sword and run the cur through. But the dagger against Noelle's milky-white throat had left Nicholas with little choice. He vowed, if Meleagant hurt Noelle in any way, there would be no place in the kingdom that the cur could hide.

For Nicholas would find him. He would hunt him down like a rabid dog, and then take pleasure in torturing him.

But what if Meleagant killed Noelle? A cold shiver ran up Nicholas's spine and a heavy feeling of dread formed in the pit of his stomach.

He would not allow that to happen!

Nicholas snatched his sword from the floor and raced out of the castle. He ran across the bailey, leaping over the bodies that lay sprawled on the ground, either dead or dying. He did not notice, nor did he care, that his men seemed to have the situation well in hand.

Tristan was fighting near the stable doors and had just finished off his opponent as Nicholas approached.

"What is wrong?" Tristan gasped, trying to regain his breath. "You look as if you could murder the next person you bumped into," Tristan said.

"And well I could," Nicholas said. His familiar mask descended once again. "Meleagant has taken Noelle hostage!"

"Then we shall go after them," Tristan said. "I will gather some men and we will follow you."

"Nay. Meleagant already has a head start. I can travel faster alone. You will be of better use by beginning the task of putting Cranborne back together. Many will be looking to you and John for help."

"Meleagant killed John," Tristan said as he followed Nicholas over to the stall.

Nicholas grabbed the first horse he came to. "I'm sorry," he said. "I would stay and help you bury John, but I fear for your sister's safety. Now that John is dead, the people of Cranborne will definitely need you. You must stay." Nicholas mounted the brown destrier. "My men will be able to help you. Does your sister know of John's death?"

"I don't think so," Tristan said, then added, "Go. I do not want the same fate for my sister," he urged, wearily sagging against the wall as if the task were too daunting to face.

Nicholas nudged his horse forward. "I will bring your sister back safe. And I will bring Meleagant's head back on my sword."

"Godspeed," Tristan called after him; then he trudged toward the castle.

As Nicholas neared the gate, he heard Dirk shout, "Where are ye going?"

"Ask Sir Tristan," Nicholas said over his shoulder, not wanting to stop and explain. "I will be back soon."

"Do you need help?" Dirk asked.

"Nay!" Nicholas shouted back. He was very capable of rescuing Noelle and murdering the bastard all by himself.

* * *

When Noelle regained consciousness, she realized that Meleagant had slowed his horse from the fast gallop they had maintained upon leaving the castle. She also realized that if she didn't get away from Meleagant he would kill her, or worse, compromise her and force her into marrying him because no one else would have her.

She wouldn't be defiled by this horrible man. And she would not allow Cranborne Castle to fall under his control. That decision made, she began to struggle, fighting for her life, her honor, and her virtue.

"Get still," he snapped.

"Never," Noelle shouted as she twisted her body violently to get out of his arms. Her jerking motions caused the horse to start sidestepping and become skittish.

Meleagant reared back to strike her, but before he could land the blow, a loud, screeching noise came out of nowhere. Noelle saw a blur as something dove at them.

The Black Knight swung his arms up over his head to fend off the attack. As soon as he did, Noelle fell backwards from the horse. It took her only a moment to regain her wits. She scrambled to get to her feet.

Meleagant bent down, trying to grab her arm. He snagged her gown instead. Noelle squealed. Then the dark blur attacked again.

She gasped at the sight before her. Boots had grabbed Meleagant's face with her talons, ripping his flesh.

Meleagant roared in pain and fury as he grabbed at his shredded cheek, but Boots showed no mercy as she dove again, this time catching the horse in the hindquarters. The horse reared, then bolted as if the Devil were after him.

Noelle couldn't believe what had just occurred. She could only stand and wonder if a miracle had really happened.

One small but very determined bird had just defeated her enemy when an army of soldiers could not. Could the falcon have remembered their adventure in the trees and was paying her back for her good deed? One thing Noelle knew for sure: she did not want Boots for an enemy.

Noelle looked around to get her bearings, then turned and started running back the way they had come. She wasn't sure that Meleagant wouldn't come after her, but if he did, his mood would be foul, and she didn't want to be anywhere within his reach. She could feel the ache in her injured leg, but she ignored the pain as she ran the best she could. She hoped her guardian bird was somewhere up above her keeping watch.

Having seen Boots in action . . . she would have the bird defend her any day.

Noelle wasn't sure how long she had run before she finally collapsed on the cold, hard ground, too tired to go any farther. Darkness was beginning to settle over the forest and the air, mild in the daylight, had taken on a decided chill. The cold seeped through her clothing and thin slippers. Sitting on the ground wasn't helping keep her warm, either. She took several deep breaths to slow her breathing as she wondered what had happened to Boots. Was she still keeping watch overhead? Noelle hadn't seen the bird since the attack.

As Noelle searched the darkening sky, she heard a noise in the distance. Was it an animal? She listened again.

Someone was coming.

Sitting still in the cold night had stiffened her joints and muscles, and Noelle struggled to get to her feet before limping off deeper into the trees. The dark shadows within the woods would hide her. She couldn't tell from which direction the rider came, but she wasn't taking any chances that it could be Meleagant.

The rider galloped past her. For some reason, Noelle looked up to see a bird soaring overhead. Boots. The rider was Nicholas, even though he rode a different horse.

"Wait. Nicholas!" Noelle shouted after him as she leapt from her hiding place in the trees. "It is Noelle. I am here."

Nicholas jerked his horse to a stop. He turned in the saddle to see what he had heard. Had it only been the wind or had he heard Noelle?

"Nicholas, I am here."

No. Not the wind. It was the Lady Noelle. Relief washed over him that he'd found her and she'd somehow managed to escape the cur.

Nicholas turned his horse and rode back toward her voice. He pulled his mount to a stop, then slid from the destrier. Nicholas had no more than touched the ground when Noelle threw herself into his arms and began to sob.

Nicholas cradled her in his embrace while he whispered a prayer of thanks that she was safe. "Shh," he crooned as he rubbed her back. "You are safe now. Did the filthy cur hurt you?"

Noelle, still sobbing, couldn't speak so she shook her head, bumping his chin.

"Where is Meleagant now?" Nicholas looked down, noting the tears that left streaks on Noelle's cheeks. Tenderly, he wiped them dry.

"He-he—" She paused, taking time to compose her thoughts. "I-I do not know where he is. Boots attacked Meleagant, and I was able to escape."

Nicholas looked at her in a peculiar way. "You jest?"

"Nay. It is too grave a matter to jest about."

A slow smile caused small creases at the corners of Nicholas's eyes. "Boots must like you. She veritably led me all the way down this path to you." Nicholas kissed the top of her head. "Let us ride back to safety." He took her elbow. "I will meet Meleagant yet another day."

Nicholas noticed Noelle's limp as she started toward the horse. "What has happened to you?"

"An arrow caught my leg," Noelle said offhandedly as if it were nothing. "I will tend the wound once we are back at Cranborne. It will be all right," she assured Nicholas, not wanting him to tear off after Meleagant and leave her out here all alone. "Now, let us ride. I long to feel the comfort of my own bed."

"Not until I check your leg to see how badly you are hurt."

"Nay. It is not decent," Noelle said, shaking her head.

"I do not care. I am going to see how bad the wound is for myself," he said and knelt down. "I will decide whether it can wait until we reach Cranborne Castle."

She didn't budge. "Do you always have to have your own way?"

"Always," he said, and not waiting for her to do so, he lifted the hem of her cotehardie all the way to her bloodstained thigh. "It's still bleeding."

"It is nothing," she insisted.

Nicholas frowned as he got to his feet, went over to his horse, removed his knife, and cut a strip of silk off his horse's trappings to use as a bandage. "This will do for now," he murmured.

When he returned, Noelle had dropped her skirt again, and he wondered how she expected him to tend her wound. She was stubborn, he'd give her that much. "If you will kindly lift your cotehardie, then I can bandage your leg to stop the bleeding," Nicholas said as he knelt in front of her.

"I still do not like this. It is most improper," Noelle protested, blushing but happy that Nicholas couldn't see it in the gathering darkness.

"Bleeding to death is not proper, either," Nicholas said.

Noelle frowned but complied with his instructions and pulled up her skirt to expose her thigh.

"You will have to spread your legs so I can bandage your wound." God's tooth! Was he mad? All his thoughts were now focused on her milky, soft skin and not just the wound. Her skin felt like silk, so smooth, so inviting. . . .

Get your mind on the wound! he warned himself as he took a deep breath, cursing his traitorous body. He wrapped her leg as quickly as possible, putting pressure on the small wound.

When Nicholas's hand brushed her leg, Noelle felt heat surge through her as a shiver rippled over her skin. His nearness was overwhelming, and she thought nothing of the pain from her wound. Nay, she was thinking about his warm flesh touching hers. She wanted so much to reach down and bury her fingers in his dark hair. Worse, she was thinking about kissing him. She couldn't help noticing the tingle of excitement she felt every time his hand passed between her thighs.

"There," Nicholas said, instantly shattering her musings as he returned to his feet. "That should stop the bleeding until we get back to Cranborne."

Noelle nodded. "Thank you," she whispered, breathless from the excitement of having him so close. If she received this kind of treatment, she would take an arrow any day. She smiled at that ridiculous thought. This man did strange things to her.

Nicholas mounted first; then he reached down, grasped her arm, and lifted her effortlessly up to the seat in front of him.

"Where is your destrier?" Noelle asked.

"I'm not sure. I took the first mount I came upon when I heard Meleagant had taken you."

Noelle adjusted her skirt as she settled herself. "I

left Thor tied to a tree. I hope no harm has come to him."

"I'm sure my men have found him and put him in the stables. Of course, if you had stayed where I instructed you, we would not be having this conversation."

"If I had stayed where you told me, you would now have an arrow in your back," she countered. "And I might still have been taken by Meleagant and had no one to come after me."

"So you acted on your own behalf. Just in case you needed to be rescued."

"Something like that."

Nicholas couldn't help but smile as he cradled the lovely young woman in his arms. She knew nothing of her place. She was determined to have the last word. Truth be told, he liked that feistiness in her.

Noelle's head rested just below his chin, so she couldn't see his smile, and that pleased him. It wouldn't do to have her know how much she affected him. He could smell the roses that now reminded him of her, and the scent nearly drove him wild.

"Have you gone to sleep, Nicholas?" Noelle prodded. "Or do you not want to admit that I saved you?"

"Your point has been made, but I had rather take the injury than have you hurt."

Noelle sighed and in a soft, hesitant voice said, "Well, I had rather have *you* safe."

Something unfamiliar and sweet ran though Nicholas, and he tightened his arm around Noelle's midriff. He was pleased by her words, for she had sought to protect him, yet his masculine pride had been wounded all the same. "Ah, Noelle, what am I to do with you?"

Anything you want, Noelle thought, but thankfully she kept her longing to herself as she rested her head on his chest. As long as Nicholas remained stubbornly silent about his feelings for her, she would not speak of love to him. Noelle continued her silence for the rest of the long journey, made more arduous by her injury. Her mind was spinning with confusion when she finally sagged against Nicholas's strong, broad chest.

It had been a long day, and she was very tired. Now that all the excitement was over, whatever measure of strength she'd had was long gone. Perhaps that was the reason for her confused thinking.

She was just tired.

But she was also very contented at the moment. Noelle rested her head against Nicholas's chest and drifted to sleep.

When they reached Cranborne, it was the middle of the night and all was quiet. Nicholas drew the borrowed horse to a halt. He hailed the castle and waited for the large portcullis to be raised. The chains rattled and woke Noelle as the gate rose slowly up, and he and his pleasant burden were admitted into the bailey.

As they rode through the dark bailey, Noelle noticed that the bodies of the dead and wounded had been taken away. All the small buildings within the castle grounds were nothing but charred rubble, and the smell of smoke lingered in the air like death as the pall of smoke hovered over the ruins. It was so late, no one was about except a guard here and there.

Nicholas rode straight to the stable where Phillip, the stableman, came out to meet them.

"You are up late," Noelle said.

"Aye. So much has happened this day, I had a hard time sleeping. It is good to have you back home. I feared you'd been lost to us when I heard that Meleagant had taken you," Phillip said as he grasped the horse's bridle. "My lord," Phillip said with a nod to Nicholas. Then he turned his attention back to Noelle. "We knew not whether you were dead or alive when Thor came wandering into the stable. He went over to his favorite stall and stood there until I let him in."

"I'm so glad you have Thor safe, and I thank you for taking such good care of him, as always. I was most worried," Noelle said. "How are you and the others faring now that Meleagant's men have been driven away?"

"Shaken, milady. I made it though the skirmish, but we lost Nigel, Frank, and several others," Phillip said, and then bowed his head. "I am sorry about Sir John."

"I want to have a word with my brother. Where is he?" Noelle asked.

Something akin to shock registered in Phillip's eyes as he looked to Nicholas. Did they know something that she didn't? She remembered that Meleagant had said something about John earlier, but she couldn't recall his exact words. She frowned at her confusion.

What had happened in her absence? A chill shuddered through her as she turned and looked at Nicholas.

"Sir John was killed by Meleagant," Nicholas finally said. "I am sorry."

Noelle gasped and covered her mouth with her hand. John was dead? True, she had been angry enough to kill him, but she'd never dreamed that he'd really been killed. Overwhelmed, she swayed, and Nicholas caught her up against him.

"I think it's far past time for you to retire, milady," Nicholas said. "You have had a most difficult day."

"Will milady be all right?" Phillip asked. His concern shone deep in his eyes.

"Aye. Your lady has had a long day, and the events have overwhelmed her," Nicholas said. "She will be much better in the morn."

When they entered the Great Hall, the guard, who happened to be one of Nicholas's men, opened the door and Nicholas stepped inside, still carrying Noelle.

"Where is your chamber?" Nicholas asked as he strode across the rushes to the stairs.

"Up the steps on the right," she pointed.

Nicholas climbed the stairs with very little effort. When he reached Noelle's chamber, he kicked open the door and headed straight for the bed. He laid her down carefully so as not to hurt her further. As he straightened, he said, "I am truly sorry about your brother."

"Thank you," Noelle replied. She propped a couple of pillows behind her back and head and watched Nicholas as he went to the hearth. "John was so different from Tristan," she said, still numbed by the news. "We were never close. I surmised from what Meleagant told me that John had promised me to Meleagant as a bride. I am beginning to wonder if John promised me to the entire Kingdom."

Nicholas, who was stooped at the fireplace stirring the embers to rekindle the fire, answered, "Nay." He glanced back over his shoulder at her with a soft smile. "He didn't promise you to me," he added with a chuckle.

Noelle gave him a weak smile. She appreciated Nicholas's attempt to take her mind off her brother's death. She and John may have had many differences, but he was still her brother.

"Be glad," Noelle finally said.

Nicholas stood. "At least, the servants thought to prepare the fire," he commented, changing the subject. "They had faith that you would return." He tossed a fresh log onto the hot embers, and sparks shot up the chimney. "We should have a roaring fire in just a moment," he said. Then he withdrew his knife and placed the tip in the fire to heat.

Noelle's eyes grew big at the sight of the long blade. "I-I know you must be tired. We can attend to my wound on the morrow. It is late."

"Nay. A wound such as yours cannot wait. I do believe that you are trying to get rid of me," Nicholas said gently as he came back to the bed.

"Nay." She smiled bravely, not knowing how to handle this different, caring Nicholas. He had actually smiled a couple of times.

"I must attend the wound tonight lest it fester."

"I know you're right," Noelle admitted. "I just dread the pain to come. I must be a bit of a coward." But at least the pain would take her mind off John's death.

"I see that you are a better physician than you are a patient."

"Agreed," Noelle said, then frowned. "I care nothing for pain."

"Well, you did such a fine job of tending me, I will see if I can return the favor. I'll promise not to cause you too much pain," he said. "If you'll remove the bandage, I shall go fetch some wine to pour in the wound."

She nodded.

Nicholas turned to leave, frowning at his small lie. He knew what he was getting ready to do to Noelle would hurt like the Devil.

Perhaps if he gave her enough wine to drink, it would dull the pain. And if he drank enough wine himself, maybe it would dull his senses.

This was going to be a very long night.

FOURTEEN

Noelle slid her gown up her leg and looked at the bandage that Nicholas had applied earlier. The blood had soaked the cloth and it was not dry blood, so she knew the wound was still bleeding. And she knew there would be no other way to stop the bleeding but to cauterize the wound.

She leaned over and retrieved her small, jeweled dagger from the bedside table, then began to cut away the bandage. Having witnessed grown men screaming when she'd cauterized their wounds, she knew what was to come and she was more than a little frightened.

Nicholas had promised not to hurt her. She knew his paltry words had been meant to comfort her, but now she didn't feel at ease at all. He'd lied. And she knew he'd lied.

She'd finally finished unwrapping most of the bindings; however, some of the material stuck to the wound, and she didn't have the strength to jerk it off. At least, not yet. The wound appeared small and would heal quickly once the bleeding was stopped, and for that she was very thankful. At least, the wound would not require stitches. Somehow, she couldn't imagine Nicholas taking nice, neat stitching. She smiled at the thought. She really couldn't picture Nicholas taking care of her at all. Perhaps he would get someone to come relieve him so he wouldn't have to perform such a task.

As if she conjured him up, Nicholas returned, carrying a bottle of wine and two gold chalices. Mary, a serving girl from the kitchen, carried a basket of supplies and a small tub of hot water.

Nicholas couldn't handle the mending; it would be left up to Mary.

"Place the water next to the fire and the basket on the bedside table," Nicholas commanded the servant.

"Will there be anything else you require, sire?" Mary asked.

"Nay. That is all for tonight," Nicholas said.

Noelle had been wrong. It seemed that Nicholas intended to care for her himself. Now she would have to be brave. She would not cry in front of him. There was more to this man than most people thought. They only saw the hard outer cover, but she was catching glimpses of the interior Nicholas, and Noelle admired his tender side. She liked what she saw.

Having poured each chalice full of dark, red wine, Nicholas handed one to Noelle. "To Cranborne," he said, lifting the goblet. "May she remain out of the enemy's hands," Nicholas toasted, touching his goblet to hers.

Noelle smiled at Nicholas's sweet toast and relaxed manner, and she finally began to relax, too, as she sipped her wine. As soon as she finished her wine, Nicholas refilled her cup and she drank that as well.

Nicholas, however, did not refill his cup. She knew she was going to need her wits dulled so she'd not embarrass herself by screaming, and he needed his mind sharp to do what lay ahead.

Nicholas looked down. "I see the bandage is stuck to your wound." He reached for one of the extra sheets that Mary had brought in and placed it under Noelle's leg. Then, he went over to the fire and dipped a cloth in the warm water. He squeezed out the excess water, then returned to Noelle.

When he placed the warm cloth over the wound, she jerked and hissed with the sudden pain, but soon she sagged back against the bed again. Nicholas was acting in a way she'd never imagined he could be. He was gentle.

"There," Nicholas said as he carefully removed the bandage. "I see that it still bleeds. It is deep." He frowned. "We will have to cauterize the wound to stop the bleeding," he said as he glanced at Noelle. She had the most magnificent green eyes—they glittered like emeralds—and the trust he saw there warmed his heart. "I am going to pour some wine on the wound. It will sting."

Noelle nodded. "It is what I would do." She jerked her leg as the wine burned when it struck the raw wound. "How did you learn the way with wounds?" she asked in a raspy voice, trying to get her mind off the pain.

"When I had no one to turn to, I learned to rely on myself. I watched how others did things." His mouth twisted wryly. "It has proven useful."

Noelle longed to reach out and touch the hurt she

had seen in his eyes only a moment before. He had so much kindness hidden beneath his gruff exterior. He wore his armor to protect himself from many things, many hurts.

"It's time," Nicholas said as he watched the many expressions flit across Noelle's lovely features.

"I am ready," she said in a soft voice that shook just a little. But Nicholas saw determination in her eyes, and he was proud of her.

Moving over to the hearth, Nicholas bent down, and with a cloth he picked up the knife and looked at the glowing tip. The knife was ready, but was he? He regretted the pain he was about to cause Noelle, but it could not be avoided.

"I will have to hold you down to keep your body from jerking. Do you need more wine?"

Noelle shook her head. Nicholas saw the fear mirrored in her eyes just before she squeezed them shut.

Nicholas took a long, drawn-out breath as he sat on the bed. Then he leaned over her middle, trying to support most of his weight on his elbow so as not to crush her with his heavier body. With his free hand, he held her thigh. He hated doing this to anyone as delicate as Noelle, but it must be done.

Taking a deep breath, he placed the hot tip of his knife against the wound. The smell of burnt skin made him wince. He removed the blade from her skin, and let his breath out. He had expected to hear Noelle utter a blood-curdling scream.

He heard none.

Finally, Noelle moaned as she reached out to hold Nicholas's back. She had actually bitten her lip until it bled to keep from screaming, but she finally had to make some kind of noise. Stars swam before her eyes, but she wouldn't pass out. She willed herself to stay alert. She must not be a weakling in front of Nicholas.

Her stomach had lurched as the fire seemed to consume her leg and reach all the way to her bones. And just when she was nearly ready to beg for mercy, it was over.

Noelle breathed a relieved sigh as Nicholas carried the knife back to the hearth. Her breaths came in rapid little gasps as she tried to calm herself. The pain was easing up some, and her breathing finally returned to normal.

Nicholas returned to sit on the bed. Noelle thought he looked as white as his tunic. He had said nothing, and he didn't look at her as he quickly wrapped the bandage around her leg.

When he was finished, his eyes finally met hers, and the concern Noelle saw in their depths amazed her.

"I believe that caused me more pain than it did you," he said, trying to lighten the moment.

"I don't think so." She managed a small smile.

"I am sorry I had to cause you pain, but there will be no more."

In a somewhat sulking voice, Noelle said, "That is what you said before."

Nicholas smiled. "I lied before. This time I speak the truth."

"Then I should trust you?"

"Aye." His voice was so husky, she shivered. "I will leave you now to sleep."

As he started to move away, Noelle reached for his arm. He swung back around and looked down at her. "Please stay with me," she whispered softly.

Had Nicholas heard her correctly? "You want me to stay?"

"Aye."

He studied her face, her cheeks wet from tears, and he saw the need in her eyes. "It would be most improper," he said with a small smile.

"I care nothing for propriety tonight," Noelle admitted. "Tonight, I need your strength," she said in such a tender tone that Nicholas couldn't deny her.

Nicholas removed his boots, then pulled back the bedding and helped her under it. He blew out the candles, then climbed into bed beside her. Nicholas pulled her into his arms, Noelle's head resting on his shoulder.

"It has been a long day," Nicholas said with a sigh.

Noelle placed her arm across him, her hand resting on his chest. "Aye. Thank you, Nicholas," she whispered before she fell asleep.

Noelle wasn't sure how long she'd slept but the pain in her thigh had eased in its intensity. She was still snuggled against Nicholas, her arm and leg thrown across him in a very unladylike manner. Slowly, she removed her leg, so as not to wake him nor cause herself a lot of pain. Then she tilted her face up so she could see him. The glow of the fireplace bathed his features with warm colors, softening the harsh lines of his face.

Nicholas was so different from anyone she'd ever known. And for some strange reason she trusted him though others said she should not. But Noelle had learned long ago to trust her own instincts.

His face was so peaceful in sleep, giving him a boyish appearance when the rest of his body suggested anything *but* a boy lying next to her.

She reached up and placed her finger on his firm chin; there was a bit of stubble where he needed to shave. Then her gaze traveled further up his face. She looked full into a pair of soft amber eyes that were open and gazing down at her.

"Is something wrong?" Nicholas whispered, his eyes never leaving hers.

"Nay," Noelle said with a smile. "For once, everything is very right," she said in a very low voice. And then the truth struck her as a battering ram would hit a door. She loved this man. Right, wrong, or indifferent . . . she loved him, and she was beginning to feel as though her insides were melting with all the feelings she had stored within her.

She knew what she had only suspected before . . . Nicholas was the one. He might not like the fact, but it had been predicted long ago by Merlin.

He belonged to her.

"What are you thinking?" Nicholas asked. "You are much too quiet."

"Are you certain you want to know?"

"Aye."

Again she raised trembling fingers to his cheek. "I

was just thinking how much I love you," she murmured.

"You know not of what you speak," Nicholas said, harshly. She could see by the tightness of his jaw that she'd irritated him.

That was not the response she'd expected. Then, she remembered that Nicholas wasn't used to being romantic. According to the rumors, he didn't have to. Women flocked to him like bees to the flowers. And now she was doing exactly the same as all the others, she realized.

But it was different, she argued with herself. Merlin had promised her that she would know when the right man came to her. She struggled to remember his exact words, and finally they came to her. . . .

You have already met your destiny, and 'twill be up to you to figure your course. Choose wisely, my child. Remember, the greatest satisfaction in life is won and not handed to you.

So, she would have to win Nicholas, Noelle remembered. She would have to melt the ice that surrounded his heart. Perhaps she could make Nicholas love her, but if he did not, it would matter not; he would with time. The only thing she knew for certain was that for now, she wanted to belong to Nicholas in whatever way he would let her. She wasn't sure if Nicholas knew how to love, but maybe, he would learn if he were shown.

Nicholas squeezed her shoulders. "You should not speak of love when it is merely gratitude that you feel for me."

She couldn't pull her gaze from his wonderful

golden eyes. "I know exactly how I feel. I have never felt this way before, but I know that the feeling is right. So don't tell me how I feel, when I have waited all my life to find exactly what I am feeling now," she stated. Her young body burned with a need that she didn't quite understand, but she knew she wanted something more. And she was determined to learn what it was all about . . . tonight.

And she wanted Nicholas to be the one to teach her.

Noelle's words slammed into Nicholas like a lance. He felt things for Noelle this night that he didn't want to feel for anyone. Noelle was so young and naive, he thought as he stroked her velvety soft shoulder.

She was also much too tempting.

Could he take her and use her as he had all the others? Nay, he could not. For she stirred something deep within him that no other woman ever had.

"I am unworthy to love," Nicholas ground out bitterly. "You had best choose another." Her eyes were so trusting that Nicholas knew he needed to say more. "I have never been faithful to any woman," he admitted, then added, "I do not want to hurt you."

"So I have heard," Noelle said and watched as Nicholas arched a brow.

"And still you tempt the beast."

"Aye," Noelle said as she looked at him with her liquid green eyes. "Maybe you have never found the right woman."

Desire exploded in Nicholas. He had never known that he could feel anything as much as he did at this very moment. He felt himself losing the coldness that had always protected him, had always kept him focused.

This was absolutely mad.

He could control men with a single glance, and yet this small woman had him completely enchanted. He should get out of bed right this very moment, he thought, as he drew Noelle up close to him so he could kiss her.

Aye, he had always been a man of stone who could handle any situation. Except, it seemed, this one woman who had started a raging fire within him.

He could kiss her. Then turn away.

He had control of his destiny.

He had a wager with the king that he wanted to win.

He could not . . . would not give up all that he sought!

Then he made the mistake of looking at the beautiful Noelle who he held protectively within his arms. Her lips were soft, full. She moistened them with the tip of her tongue as if she were waiting for him.

He groaned. God help him; he was a drowning man.

His vow of chastity made so foolishly before the king shattered. He could no longer deny what his body yearned for. And then he smelled the roses . . . those damned roses. Sir Nicholas the Dragon had just crossed into the valley from which there was no return.

"Noelle," he whispered achingly. "What have I done to deserve you?"

His lips met hers and lingered as he tasted her intoxicating essence. He explored the softness of her mouth. But he wanted more. . . .

He wanted her body, her soul.

He drew back just enough to coax her lips to part so he could deepen his kiss. Her mouth was sweet and she innocently knew how to please him with her tongue when it tangled with his. He could see in his mind's eye his tongue traveling over other parts of her body.

Oh, how he was going to enjoy showing Noelle how to make love. He deepened his kiss as a hunger in him took over, and now that it had, he couldn't wait to touch Noelle's delicate, soft skin. He began to tug on her clothing until he'd removed it all.

Accidentally, he touched her wound, and Noelle groaned. "I'm sorry, my love. I had forgotten your injury." He felt like an animal, too crazed to stop though he knew he should. Nicholas forced himself to speak. "Do you want me to stop?"

She shook her head and reached to draw his face closer to hers. "Nay, I want to kiss you."

Her sultry words made him throb with desire. He glanced at her skin, now bared to him. "You are so very beautiful," he whispered hoarsely. Her body was perfect—her waist small, her hips large enough to bear many sons.

Suddenly, he felt like a wild man. He had to have her, to possess her, to make her his own. There would be no stopping him. His tongue explored her mouth while his hand cupped her full breast. His hot kisses trailed down her neck, pausing at the soft spot on her throat. He heard her moan, and he was pleased that she responded. He wanted her to enjoy every minute of their time together. His kisses moved lower until he found what he desired. His mouth was on her breast, pulling the fullness into his mouth, then sucking the tip until her moans of pleasure grew louder. His tongue flicked both nipples until they tightened into firm little buds, and Noelle writhed beneath him.

"Nicholas, I-I," Noelle whispered.

"Just a moment now, my love," Nicholas said huskily as he left her to remove his clothes with great speed. When he turned back, he saw that she gazed lovingly at him. Her eyes had grown wide, and it made his manhood grow longer and harder and thicker.

My God, was all that Noelle could think. Nicholas was so big, like one of her brother's stallions at rut. She'd never imagined that anything could be that big! Her breath caught in her throat as wild pleasure shot through her. Could she handle him? Would he fit? She thought to ask him, but was afraid he'd laugh at her.

The light from the fire caught the blond in his hair, and his gold eyes glowed, making him look fierce, like the warrior she knew he was. Like a predatory animal. She shivered in anticipation.

He lowered himself carefully to cover her and returned his attention to her breasts. Noelle instinctively arched to his mouth as her fingers tangled in his hair. She had never imagined that anything could feel so wonderful, so right. Heat engulfed her, and a strangeness that she couldn't quite name was in the pit of her stomach. Then Nicholas began to move, sliding lower across her stomach until his mouth was at the juncture of her legs.

Noelle gasped. What was he doing? She squirmed to get away from him.

"Don't," he commanded, then added, softly, "let me show you pleasure you have never imagined." She could feel his breath on her thighs. "Let me love you, Noelle."

She stopped moving and allowed Nicholas to kiss another part of her body. He licked her tender parts as the most delicious passion pumped the blood through her body, causing her to want and hurt all at the same time. He was driving her wild. "Nicholas," she rasped between parted lips.

The surge of tenderness that Nicholas felt for Noelle at this moment was overwhelming. He'd never expected to feel anything like this for her . . . for any woman, but he did.

God help him . . . tonight he felt something other than pain for the first time in a very long time . . . and it felt good. His body craved the feeling.

He took her in his arms and captured her mouth in a long kiss that made her grow dizzy.

Noelle kissed him back with a wild, primitive need. She knew she wanted more of him, but she wasn't sure what to do. She ran her hand along the length of him, feeling the thick hair on his broad chest, across his belly, and lower. He sucked in his breath as her hand moved along the tender skin of his inner thigh.

What was she doing?

Noelle knew she should stop now. Nicholas would

only break her heart as he had so many before, but she was helpless to end this closeness that she sensed was meant to be.

Nicholas pulled her back up to his mouth where he kissed her senseless.

"I-I do not know what to do," Noelle whispered. "I want to please you."

"You will, my love," Nicholas said as he covered her. "You are doing just fine." He parted her legs with a nudge of his knee. "This will hurt a bit, but I promise if you trust me it will only last a moment."

"Will it hurt as much as the last time you promised me it wouldn't hurt?" she asked with a teasing frown.

He chuckled. "Nay."

She nodded her consent, and Nicholas shifted into position.

He poised his throbbing shaft at the moist spot between her legs and positioned his hands beneath her hips, lifting her to fit his hot hardness. He eased in until he felt the tightness all around him. He knew the time had come, and he plunged into her with such force that she gasped, calling his name.

Nicholas stopped. He hadn't wanted to hurt her, but it couldn't be helped.

"What is wrong?" Noelle asked.

"Nothing is wrong, my love."

She moved beneath him. "I want to feel you move. I want to feel all of you inside me," she murmured.

With those words she robbed Nicholas of all reason. He began to proceed slowly in hopes of not causing her further pain, but it could not satisfy his urgent need. He increased his rhythm, all the time watching her face to see if there was discomfort. Then he drove full-length into her. But what he saw was not pain. He saw pleasure.

He saw love. He saw trust.

His breath came harder now as he stroked and pushed harder and harder until his shoulders ached and his heart felt as though it would burst. "You are mine, Noelle," he cried triumphantly as he climaxed with a shuddering explosion that rocked him to his very core.

Ecstasy ran through Noelle's body as stars exploded before her eyes. She seemed to be falling, yet floating at the same time. She tightened her arms around Nicholas as he collapsed on her, almost knocking what breath she had left from her. After a moment, he eased himself to the side but drew her over in his arms.

Nicholas gently rubbed her arm as he waited for his body to calm down and his sanity to return. As it slowly did, he wondered just what he had done. When his usual custom was to get up and leave, he found he had no desire to leave this bed nor this woman.

He really could never remember such a contentment and it was not a feeling he disliked. But what to do about this woman? Unfortunately, he still lacked his answer.

"I am sorry, Nicholas," Noelle said and felt him tense, and she knew that he misunderstood her apology. "I do not mean that I am sorry that I mated with you. I'm sorry that you will lose your wager with the king."

Nicholas relaxed, but asked, "How do you know about such?"

"Guinevere told me when she warned me about you."

Nicholas dipped his chin down and smiled without humor. "Our queen warned you?"

"Aye."

"Yet, you did not listen."

She finally looked up at him. "Nay, I did not."

His brows drew together in puzzlement. "Why?"

Noelle had known there was something special about Nicholas from the very moment they had first met at the pool in the woods, and now her heart told her this was right. "Because I love you."

Nicholas didn't know how to respond to her softly spoken words. "We have a far more weighty problem than just the wager," Nicholas said. "You are promised to another."

"I do not love him."

Nicholas's cheek rested against the top of Noelle's head. "I'll not let him have you," he murmured fiercely, and then he grew quiet as he fell asleep with Noelle still held in his arms.

The next morning Tristan stood just outside of Noelle's chamber, trying to wipe the smile from his face. Finally, with an effort, he resumed his stern expression.

Tristan had been told last night that Nicholas had returned, having rescued Noelle. Tristan had wanted to go and see her right away. Instead he'd stayed away purposely. Noelle had told him that Nicholas was the one, and Tristan wanted to give her a chance to find out before she married another.

However, if Sir Nicholas was the one, what were they going to tell the king? Not a pleasant thought, but Tristan would deal with that matter later.

Now, if his hunch paid off, Noelle had the time to find out if she'd finally found "her" knight.

If she had, Christmas might never come to Camelot when King Arthur heard about Noelle's liaison with Nicholas. Tristan could just imagine that the king's ire would be far, far worse than Noelle's stubbornness.

Tristan took a deep breath, and shoved Noelle's chamber door open.

The door to Noelle's chamber flew open and Tristan burst through. "Noelle. Are you—" Tristan stopped. He still wasn't prepared, even though he thought he was, to see his sister in bed with a man. He frowned. "This is your idea of rescuing my sister?" Tristan demanded. "You have broken your oath, sir? She is promised to another."

Nicholas sighed. "I broke many things last night," he said with little remorse as he sat up in bed.

"Do you have no shame, Noelle?" Tristan asked.

"Nay," Noelle admitted.

Tristan finally smiled. "Then he is the one?"

Noelle nodded.

"And you would marry him?" Tristan asked.

"Aye."

Tristan was frowning again. "Who is going to tell the king?"

"I will speak with Arthur," Nicholas said as he slid out of bed, taking one of the blankets with him. "Leave us now so we may dress."

"Well, I cannot say I am unhappy, though Sir Gavin is a good knight as well. But I cannot say the same of King Arthur. I believe he will be very angry."

Nicholas smiled grimly. "I do not anticipate the meeting with the king to be pleasant. He cares nothing for having his orders disobeyed. Of course, he will be glad that he has won his wager."

"What wager?" Tristan asked.

"It is between the king and myself."

Tristan turned to leave. "What do you think King Arthur will do?"

Nicholas thought a moment. "He could very well have me put to death. Or relieve me of my title and banish me from the kingdom."

When the door had shut, Noelle protested, "Nay! This is not all your fault. I will explain to our king."

Nicholas reached over and placed his hand on the side of Noelle's face. "I will fight my own battles. I don't want you fighting them for me."

"But we are in this together."

"Then I will face the king for both of us and accept whatever punishment he deals out."

"But what if the punishment is death?"

Nicholas leaned down and brushed her lips. "Then I will die a happy man."

FIFTEEN

The next two weeks were spent putting Cranborne Castle back together. Where once a small city thrived behind the high walls, only shells of huts now stood. They would have to be reconstructed, and since so many of Cranborne's men had been killed, Nicholas, his soldiers, and Tristan decided to stay and help in the rebuilding.

Tristan and Nicholas walked along the tops of the outer curtain checking for damage so they would know where to direct the masons for the needed repairs.

Nicholas spotted a small section of the battlement that had crumbled and would need fixing. He glanced over the battlement toward the base of the wall. "Tristan, come here," Nicholas called, then waited for Tristan to join him.

"See the base of the wall," Nicholas said, pointing down below. "If you will have your masons construct a batter, a sloping base, it will strengthen the structure and give better defense."

Tristan straightened back up. "How so?"

"When the stones and missiles are dropped from

the top of the battlement they will bounce toward the enemy and roll away from the castle."

"I admit, since much of the castle's care was in John's hands, I have much to learn," Tristan said. "I appreciate all that you point out to me."

Nicholas smiled. "You will do admirably—much better than John ever did, I wager."

Tristan beamed at the senior knight's praise. "Let's go down below and see what needs to be done there. I'll have the masons repair this battlement and construct the batter."

Once down in the inner ward, Nicholas told Thomas, the master shoemaker, that he wanted to help the old man restore his building.

"But sire, we are capable of making the repairs ourselves," Thomas protested. "You needn't bother if you have something else to do."

Nicholas looked at the friendly, white-haired man. "I have nothing else to do and would be honored to lend you a hand putting your shop back together. When I was young, I spent many an hour working on the huts in the village." Nicholas didn't add that was the only way he could earn his meals.

Thomas went back to stirring the clay he would use to rebuild his hut, so Nicholas moved over and picked up a wattle, which was a mat of woven sticks and reeds. Nicholas hoisted the wattle up and held it in place so Thomas could smear the clay on the mat to strengthen and seal it in place.

Nicholas liked this physical work because it kept his mind off the other problems he needed to face.

So he stayed with Thomas all afternoon, working hand in hand with him.

By the end of the day, they had completed the cobbler's shop. Thomas turned to Nicholas and said, "I misjudged you, sire. You are truly a fine man. May I mend some shoes for you?"

Nicholas waved his hand. "Nay, you have done a good day's work. But I'll bring you some work soon," he said as he turned to leave. "You will have ample opportunity to repay me."

Tristan joined Nicholas as they walked across the bailey. "I must ask you something," Tristan said.

"Go ahead, ask," Nicholas replied.

"The past few days, as we have been working, you have yet to ask me anything about my sister," Tristan said and then looked sideways at Nicholas. "You do plan to marry Noelle?"

Nicholas resisted the urge to curse. He had successfully kept his thoughts off Noelle all day, and now Tristan had to remind him. "Noelle is very special. If I did what was best for her, I would leave her now, for she needs someone far better than I."

"Nay," Tristan said and added, "she wants you."

"Why me?" Nicholas asked. "Surely, she knows my reputation for never being faithful to anyone."

"Then you are willing to let Sir Gavin marry her?"

"Nay! But I want you to tell me why she has set her heart on me," Nicholas said.

"This goes back to when Noelle was a small girl. Merlin predicted that she would meet her knight-in-armor, and she would know that he was the one. There would never be another for her, and you, my friend, seem to be her chosen knight." Tristan chuckled and then added in a very serious tone, "Do not hurt her."

"That is what I am trying not to do."

Noelle took charge of putting the Great Hall back in order. The hall hadn't been as severely damaged as the bailey, but several of the chairs had to be replaced, and the rushes smelled so smoky that they all needed to be thrown out and new ones brought in. Plus all the tapestry that had been torn down had to be placed back on the walls.

The servants were still jittery, so Noelle had to constantly tell them that there would be many men left behind to protect them in the castle.

Nicholas slept with his men in the barracks. With his many unanswered questions, he had some thinking to do, and he didn't need the distraction of having Noelle so near.

Of course, he had his meals with Tristan and Noelle. They would sit and talk after their meal until it was time to retire, and much to Nicholas's regret the time would always pass too quickly. Noelle was interesting and smart, and he reluctantly admitted to himself that he enjoyed her company.

Tonight he lay on his cot, staring at the ceiling. However, his thoughts kept drifting back to Noelle and how much he'd enjoyed her body, and how he would like to forget that she was a lady and seduce her all over again.

So what was the problem? He'd never had a problem with seducing damsels before.

Noelle deserved better. That was the problem. She deserved someone who could give her children. He had decided a long time ago that he would not father any children. She deserved someone who could make a commitment. He couldn't do that, either.

They damn well needed to talk.

Perhaps if they talked, he could convince her to change her mind.

A momentary look of discomfort crossed Nicholas's face. He bent over, his arms resting on his knees. His life used to be so simple when all he had to worry about was which sword to use in battle, or decide which battle he needed to fight next.

"I take it something has displeased ye?" Dirk asked from the cot across from Nicholas's.

"Nay," Nicholas said.

"Are ye ready to return to Camelot, then?" Dirk asked as he leaned back against the wall.

"It is time," Nicholas said.

"What do ye think of Cranborne?"

"With a little work, Tristan will have a fine holding."

"Aye." Dirk nodded thoughtfully. "I wager Tristan will lose some of his land to Sir Gavin once he marries Lady Noelle, though."

Nicholas straightened and glared at Dirk.

Dirk looked surprised by the scathing look. "Had ye forgotten that small fact?"

"He'll not marry her," Nicholas said, a slight edge

to his voice. If he couldn't have her, no one else could either.

"Is there something ye'd like to tell me?"

With a long, exhausted sigh, Nicholas stood up. "Nay."

Dirk was beginning to lose his patience. "Then ye intend to sit here and simmer until ye explode?"

Nicholas glared at Dirk.

"And glaring at me won't help ye either. Ye need to face your problem. Are ye goin' to marry her?"

Nicholas stood. "You are not going to leave this alone, are you?"

"And ye are avoiding the question. Are ye goin' to marry her?"

Nicholas started toward the door. Before he went out, he glanced back at Dirk. "I wish I knew."

Once outside, the crisp air helped clear Nicholas's mind. He glanced up at the sky and noticed that the stars were brighter than usual this night. He realized he was walking in a direction he shouldn't go, but he kept moving anyway, covering the short distance across the bailey to the Great Hall.

He knew what he had to do. He needed to speak with Noelle. It would be the last time he had a chance to speak with her alone, if at all. For when they returned to Camelot, he wasn't sure what would happen.

His life could suddenly become worthless.

Nicholas nodded to the guard at the door. He was one of Nicholas's men, and he knew the guard wouldn't dare question where he was going, so Nicholas continued on his way, deep in thought.

He should have known better than to get in this situation, he berated himself. Not only had he betrayed a fellow knight, he'd lost the chance to win Briercliff, and he more than likely had angered the king.

Willpower. Nicholas almost laughed at the word. He'd always been the man of steel who could resist or overcome anything.

So what had happened?

How had one mere slip of a woman undone him?

Evidently he'd thought with another part of his body, he told himself ruefully.

Arriving outside of Noelle's chamber, he rapped on the door and waited, knowing it was not proper to seek her out there. But who was going to stop him? He smiled at the very idea. Where Noelle was concerned, he had never done anything proper, and that was the crux of the problem.

Noelle wasn't like any of the other women he'd known. If she were, he wouldn't be in this dilemma.

"Nicholas?" Noelle greeted him, her surprise evident as she opened the door a crack.

"We need to talk," Nicholas said.

"Do you want me to meet you down in the hall?"

"Nay," he said as he entered the room and shut the door with a backward shove, giving Noelle little time to get out of his way.

"Do you think it wise to be in my chamber?"

"Probably not," he said with an ironic smile. "I will be leaving on the morrow for Camelot. My men have been hunting and have brought back fresh game for the holding. You will be adequately provisioned until Tristan can restore order here."

"Thank you," Noelle said as she stood before him. "We could not have saved Cranborne had it not been for you and your men."

"Noelle, I would never have let Meleagant harm you or your home," Nicholas said, and at the same time cursed himself. Here he'd come to tell her he was not the man for her, and somehow he had already gotten twisted up in his thinking. He must stay steady on his course. "When I return to Camelot, I will go and speak to our king who, I grant, will not be happy."

"And I will not be happy if he punishes you."

"Nay." Nicholas shook his head. "It was my wrongdoing. It is I who shall pay."

Noelle frowned. Nicholas stood before her as still as a tree. He was acting strange . . . as if he was afraid of her. This wasn't the Nicholas she'd made love to, who'd taught her the pleasure of physical love. Noelle took a step toward him. "You have regrets?"

Nicholas stared at her, completely dumfounded by her question.

Noelle wanted to smile at the fierce knight who, at the moment, seemed very leery of her. For once, Nicholas didn't hide his emotions, and she could read each one of them, and there were many. However, the one that seemed to draw his brow together was uncertainty.

Aye, Sir Nicholas was afraid of her.

"I am not worthy of your love," Nicholas said finally in a voice void of emotion.

Noelle took another step closer until she stood right before him. "Do you not think that I should be the judge of whether you are worthy of my affections or not?"

"Nay." He shook his head with the certainty of a man who knew everything and was never wrong. "You are young and know nothing of the world."

Noelle reached out and touched him.

He jumped.

She smiled.

"I might be young, as you say, Nicholas," Noelle said in a velvet-sounding voice as she placed both slender, white hands on his chest. "But rest assured, I know exactly what I want."

Her husky voice sent shivers running rampant down Nicholas's spine. Damn his traitorous body for wanting her. Damn him for not being able to resist. Nicholas reached out and pulled her next to him. "Do you not understand? I cannot marry you. There is so much you do not know about me."

Slowly, Noelle slid her arms around Nicholas's neck. His frown increased and he tried to draw away. "You are not listening, Noelle," Nicholas insisted.

"Nay, I am not," she said as her lips brushed his, teasing his lower body to life.

Damn! He'd never known a creature as wanton as the woman he held in his arms. His hands splayed across her back as he clasped her against his hardened body. His mouth found hers, and his lips were hot and demanding as his tongue slid smoothly into her mouth, probing with passion, savoring all her sweetness.

She offered him all of her, and Nicholas groaned with need. He'd never let her go. He could fool himself no more as his tongue plunged into her mouth, causing her to wrap her arms more securely around his neck.

Her response was as hungry as his.

Nicholas scooped Noelle up and carried her to the bed. They parted only long enough to hastily remove their clothes.

Noelle held her arms up toward Nicholas. His eyes had darkened with lust as he joined her, his hot body pressed against hers, creating an exquisite harmony. She snuggled against him as their legs intertwined, and she could feel his hardness between her legs. She kissed him long and hard as heat rippled under her skin and Noelle realized just how much she wanted to feel Nicholas inside her.

Nicholas also felt the urgency of the moment. Later they would make love slowly and leisurely, he promised himself, but for now they needed each other and the waiting was torture. The force, he thought as he entered her, robbed him of his breath, his wits, his thoughts.

They were so much a part of each other. There was no beginning and there was no end. Instinctively, each seemed to sense what the other needed. Nicholas thrust into Noelle's warmth over and over again until they both cried out their pleasure at almost the same time. Then Nicholas collapsed, spent on her warm, soft body. He felt as if someone had sucked the life from him.

Nicholas was so sated that he didn't have the strength to move. He could stay like this forever, he thought, buried in her warmth.

Their breathing, matching breath for breath in an instinctual rhythm, was the only sound in the room as they clung to each other. When they finally floated down to earth, Nicholas rolled to the side, cradling Noelle in his arms.

He took a deep breath and said, "I promised myself that this would not happen again."

"I know," Noelle said in a small voice. "But sometimes there are other forces at work."

"But my blood may be tainted, Noelle. I would not wish that on anyone."

Now was the time to tell him that she knew, Noelle realized. "I know about your mother."

Nicholas leaned up on his elbow and looked down at her. Puzzlement replaced the desire in his eyes. "How do you know such?"

"You spoke of your mother when you were afflicted with the fever. In your delirium you relived the entire tragedy of the fire." Noelle sighed, her breath moist and sweet against his sweaty skin. "I heard everything from the small, scared lad you were then." She paused. "The pain that you felt . . . I felt also. It must have been so hard for you to understand as a wee child?"

"Being a grown man has brought no answers either," he said, and then caught himself. "It is something that I have tried to put out of my mind," Nicholas said in an offhand manner as if it bothered him no more. "For whatever reason, my mother didn't love me. Perhaps, I was not lovable. I do not know, nor will I ever."

Noelle shook her head, denying what she heard him say. Gently, she placed her hand on the side of his face. "It was not you, Nicholas, but your mother who was unable to love. You are a very good man, and I love you. That is all that matters to me."

"That does not change the fact that my blood is tainted."

"You do not know that for sure. But it would make no difference to me."

"But it does to me," Nicholas stated. "If we marry, we could not have children."

"Because you don't want them?"

"Nay, because . . ." He looked away. "It is hard to explain how I feel."

"Are there others who have had your children already and you know nothing of them?"

"Nay, I have always taken precautions not to father children."

Noelle looked at him, not understanding his meaning. Other than withdrawal, how could he accomplish such a deed? "How so?"

"I have always withdrawn so that my seed spilled elsewhere."

"But you didn't do so with me."

"I know."

"Why?"

"It is not important," he snapped, but softened his

words by kissing the palm of her hand before she withdrew it.

Noelle gazed at him long and hard, saying with her eyes, *you must trust me.* Finally she said, "It is important to me."

Nicholas sighed deeply. "Because I love you, Noelle. I did not want to stop."

Noelle smiled up at him. "That is all you need say, my love. With love, we can overcome anything else."

"Will we be able to overcome King Arthur and Sir Gavin?"

Noelle frowned, having completely forgotten about that problem for the moment. "I do not look forward to what is to come. But I will tell the king how I feel, and surely he will understand."

"Do not count on such. Sir Gavin cannot be made to bear any shame," Nicholas said. "If I am allowed to live, Sir Gavin may challenge me for your hand."

"I will not let them hurt you," Noelle said, her conviction strong.

Nicholas laughed. "I can fight my own battles, my love. The problem is that I know not what our king will do."

"I pray that Arthur will understand."

"You should keep those prayers up, for I have a feeling I will need all the help I can get," Nicholas admitted in a voice that sounded far away.

"I am sorry for all the problems I have caused you."

"Do not be. I would do everything again to have you. If only for one night." He leaned over and kissed her and Noelle felt as if she were in heaven. Now she would not have to worry that Nicholas had regrets, but his next words brought a black cloud over her happy thoughts.

"We will depart in the morning," Nicholas said with far more conviction than he felt. "Together we will face what we must when we reach Camelot."

SIXTEEN

Blackness surrounded the procession as they made their way through the sleeping countryside toward Camelot. The torchbearers were spread throughout the procession to provide light for the column of Nicholas's men.

The brisk wind blew the white banner with the scarlet-red dragon, making the dragon look as if he were alive as they rode. Noelle drew her mantle closer around her to ward off the nighttime chill. She wished she had Nicholas to warm her, but he was nowhere near, having chosen to ride near the front. Which was just as well.

What could they say to each other? They knew nothing of what lay ahead of them, and it was better not to dwell on it.

Noelle could see Thor's foggy breath as it curled from his muzzle. Even the horse was impatient to reach his destination and find someplace warm to sleep for the rest of the night.

A screeching noise came from overhead—a sound that Noelle had come to recognize. She looked up to see Boots flying overhead, keeping watch. Noelle found the bird's presence very comforting, even among this army of soldiers. After all, she had seen the bird in action and knew how well she could defend her.

Finally, they topped a hill, and Camelot came into view. The castle appeared like a bright, twinkling star amidst the dull blackness. Noelle wasn't sure whether she was frightened or happy to see the holding, and then decided it was a mixture of both. Nicholas would smooth everything out with King Arthur; she had to believe that. It was the only way she could go on.

The sound of chains rattling shattered the brittle darkness as the drawbridge lowered and the portcullis rose. The guards had recognized Nicholas's banner, and had opened the gates without challenge. The drawbridge touched the ground with a loud thud, and the procession started across the long bridge.

Noelle took a deep breath for courage. The time was near.

Most of Nicholas's men stopped at the stables in the outer bailey. A few rode into the inner bailey with their leader, as did Noelle. The yards were quiet, as everyone had gathered in the Great Hall for the evening meal.

Noelle looked around at all the greenery on the small huts and the tiny red ribbons tied around the many torches that hung from the walls. She'd almost forgotten it was Christmas. But on the morrow it would be Christmas Eve and then the next day would be her wedding day.

The question was, Who would be her groom?

She didn't want to think about that, but she knew she must prepare for whatever lay before her. The morning would also bring the great tournament for which all the knights had been practicing. Noelle vowed to keep her mind on the joust. It would be colorful and diverting and there would be honor for whoever won.

Nicholas stopped his destrier and held up his hand, signaling the retinue to stop. Noelle and the rest of his company halted beside him.

"I hope they saved us some food," Dirk grumbled from behind her.

"If I know our king, the food will be plenty," Nicholas said. "Let us go and see what has been placed on the table."

When they entered the hall, the smell of roasted pork filled the air. Everyone was still seated, laughing and talking as if they were in a festive mood.

King Arthur spotted Nicholas the moment he and his party entered. Arthur rose and held up his golden chalice. "They return. Raise your cups in a toast to their successful siege." Arthur paused and sipped his wine. "Now our tournament will be complete, for all my brave knights have returned. Come, Sir Nicholas and Sir Tristan, join the feast and replenish yourselves."

Nicholas leaned down to speak to Noelle. He hadn't realized he'd been holding her hand, which was hidden in the folds of her skirt. He let it go, and said in a low voice, "You should join your ladies, and I will seek King Arthur's counsel after we eat."

"But I want to be with you," Noelle protested in a whisper.

"Do as you are told, for once," Nicholas said, the

irritation evident in his voice. When he straightened, he saw Sir Gavin approaching. This was exactly why Noelle couldn't remain by his side, Nicholas reminded himself when he thought he might waver. Did she not see that he and Arthur would have to work out many things first?

"I heard you have been very busy in my absence," Sir Gavin said, then chuckled. "Thank you for looking out for my interests, Sir Nicholas. Are you both unharmed?"

Noelle could feel the heat seep through her body, as well as the guilt. She hoped the guilt didn't register on her face, for it would not do to have Gavin suspect. Then she wondered why she should feel guilty. She'd never loved Sir Gavin. She had never pretended that she did. But then, her feelings were not supposed to matter. What the king said was so, and by loving Nicholas, she had defied the king.

She swallowed hard. What had she done?

"Aye," Nicholas said. "And how did you fare in the south?"

Sir Gavin's gaze shifted from Noelle to Nicholas. "We finally drove Meleagant's men away, but there was no sign of Meleagant himself."

"Probably because I had the pleasure of doing battle with the cur at Cranborne," Nicholas said in a disgruntled tone.

"And what of Cranborne?" Sir Gavin asked Tristan, who'd just walked up to join them.

"We will rebuild. Sir Nicholas has been indispensable in giving me suggestions on how to make the fortress stronger."

"Let us speak later," Sir Gavin said. "You have been busy, and your journey long. You must be famished." He gestured toward the heavily laden tables. "Come, let us partake of the feast." He took Noelle's elbow and escorted her to where he had been sitting. Tristan followed.

Nicholas had to clench his jaw to keep from telling Sir Gavin to get his hands off Noelle. The next couple of days would be miserable until he and Arthur and Gavin settled their affairs. If it were possible to do so.

Nicholas joined King Arthur at the dais and related to him all that had transpired. Though Nicholas ate, he tasted very little of his food. He had no desire to sit here and make idle conversation when he had more important matters to discuss with the king. He both longed for and dreaded what was to come. He just wanted to get it over with.

Matilda appeared by Nicholas's side and poured him another cup of mead. "I have saved some meat scraps for Boots," she said, and placed a small leather pouch beside Nicholas's trencher.

"Thank you, Matilda. You have always looked out for us," Nicholas said and then smiled at the kind older woman.

"You were not hurt?" she asked as she scanned his body, making certain for herself.

"Nay. Lady Noelle's brother John was killed, but Tristan and I were unharmed."

Matilda looked at Nicholas with compassion in her eyes. "I am sorry for your lady, but I am glad that you are unharmed," she said in a whisper. Then she hurried off.

His lady. Was it so obvious that Matilda could see his very thoughts in the depth of his eyes? And what was it about that old woman that he liked so much? It had seemed as though Matilda had been around from the time he was small until the family castle burned down, and then he'd lost touch with her until he'd come to Camelot.

He liked the fact that Matilda really could handle King Arthur. And now Nicholas wished he had her skill as he prepared to deal with the king.

"Sire," Nicholas said to Arthur.

Arthur nodded.

"I would like to speak with you in private, at the Round Table," Nicholas said.

"You sound serious, Nicholas," Arthur said with a frown. "Go, and I will join you there anon."

Nicholas rose, bowed to the king and queen, and then strode out of the hall.

Guinevere looked at her husband. "Something is troubling him."

"Aye." Arthur nodded as he rose. "And I have a feeling I will not like it at all."

Noelle almost choked on a slice of meat. She hadn't been able to keep her eyes off Nicholas, so she saw him speak to the king, then leave, and she knew exactly why he had gone.

Her food no longer tasted good. What was going to happen? She had never been in this much trouble before, and she had no earthly idea how to handle the situation.

Tristan reached over and put his hand on hers. She glanced at him and he said, "It will be all right. There is nothing you can do but pray."

That was the problem, Noelle wanted to shout. She felt so helpless. "Excuse me," she said as she stood. "I must go to my chamber."

"Do you need our assistance, milady?" Isabelle asked.

Noelle looked at Isabelle, who was sitting next to Dirk, and Carolyn, who sat next to Sir Gavin. Why deprive them of their fun? It was Noelle who had the problem, not her ladies. "Nay. It has been a long day for me. You may come later."

Noelle hurried from the hall. She needed to get away from everyone. What if King Arthur ordered Nicholas put to death? How would she bear it? No, she told herself fiercely. She would find some way to free Nicholas even if it meant disobeying the king.

Having paid no attention to where she was going, she ran headlong into someone. "I am so sorry," she said as she backed up—then she realized she had bumped into Merlin!

"Where are you headed with such haste and with such a frown?" Merlin asked.

"Oh, Merlin. I'm so afraid."

He reached down and took her hands in his gnarled ones. "What of, my child?"

"Afraid that King Arthur will be so displeased with Sir Nicholas that he will do him harm."

"I see you have found the one."

Noelle managed a grim smile as she looked up at Merlin. "Aye," she said, nodding. "Thank you. He is all that I dreamed of, but as you know I am promised to another who I want not. I cannot lose Nicholas after finally finding him."

"I told you that the path may not be easy, but if you trust the turns that you take, all will be well at journey's end," Merlin said and then released her hands. "Now, go and worry no more."

Noelle smiled at the wise old wizard. She felt a little better as she turned and headed for her solar. Perhaps a small prayer would help also.

Nicholas arrived in the smaller hall first. He found his seat at the table and waited for the king. He glanced up at the roof overhead that had been painted to look like the sky, all light blues and fluffy clouds, and in the middle, the image of the sun shone down over the table.

The room, no matter how glorious, was too quiet. Nicholas could swear that his very heartbeat echoed off the walls. He wanted to get this meeting over with.

The door opened with a loud whoosh, and King Arthur swept in and headed for the Seat Royal. Nicholas watched silently and waited for the king to take his seat before he said, "You have won the wager, sire."

The king grinned. "So you have found it hard to abstain," he said with satisfaction. "But I wonder that you have gone this long to fail now. Are you sure?"

"Aye, sire. You have won the wager. I cannot lie to you."

"I saw you with no one at the castle. Was it someone at Cranborne? That was it, was it not?" Arthur shook his head, having answered his own question. "Such a shame, since you were only a few days away from triumph. And well I know how you would have savored another victory over me."

Nicholas did not blink as he stared at the king. "It is worse than that, sire."

King Arthur frowned. "I am sure I do not want to hear this, but I must. What have you done?"

"I want to marry the Lady Noelle."

"What?" Arthur leapt to his feet and braced his hands on the table as he stared at Nicholas. "She is the one woman you cannot have. She is promised to another."

"How well I know, sire. But I love her," Nicholas confessed, the words still sounding strange to his own ears. And evidently incredibly strange to the king as well. "I will not give her up."

Arthur sank back slowly to his chair, his brows drawn together in a frown. "She has been promised to Sir Gavin. Or have you forgotten?"

"No, I have not forgotten, though I did not think of Sir Gavin at the time," Nicholas admitted.

Arthur grimaced. "What happened to the boastful knight who told me women were of no use to him?"

"It is what I believed for many a long year. But, as you well know, Lady Noelle is different from most women."

"Do you say that now, then later regret your words?"

"Nay. She is unlike anyone I have ever met. Surely you must remember how you felt when you first met our queen. Would you give her up?" Nicholas countered.

Arthur smiled and gave a slight nod. "I knew I had to have her," he admitted. "Nay, I would not have given her up. Are you willing to fight for the lady?"

"Aye."

Arthur rose and went to the door, where a servant stood waiting. "Go and bring Sir Gavin and Sir Tristan to me."

As the servant scurried off to do the king's bidding, Arthur returned to his place. "I had forgotten how dull Camelot can be when you are not here, but it took you only a matter of hours to remind me." He didn't wait for Nicholas to answer, but went back to his chair.

They said no more as they waited. Soon the other two knights arrived at the door, and the king motioned them in. He turned to the servant. "Stanley, go and fetch the Lady Noelle. Have her wait outside the small hall until I summon her." King Arthur gestured for Tristan and Gavin to sit.

"What is wrong, sire?" Sir Gavin asked. "You look troubled."

"And well I am," Arthur said, then looked to Nicholas. "Nicholas." Arthur held his hand out.

Surprised, Nicholas stared at the king. Evidently, Arthur was going to let Nicholas do all the explaining. Nicholas wasn't sure how to handle this situation, but talking in circles had never been his style. "I wish to marry Lady Noelle."

Of all the things to happen, Nicholas did not expect Sir Gavin's reaction.

Sir Gavin was laughing.

"You cannot be serious," Sir Gavin said as he tried to get his mirth under control. "You have never had a serious bone in your body where any lady is concerned. And to think you are serious about my intended—" He paused and chuckled. "Thank you for the jest." Then Gavin sobered when he saw the serious expression on Nicholas's face. "Wait. You are serious." Sir Gavin came to his feet. "Noelle was promised to me! Now I see how you have been taking care of what is mine."

"Aye. But you do not love her," Nicholas stated, trying hard not to raise his voice. A shouting match would only make everything worse.

"And you proclaim to love her?" Gavin challenged archly.

"Aye."

"By the saints, you just want that which is mine," Sir Gavin roared, bristling with indignation. "I will not give her up easily. And when have *you* ever fought for a woman?"

"There is always a first time." Nicholas stood, his voice growing angrier. He'd finally lost the tight grip he'd held on his emotions as he said, "Can not a man change?"

"Nay," Sir Gavin shot back, shouting at Nicholas. "Not where you are concerned."

King Arthur cleared his throat. "Silence! Cease

your shouting and take your seats. I am not deaf, nor is anyone else at Camelot. Tristan, what say you in the matter?"

Tristan had no desire to get in the middle of this, but it looked as though Noelle and Nicholas had created a very unusual situation. Christmas may never come to Camelot, he thought, but he was careful not to smile because no one else at the table would find anything amusing at the moment. "The last time I spoke to my sister, she didn't want to marry anyone. The marriage to Sir Gavin was my brother's doing. John is now dead, so the matter falls to me. I want only that my sister be happy, and I can tell you that only she can choose the one that she truly loves. I think if neither man will give her up, then they must compete for her hand in the tournament. The winner can take her."

"I agree," Arthur nodded. "That way no knight is shamed. I presume that you have not fallen in love with the Lady Noelle, Sir Gavin?"

"Nay, I have hardly had the chance to be with the lovely lady," Sir Gavin said with sarcasm. "It seems that Sir Nicholas spent much more time with my intended than I. However, she was promised to me."

Nicholas said nothing, nor did he bother to look guilty, Arthur noticed. "Do you both agree to abide by my rules?"

They both nodded. "Aye, sire."

The king nodded and then told Tristan, "Bring in your sister."

* * *

Noelle stood outside the double doors wondering what was happening on the other side. Everything would work out—it would, she reminded herself. She tried leaning closer to the door so she could hear what was being said, but it was for nothing. The room was well constructed, the thick walls blocking out all the noise.

Unable to remain still, she began to pace back and forth in hopes of easing some of her nervousness. She had thought that finding love would be the answer to all her problems. But she'd been wrong; she had never dreamed that love would bring on yet another set of problems.

The door swung open and Tristan beckoned her. "Come forth," he said.

"I had rather not," Noelle admitted in a whisper.

"The choice is not yours," Tristan told her.

Noelle swallowed, gave her brother a desperate look, then swept past Tristan. When the door closed behind her, she remained just inside, unsure of where she should go. She wanted to run to Nicholas and throw her arms around him, but that would not do.

"Come, Noelle," King Arthur said and motioned for her to come and sit beside him. When she had done so, he said, "Sir Nicholas has asked for your hand in marriage."

She nodded.

"Since the banns have already been posted for your wedding to Sir Gavin on Christmas Day, we have a problem to resolve."

Noelle nodded again.

"The suggestion has been made for the two men

to joust for your hand. The winner will be allowed to marry you. I trust you see the wisdom in having this settled thusly?"

"As you wish, sire," Noelle said.

"Good. Then let us prepare for the 'morrow. I expect this to be the best tournament we have had in a long time."

After everyone had left, the king sat for a long time staring at the door. Some men went to war for excitement. Evidently, he didn't have to do anything; excitement seemed to find him at home. Over the next few days there would be plenty of it at Camelot.

He leaned back and breathed a long, deep sigh. He hoped that everything would end as it was supposed to.

SEVENTEEN

When the first beams of light entered her chamber, Noelle welcomed the morn. Her eyes were scratchy and swollen from little sleep and her body ached from head to toe with her tossing and turning. Her mind just wouldn't quit thinking *what if* Nicholas lost the tournament?

She scurried out of bed and hurried to the washstand, where she placed the porcelain bowl on top. Then she went to get the pitcher of water that she'd placed near the fire the night before. She had begun to wash her face when Carolyn and Isabelle swept into her chamber, already dressed and ready for the big day.

"Good morn," Carolyn said.

"Are you excited about the joust? Everyone will be dressed in the finest silks and colors, and the horses will have on their best trappings. Should be very colorful indeed," Isabelle added.

Noelle drew in a long, deep breath. How did she feel? "Truth to tell, I think I am numb," she finally said. "I did not tell you last night, but King Arthur has decided that the winner of the joust will have my hand in marriage."

Isabelle and Carolyn squealed in unison.

"How romantic," Isabelle gushed.

Carolyn rubbed her hands together with glee. "And exciting."

Noelle dried her face with a soft sheet, then turned toward them. "It is only romantic and exciting if the right knight wins," she reminded them. "What if Sir Gavin wins?"

"I have heard that Sir Nicholas is unbeatable," Isabelle said as she searched through Noelle's trunk for a gown. Then she turned and looked at Noelle. "What happened while you were at Cranborne?"

"I was captured by Meleagant and dragged from the castle! I thought he would kill me," Noelle said with a shudder of revulsion. "And he probably would have if it had not been for Boots. Meleagant was ready to ravish me as well when Boots attacked."

"How dreadful," Carolyn exclaimed with her hands over her mouth. "What happened next?"

"And who is Boots?" Isabelle asked.

"You remember Nicholas's falcon. The one I climbed the tree to save."

They both nodded.

Then Noelle told them the whole story, and they listened eagerly, their eyes growing large at some of the things she told them about how gentle Nicholas had been when he had tended to her wound. After she finished the story, she added, "I realized that I love Nicholas." She smiled, still excited every time she thought about him holding her in his arms. He hadn't declared his undying love, but she was certain that he cared for her. Whether he wanted to or not. And that small fact pleased her a great deal.

She wanted to tell them about making love with Nicholas, but that was too private to tell anyone. She just hoped one day they would both feel the way she felt.

"We knew you loved him before you left," Isabelle reminded her.

A small smile drifted across Noelle's face. "But you didn't know that he feels the same."

"Was it wonderful kissing him?" Isabelle asked.

"It was so much more, more than I ever imagined. Just the thought of kissing him makes me tingle." Noelle blushed.

Carolyn hugged her mistress. "It's marvelous. You know that Sir Nicholas is the best knight. Maybe you worry over nothing. Was Sir Gavin angry?"

"I could not hear his response. But he didn't look too happy when I entered the hall," Noelle said. "He cannot admit that he's been disgraced. I was promised to Gavin first, and he does not want to let go of his claim. I feel like a blanket being pulled between two knights."

Isabelle grinned. "Sounds heavenly."

Noelle frowned.

Isabelle ignored her as she pulled out a soft cream cashmere gown. "How about this for a wedding dress? It is quite lovely and the finest piece that you own."

Noelle looked at the beautiful cotehardie. "Nay, I will wear that gown today. Pull out the red velvet. That is what I will be wed in."

Carolyn looked a little surprised. "Well, it will be different, I must admit, but will look lovely on you," she said as she took the red gown from Isabelle and shook it out before placing it on the bed. She smoothed out the wrinkles with her hands. "It is lovely."

Isabelle held up the cream-colored, cashmere cote-hardie and Noelle stepped into the garment. The material felt warm and soft as it slipped over her body. "Since these sleeves are tight-fitting, I think I will wear my purple surcoat."

Carolyn brought the coat and Noelle slipped it on. The fit was perfect, fitting her hips snugly, and it would also provide more warmth.

She stepped over to the window to look out onto the bailey. It was getting to be a familiar sight. The merchants wouldn't open their shops today, as all would attend the joust. "It's cloudy. Let us dress warmly for this day."

Queen Guinevere met the three women in the Great Hall. "It is time to go to the tournament." The ladies-in-waiting went ahead but Guinevere hung back with Noelle.

Guinevere placed her hand on Noelle's arm. "Are you all right? Arthur told me of the meeting last night. I can well imagine how you must feel this morning."

"I truly do not know. *Frightened* would probably be the best answer," Noelle admitted. "Though you warned me against it, I fell in love with Nicholas.

But I wish no shame upon Sir Gavin. He does not deserve such treatment. If John hadn't promised me against my will, none of this would have happened," she murmured.

"Aye, but then you might not have met Sir Nicholas. Fate has a queer way of steering us along the proper path."

"I hadn't thought of it that way. I just pray that Nicholas is the victor."

Guinevere gave Noelle a sympathetic smile. "I think I would feel the same. Let us hope that this day will bring you all that you wish for."

"I guess we should go to the field," Noelle said with a sigh, wrapping her full-length cloak around her. "I think I would walk today rather than ride, if you don't mind."

"Nay, I mind naught," Guinevere said as they left the Great Hall. "I will walk with you."

Their ladies-in-waiting were watching for them outside.

As they started across the bailey, their ladies fell into step behind them. Many of the castle serfs walked ahead of them, jostling boisterously, laughing and chatting.

"I see everyone is in a festive mood today," Noelle said. "I wish I felt the same. It is the uncertainty that scares me."

Guinevere nodded. "Cold weather is good for curing one's soul, and today feels much like Christmas."

The day was cloudy, the wind cold as they walked across the bailey to the gatehouse. They nodded to the guards as they passed through the gatehouse, leaving the castle walls.

Isabelle and Carolyn chatted behind them with Guinevere's ladies.

"Have you noticed how gray the day looks?" Carolyn asked.

"Aye, it reminds me of the day we went searching for mistletoe," Isabelle replied as she and Carolyn trudged on. "We will have to keep an eye out for our lady. It seems she tends to get lost when looking for mistletoe."

"That is quite enough, Isabelle. I have been teased aplenty for my misadventure," Noelle snapped. Then she added in a softer tone when she realized she was taking out her mood on Isabelle, "Maybe it will snow again." Noelle had always imagined her wedding with snow on the ground. Of course, having the correct husband would be necessary to make the day perfect.

They approached the meadow where all the brightly colored tents and pavilions had been pitched. She could tell that there were more tents than in the days previous.

Squires and pages bustled to and fro, dashing everywhere as they prepared for the day's events. Several countries would be represented.

Flags and pennons fluttered in the wind. The colors were many: bright green silks, golds, reds, and blues. And the coats-of-arms were displayed on all the pennons. Noelle and her party strolled past a green silk pennon bearing the symbol of the Czech lion. But none of the banners were as bold as the flag belonging to Nicholas. Always . . . even in her dreams . . . she could see the fire-breathing dragon.

The ladies passed by several tents where young men sat proudly polishing helmets for the knights they served. Noelle nodded to Tristan's squire, who she was glad to see had fully recovered from his ailments. It would be difficult to play the squire today, Noelle thought.

"Are you going to give one of the knights your silk handkerchief?" Guinevere whispered for Noelle's ears only.

"I would like to, but under the circumstances I think not." They moved past the pavilion displaying the fire-breathing dragon. *Please let Nicholas win*, Noelle prayed.

A huge crowd had already gathered at the viewing stands when they arrived. There were seven dukes and three kings on hand, and most were already seated. The tournament was considered serious business, for this was the way the men trained for battles.

Noelle followed Guinevere to the central viewing stand. A purple canopy stretched over the platform, indicating where King Arthur's throne had been placed along with Queen Guinevere's. They would be able to watch the contest and enjoy the best view. Noelle and her ladies sat in the first row beside the queen.

King Arthur joined them after they were seated. "I believe this will be the best tournament we have had in a long time," he pronounced, and then he glanced at Noelle and the other ladies. "You look lovely."

"Thank you, your majesty," Noelle said as the king

moved to his throne. She glanced back to the lists, the field where the jousting would take place. The brown grass had been trampled into the muddy ground from all the practicing, so there was nothing left but dirt. Down the center of the lists was a long fence barrier to prevent the horses from colliding with one another during the match. She knew that the rules of the joust were strict. The knights wore full armor in place of their mail shirts. This would give the men as much protection as possible, in hope of preventing injury.

This was the first real tournament that Noelle had ever seen, and she was unsure of the rules as she watched the squires and pages running around the field, each seeming in a hurry to accomplish his task. She leaned over to Guinevere. "Can you explain the rules of the tournament?"

"I think so," Guinevere said with a smile. "This is my third match, so I have learned a few things. "The knights earn points. One point is given when a knight strikes his opponent hard enough to break the spear. You can well imagine the jolt they receive."

Noelle nodded.

"It takes three points to win the match. If a knight unhorses his opponent, he is given three points and automatically wins the match," Guinevere said and then she thought of something else. "Oh, in this tournament the spear heads will be blunted with protective coronals. Since it is Christmas, we do not want any bloodshed. And the men over there—" Guinevere pointed, "—are the constables. They are checking the saddles to make certain no knight has used strapping to tie them into the saddle."

A young man dressed in purple and gold, a trumpet tucked under this arm, marched onto the field. He was the herald, who acted as the master of ceremonies. The crowd cheered, and he had to wait until they were quiet again. He stopped in front of the king and bowed.

When Arthur indicated that he should rise, the herald shouted, "Here ye, Here ye! Camelot's Christmas tournament shall begin. The rules are as follows," he announced and then began listing them. When he was finished, he placed the trumpet to his lips and blew a long, loud blast, much different from the earlier sound.

The knights poured onto the field from two different directions. Soon the field glittered with shiny armor and bright pennons as the knights lined up for the king's inspection. They all turned and faced Arthur, then saluted him by raising their lances.

King Arthur rose. "Go forth and have a good tournament. Do your utmost to win. There is a special prize for Sir Nicholas and Sir Gavin," the king announced. "They have decided between them that the winner of the two will win the hand of Lady Noelle." Arthur pointed to Noelle.

All the knights cheered, raising their lances in salute. Everyone in the gallery turned to look at Noelle; they began to cheer.

Noelle wanted to get up and run. Instead, she lifted her head stubbornly, raising her chin, refusing to be embarrassed with so many eyes upon her. Without realizing she'd done so, she had found Nicholas and was looking directly at him. He looked magnificent. His snow-white horse wore white trappings with a blood-red dragon on the side, and the horse's bridle and reins were studded with bosses of silver. Nicholas had red plumes on his helmet, which he had tucked under his arm. He did not smile at Noelle. His expression was fierce.

Then he looked at her. Slowly and seductively, his gaze slid over her face, and she felt as if he had reached out and touched her for only a moment before the stony mask slid back into place.

He looked determined.

He looked focused.

How Noelle's body ached for his touch, and she told Nicholas with her eyes how much she loved him. It would have to do since she could not boldly give him her sleeve.

The herald raised the trumpet to his lips again. The knights turned their mounts and left the field, but Noelle couldn't tear her gaze from Nicholas's profile. He sat so tall and proud in the saddle.

It was time to begin.

Knight after knight fought one another, lances splintering as the knights earned their points while others were eliminated. Only one tragic accident had happened so far. One knight was knocked from his horse, which bolted and dragged him across the list and out into a field. Noelle heard later that he had a broken leg and arm.

Nicholas had won all his matches so far, and Sir Gavin had won his. The field began to narrow down, and Noelle's stomach tightened.

Tristan was up next, having defeated his last five opponents. Noelle was proud as she watched her brother take the field. His next opponent took his place, but before the herald could drop the flag, a group of riders came galloping through the open field and onto the list.

One of the riders had a scrap of white silk on the tip of a lance. Noelle wondered where these knights had come from. She didn't have long to wait to find her answer as the riders stopped directly in front of the king.

The first knight, dressed all in black, raised his visor. It was Meleagant who sat smugly confident upon his black destrier.

Murmurs ran through the crowd. The king's knights started for Meleagant, but Arthur held up his hand. "The Black Knight comes under a flag of truce. Let him speak."

"I am glad to see that the king still abides by the rules of chivalry and allows a good knight to speak. After all, I was one of you."

"You *were*. Say what you will, Meleagant, and then be gone," Arthur said, the impatience in his voice evident.

"I heard that the tournament was open to all knights." Meleagant looked around. "I see several countries represented. I have come to compete as well."

"You are not welcome in Camelot," Arthur said, his voice striking out like a savage lash.

Meleagant gave a half smile. "Are you afraid I will show up your noble knights?"

"Let him compete!" Lancelot and several other knights cried out.

"I will be happy to joust with the Black Knight first," Tristan shouted.

"My knights have spoken. But only *you* can compete, Meleagant. Your men will have to wait outside, but your squire may stay to assist you."

"So be it," Meleagant said with a curt nod. He turned and said something to his ten guards. They turned and rode out to the open field to await him. Meleagant rode to the far side of the jousting field and took his position. He was followed by his squire.

Meleagant looked at Peter, his squire, who had dismounted. He selected a lance from his pack and brought it over to Meleagant.

"They are such a stupid lot," Meleagant sneered. "Their arrogance would not let them decline my offer. Though each one of them would like to kill me, they could not do so unless we were at war. Aye, I am going to enjoy this match right down to the moment I kill their best knight."

Peter laughed. "And then we will have to make a mad dash to safety. There is no doubt you will win, for we know you have never been defeated in a match."

Meleagant nodded and lowered his black shield. As he looked at his opponent on the other end, he lowered the visor on his helmet. This would be easy.

What a good way to extract revenge from these mightier-than-thou knights.

And when had Tristan of Cranborne become a knight? Tristan wasn't as worthless as his brother, but he was definitely inexperienced. Meleagant would be happy to teach the young knight a lesson.

Noelle couldn't believe how somber the crowd had become. Even the sky had turned a darker gray to match the mood. She was appalled that Meleagant had the arrogance to appear here so soon after murdering her brother. There were many here who wanted to see the man dead, and she was among them. If she had a bow and arrow, she would gladly put a permanent end to his jousting this day.

And if by some chance he won the tournament, she would die before agreeing to marry the cur.

The two knights were poised, their lances lowered as they awaited the signal to start. The contestants glared at each other, then Tristan lowered his visor.

They were ready.

Noelle squeezed her hands. The herald dropped the flag. Both riders charged forward.

Tristan's lance caught Meleagant in the shoulder, knocking him backwards, but it did little damage. Both riders pulled their mounts to a halt, swung around, and prepared for the second round.

They charged at each other again. This time Meleagant's lance hit Tristan's helmet, knocking him sideways on his horse, the helmet wedged half on and half off his head. When Tristan's horse reached the end of the field, Tristan fell to the ground, unable to keep his grip.

Noelle stood on tiptoe to see better. Several squires raced to help Tristan to his feet. He stood, wobbling a little, but his helmet was still stuck, so he raised his hand to forfeit the match.

Noelle let out her breath. At least her brother wasn't hurt. It was a vicious hit, she thought as she watched the treacherous Meleagant leave the field to prepare for his next match.

The next match was Nicholas and Sir Gavin, who had just gotten into position when Meleagant rode back onto the field and spoke to Sir Gavin, who nodded and moved out of the way.

"What has happened?" Noelle asked Guinevere.

Guinevere shrugged and looked to her husband. King Arthur leaned over. "Meleagant is the senior knight, so he just pulled rank on Sir Gavin to joust Sir Nicholas," Arthur explained.

Nicholas watched the two men. "So Meleagant wants my blood," Nicholas said out of the corner of his mouth to Dirk.

"So it seems," Dirk said with a nod.

"Well, I am ready for him. Nothing would suit me better than to see him lying facedown in the dirt."

"He is sly and crafty, so be careful," Dirk warned Nicholas and moved away.

Nicholas grasped the ash-wood spear from his squire and nestled it under one armpit. His gauntleted hand grasped the spear where it had been thinned down for a handhold. He held his knees firm against his mount, steadied his breathing, and focused on the opponent.

The flag dropped.

They spurred their horses and charged. The horses sounded like rumbling thunder as they sped across the field. Nicholas's lance stuck Meleagant in the chest, shattering the lance and sending Meleagant sideways. However, he regained his balance before falling.

They readied themselves and charged again. This time Nicholas's spear hit Meleagant's shoulder, but did not unseat him.

"That is two points for ye," Dirk said as Nicholas returned to the starting position. "Aim right in the center and unsaddle the cur this time. Look how his arm hangs—ye might have dislocated it."

"That is exactly what I intend to do," Nicholas said.

Peter ran to Meleagant, grabbing the horse's bridle. "Are you hurt, sire?"

"Just a little bruised," Meleagant said through clenched teeth as he straightened his breastplate.

"One more point, and Sir Nicholas wins," Peter said.

"Do you not think I know that?" Meleagant snapped. "But Nicholas will not win. This time I will stop him." He held his lance high. "I will come under him and throw him from his mount."

"I do not know." Peter shook his head. "He is fearfully strong," Peter said, looking at Sir Nicholas over his shoulder.

"But I am craftier," Meleagant sneered. "Loosen the coronal on my lance."

"But, sire. It is illegal. They will stop you," Peter pointed out.

"Not if they don't see the spear until it is too late."

Noelle watched the two men preparing to make their final round. All Nicholas had to do was strike Meleagant, and he would be the winner. Then he'd have his match with Sir Gavin. And now that she'd seen Nicholas in action, she had little worry about who the victor would be. Nicholas would finally be hers. She sighed, and a giddy feeling settled over her.

The two riders tucked their lances under their arms and crouched down low on their mounts. Meleagant lowered his spear and then adjusted it again just as the flag was lowered. Noelle wondered if he was getting too tired to hold the spear as she watched Meleagant. He dipped his lance again and Noelle thought she noticed something odd about the lance.

And then Meleagant charged. Dirt flew from his horse's hooves.

Noelle's eyes widened. Now she knew what she'd seen that was odd. The cur's lance had lost its protection.

She jumped to her feet. "No, Nicholas! Meleagant's lance is uncovered!"

* * *

At the sound of Noelle screaming, Nicholas turned his head. Then everything seemed to move as if time itself had slowed to nothing. Meleagant's lance hit and stuck in the armor of Nicholas's left chest.

Nicholas leaned to the left, grasping for the lance, struggling to pull it free. Unbalanced, he fell from his horse.

Nicholas staggered to his feet, then slowly sank to his knees and collapsed.

The crowd came to their feet as one and, for a moment, the spectators were deathly quiet. Everyone stared at the downed knight with a lance protruding from his body.

No one was moving. No one was trying to help Nicholas.

Noelle raced down the steps to the field. "Help him! Help him," she screamed when no one moved.

King Arthur shouted. "Get Meleagant! He has broken the rules of the joust. He is escaping. And someone get help for Sir Nicholas."

Several knights tore off after Meleagant, who raced across the list and out through the far side of the field.

A squire had just reached Nicholas as Noelle ran around the fence in the middle. She noticed that Guinevere, Carolyn, and Isabelle had followed her.

"I hope he is not hurt," Guinevere said, holding her skirts up out of the mud.

Noelle could no longer find her voice as she raced across the field to Nicholas.

The page had just removed Nicholas's helmet as she knelt down beside him. Sir Gavin grasped the lance and jerked it free from Nicholas's chest. Blood seeped through the hole.

"We must get this armor off," Noelle said. "Nicholas," she said. "Nicholas, you must awaken." He did not answer. She pushed the hair, damp from sweat, from his face. "Please talk to me, Nicholas."

"It is snowing," Guinevere said. "We must get Sir Nicholas off the frozen field."

Noelle looked up to see the white, fluffy flakes coming down.

Dirk had just removed Nicholas's breastplate. His tunic was soaked with blood where his heart was located. Noelle took her scarf, folded it, and placed it over the wound. She pressed hard on Nicholas's chest, trying to stop the bleeding. "Take him to his tent," she ordered the men who had gathered around. "The wound is serious. We must hurry or my lord will bleed to death."

"Dirk, keep pressure on his chest," Noelle hissed. She looked at Sir Gavin. "We must find Merlin."

"I am off to do your bidding, milady." Sir Gavin ran for his horse.

Noelle clambered to her feet as they carried Nicholas off the field. Tears poured from her eyes and ran down her cheeks, and all but blinded her.

The snowflakes coated her hair, and she remembered Nicholas's dream of snow. His words came back to her, producing a chill much colder than the falling snow. She felt the cold hands of fear.

"He will be all right, you will see," Guinevere said, placing a hand on Noelle's shoulder.

"Aye, milady," Isabelle said. "You can make him well again."

Noelle turned eyes brimming with tears toward her friends and whispered, "Nay, I cannot. Nicholas is dying."

EIGHTEEN

They carried Nicholas toward his pavilion.

Noelle followed with Guinevere, Isabelle, and Carolyn. Noelle was truly frightened. She'd never felt so cold and empty before. She had to hold her hands to keep them from shaking.

"What did you mean, he is dying?" Guinevere asked.

"It was a dream Nicholas had," Noelle said. "When we were lost in the forest, he told me about this recurring dream of him dying in the snow."

"But you can save him," Isabelle said. "You have taken care of everybody, and you have saved him before."

"I hope you are right," Noelle said. "But the last time was so minor compared to this. I don't know if my knowledge is enough for a wound so grave."

The snow fell faster, obscuring everything but Guinevere, Noelle's ladies, and the litter carrying Nicholas. They walked faster toward the tent, through the big, beautiful flakes. But instead of seeing the beauty as Noelle normally did, all she could think of were Nicholas's words. . . .

I dreamed I lay upon a field dying and I could

see the white, fluffy flakes falling. They landed upon my face, but I could not lift my hands to remove them. It was a helpless feeling.

Noelle knew not how, but she was going to save Nicholas. His dream would not come true.

Once inside the tent, the men placed Nicholas on his cot then stepped back, and Noelle pushed her way to him. She ripped open his tunic, removed the bloody cloth. Quickly, she tore his tunic in strips. Then she folded them, placed the fabric over his wound, and applied pressure with her hands. Dirk stirred the small fire in the pit behind her to provide much-needed warmth. Noelle didn't hear her ladies. Evidently they had remained outside to give them more room.

Noelle wrapped her fingers around Nicholas's wrist, pressing against the veins. His pulse was not strong at all. "Please, Nicholas, look at me," she pleaded. The tears blinded her eyes and choked her voice.

"You must fight to live," Noelle begged Nicholas. "You must live for me."

She had to convince him that he had to struggle to stay alive, for Noelle didn't know what to do next. Panic like she'd never known welled in her throat and threatened to engulf her. She shut her eyes and lifted her face to heaven. *Merlin, please come to me. I cannot do this alone. If you can hear me, please hurry.*

When she opened her eyes and gazed down at the wound, her hand and cloth were covered in Nicholas's blood. Nicholas was losing too much blood and she was helpless to stop the flow. It was as if his very existence was slipping from her.

Hot tears poured down her face. She reached up to brush them away and left her cheek smeared with sticky blood. She cared naught. "Do not leave me, Nicholas."

"Can ye do something for him, lass?" Dirk asked, and Noelle looked up to see that the brawny Scot's cheeks were wet with tears.

"We are losing him, Dirk. We must find Merlin. Only Merlin can help Nicholas now. The wound is fatal." She glanced at Dirk and saw that he'd gone completely pale. And at that moment, she could see how much Dirk loved Nicholas, too.

"I will get Merlin," Dirk stated firmly. "One way or the other . . . he will be here."

Nicholas knew he was dying.

It was not a bad feeling, really, he thought abstractly. Rather pleasant. Warm and soft.

At least the pain was starting to leave his body as the blood seeped from his chest. How in the hell had he gotten back into his tent? And then he remembered. He could not believe he'd let Meleagant best him. Oh, how Nicholas wished he could have gotten his hands on Meleagant and run him through. Of course, Nicholas had been stupid enough to trust the Black Knight. He should have known that Meleagant would do nothing the fair way. Perhaps if Noelle hadn't screamed, Nicholas would have seen the spearhead and avoided death.

It was too late now.

Vaguely, he could hear someone talking to him. What was she saying? He just needed to concentrate more.

Noelle looked down at him. Her flaxen hair had come loose and hung around her shoulders, tumbling down her back. Her green eyes sparkled like rare gems, her thick lashes were spiked with tears. There was a red smear across her cheek. Why was she crying? And what was she saying?

She was begging him not to die. Did she think he wanted to die?

Hell, no! Nicholas would not let the warm softness seduce him. He was a fighter. He was determined to fight death to the very end just so he could be close to Noelle a few moments longer. He didn't want to leave her.

He had known there was something special about her from the very first time he had found her at the lake spying on him. He remembered her falling from behind the bush she'd hidden in, and his heart warmed. A little too late he realized how much he loved this woman who held his hand. She was a stubborn one, but with time, he probably could have taught her to obey. And if the stars were right, to hold her tongue. He wanted to smile over that thought, but he couldn't. He couldn't move at all, no matter how hard he tried.

Oh my love, Nicholas sighed. If only we had more time together. We couldn't have had children, for I would not wish the possibility of my mother's madness on anyone, but we could have loved, and I would have tried to make you happy. You must understand, Noelle, for I cannot speak, and I do not have much longer. I can feel my life ebbing away no matter how much I fight it—I grow weak.

But know this, until the end of time I will love you as much as any man could love a woman.

Please do not weep, my love. If only I could speak to you and make you understand how very much I love you.

If only . . . Nicholas felt strange. He could feel himself coming out of his body. . . .

Nicholas's eyes were open. But he acted as if he couldn't see her. Noelle waved her hand in front of his face, hoping he would blink or something, but she received no response.

He was dying.

Noelle could feel him leaving her, no matter how much she begged him to live.

"NO!" she screamed, a bloodcurdling sound that sent chills up everyone's back. "Please, Nicholas!" Tears choked her voice. "I love you. Please fight harder. I know you can do it."

A commotion sounded behind her as Sir Gavin entered the tent, followed by Dirk. Noelle's spirit sank. They had not found Merlin. Oh God, no! Merlin had been her one last hope.

"Just a moment," someone called from outside the tent. Then Matilda pushed Merlin through the flaps.

"Matilda had heard what happened and she went

for Merlin," Dirk explained. Then he stepped back and stood with Sir Gavin and Matilda.

Merlin immediately went to Noelle and knelt down beside her. "You are sure he is the one you sought?" he said softly with eyes filled with wisdom hundreds of years old.

Noelle nodded her head as the tears tumbled down. "But he is leaving me. You must help him live. I will do anything. Please, Merlin."

"Would you give him up?"

Noelle glanced sharply at Merlin, completely shocked by his words. She looked back at Nicholas, her gaze lingering on his face, and then she answered, "If I have to, aye."

"That is what I needed to know. Now stand back."

Matilda helped Noelle to her feet and placed her arm around her, cradling Noelle's head. As if through the fog of a dream, Noelle noticed that Nicholas's sticky blood still dripped from her fingers. Her gown, once white, was splotched with bright red stains. Despair wrapped around her and threatened to squeeze the very life from her, but she no longer cared. All she had ever dreamed about lay before her dying, and she cared not to live.

"It is not his time," Matilda said in a motherly voice to Noelle. "He is too good to die."

Noelle wrapped her arms around the old woman, and they stood there watching Merlin and praying for a miracle.

Merlin sat on the small bed. He shook his head, his white hair falling around his face. He lifted one twisted and gnarled hand and shoved his hair over his shoulder. Then he pulled up his long sleeves and placed his hand over Nicholas's heart.

Merlin began to chant.

Nothing happened.

Noelle was breathing so rapidly she was feeling faint, but Matilda held her up.

And then the strangest thing happened. As the chanting grew louder and louder, something akin to a whirlwind began to spin in the top of the tent. It looked very much like bright stars as it spun faster and faster, all the while getting lower and lower and colder and colder.

Soon the whirling stars were swirling around Nicholas and Merlin, until Noelle could see neither. It was as if they were lost in a blizzard that encompassed only them.

Noelle couldn't believe her eyes as she stared and prayed. Her tears had been dried by a gust of wind colder than anything she had ever experienced. The wind swept in through the tent and knocked it from around them. Matilda and Noelle clung to each other to keep from being swept away with the tent.

The snow came down harder, settling upon Nicholas and Merlin until they were completely blanketed in white. Noelle blinked and realized that the snow had only fallen on the cot.

Then an eerie quiet settled over them.

No one in the tent had moved; many had ceased to breathe in the last few minutes as they all gaped at the sight before them.

Merlin shook the snow from his body and raised his hands above him, his long fingers pointed toward heaven; then he shouted, "Fire of the dragon!" before leaning down and breathing fire into Nicholas's mouth.

Nothing happened.

Noelle looked around her. Sir Gavin, Tristan, and Dirk had tears in their eyes. Everything was for nothing.

It was too late.

She had lost Nicholas.

She had lost everything.

And then a miracle happened. . . .

Nicholas bolted straight up, knocking Merlin to the ground. The hole in his chest was completely gone. In its place was a mark that looked like the dragon's breath.

"God's tooth, why do I not have any clothes on out here in the snow?" Nicholas bellowed. "It is cold."

Noelle ran to Nicholas. He took her in his arms as he tried to soothe her. "You have been crying. Who has caused these tears?"

"You have," she said in a small voice.

"I have not lost the match, have I?" Nicholas looked at everyone around him. "Why is everyone in my . . . and where is my pavilion?"

"Nay, you still have a match to go," Tristan said. "Do you not remember your match with Meleagant?"

Nicholas frowned as he held Noelle in his arms and slowly everything came back to him. "Aye, I must kill the bloody bastard. His spear carried no coronal upon it. Let us continue the match."

King Arthur, who had just walked up said, "You

need to be clothed Nicholas, before you catch your death. We nearly lost you once. I do not think that any of us could bear it twice in one day."

"I am still muddled on the details," Nicholas admitted.

Noelle pulled herself away from Nicholas and turned to see that Matilda held Nicholas's surcoat and tunic in her plump hands. Noelle took the garments with a smile, and then handed them to Nicholas, who slipped the tunic over his head.

"I think I have just met death, sire. And I see my premonition of snow was not so farfetched," Nicholas said as he dressed himself. He looked at Noelle, who was the only one who knew what he meant.

"What does that mean?" the king asked.

Nicholas gave Noelle a small smile. "Nothing, sire." He looked at Merlin. "Thank you. I will try and make good this life you have extended to me."

"Aye, yet know that the dragon lives within you," Merlin said as he went to stand beside the king.

Nicholas stood. "I believe we have a match to finish," Nicholas said to Sir Gavin.

"Nay," Noelle said. "I will marry Sir Gavin, for I do not want you on the field again this day."

Nicholas looked at her and frowned. "Are you saying I am not fit to fight for your honor?"

"Nicholas, you almost died." Noelle stepped back and looked at the stupid man. Did he not realize she had almost lost him? She would lose him this way, as well, but at least he'd live. "I will not put your life in danger twice this day."

"Woman, it is not for you to say."

Nicholas was so stubborn, Noelle thought. But she could not take the chance that anything would happen to him again. Because she loved him thus, she would give Nicholas up though her very heart was being wrenched from her body.

Sir Gavin stepped up. "I can settle this argument," he said. "I will not joust you, Nicholas. It's not necessary."

Anger was starting to cloud Nicholas's face. "Have I lost my voice that I cannot speak for myself?"

Sir Gavin held up his hand. "Let me speak. I have just witnessed the most marvelous thing."

"And that being?" Nicholas's voice was edged with steel. He didn't like being made the fool. He would finish the match as was agreed. He would not let Noelle go so easily.

"I have witnessed true love. When one will sacrifice his happiness for another, then I know of no truer love. And I hope one day that I, too, will find such a love." Sir Gavin paused and took Noelle's hand. "So I rescind my offer of marriage and give Noelle to you with my blessings." He took Noelle's hand and placed it in Nicholas's.

Noelle smiled until she heard Nicholas's next words.

"What if I have changed my mind?"

Noelle looked at him with such a startled expression that Nicholas thought she was getting ready to swoon or hit him. He wasn't sure which, but decided to ease the pained look upon her face. "I have not changed my mind, for I love you, Noelle." He gave her a teasing smile.

"Then tomorrow we will have a wedding," King Arthur boomed in the background.

Noelle faintly heard the king, but she couldn't be sure. For nothing mattered but the fact that Nicholas held her, his lips brushing softly over hers. Then he kissed her with the warmth of the dragon. A kiss that was meant for a private chamber, but Noelle cared not for she had found her own true heaven in Sir Nicholas's arms.

NINETEEN

Nicholas and Dirk had already attended the Shepherds' Mass early this morning. It was the second Christmas Mass; the third would come tonight. Nicholas had not been allowed to sit with Noelle. As a matter of fact, he'd not even seen her in the church, which still irritated him. They had probably brought her in after he was seated. Probably Arthur's doings.

But they could not keep her from him much longer, Nicholas thought with a scowl.

Dirk stood in the opening of the tent, grinning at Nicholas.

Nicholas had just finished dressing and was leaning against a table in his tent. "I can always tell when you are dying to say something. Are you going to stand there and look like a simpleton, or will you enter and say your piece?"

"Ye looked a little out of sorts at Mass," Dirk said with a chuckle.

Nicholas glared at him.

"I didn't believe ye were truly going to marry the lass," Dirk said as he entered and stood across from Nicholas.

"I am not at all certain that I believe it either," Nicholas admitted.

"It is a good thing." Dirk nodded. "The men are happy to be preparing for the wedding instead of war. We are going to have one hell of a Christmas celebration this year."

Nicholas finally smiled. "I believe I am going to enjoy this day, as well. But to more serious matters . . . exactly what happened yesterday? I remember nothing but falling from my horse."

"Meleagant did not have his lance protected with a coronal. His intention was obviously to kill you. Which he would have done, if not for Merlin's magic."

"You know, I believe I did die yesterday. It was a strange feeling, but I could feel myself coming out of my body. I cannot say it was an uncomfortable feeling, but I kept hearing Noelle's voice begging me not to leave her."

"Lady Noelle is very extraordinary," Dirk said as he folded his arms across his chest. "And she loves ye a great deal, though I cannot fathom why."

"Aye," Nicholas agreed. "But getting back to the match. I don't understand why I did not see the lance and avoid it. I have never slipped and been so careless before. It's a flaw that I cannot abide."

"I believe milady called yer name and distracted ye," Dirk said with a smile.

"God's tooth. I remember now. Noelle could be a problem. I cannot allow such distractions. I must figure out how to deal with her in the future."

Dirk's laughter made his shoulders shake. "Ye are

going to have a lifetime of *trying* to deal with yer lady. And I have a feeling it will take ye that long to figure her out. Good luck."

Nicholas frowned. "I will work out how to handle that problem later. After all, she is merely a damsel." He paused, then remembered something else. "Did they catch Meleagant?"

"Nay. He escaped unscathed."

Nicholas expelled a long, low breath. "Well, one day Meleagant's luck will run out, and when it does, I pray I am there. For I will not rest until the deed is done," Nicholas promised.

"And I will be right beside ye," Dirk said, moving over to clasp Nicholas's arm. "I am truly happy this day. This marriage to the Lady Noelle is a good thing."

"You have been my friend and right arm, Dirk, for a long time. Thank you. Your blessing means much to me."

"My Lord," Ector, Nicholas's squire, called.

"Enter," Nicholas commanded.

Ector entered and said in a rush, as if he'd run all the way from the castle, "King Arthur has requested that you return to the castle."

"Well, my friends, maybe the time has finally come," Nicholas said as he grabbed his red surcoat and left to do the king's bidding.

When Nicholas reached the castle, he was told that Arthur awaited him at the Round Table. Nicholas made his way to the small hall, wondering why Arthur would want to meet him there.

When Nicholas entered the room, he found not only King Arthur, but all his fellow knights sitting at the table.

"Here he is now." King Arthur didn't bother to stand. He held out his hand and gestured. "Take your seat."

"Sire," Nicholas said with a nod, and then went to his chair. "Has something happened? Were we supposed to meet today?"

"Nay, Nicholas. We have gathered to offer you our congratulations, brother to brother," Arthur said.

"Hear, hear," the other knights said as they struck the table with their forearms.

Confused, Nicholas stared at the king. Arthur was smiling far too broadly. It meant he was up to something, and Nicholas wondered what. "Thank you," Nicholas finally said.

King Arthur rose. "I would like everyone here to know that Sir Nicholas has given up much for the lady he loves, for he and I had a wager." Arthur's lips quirked in a sly grin.

"What was the wager, sire?" Sir Lancelot asked.

"That our most illustrious knight . . ." Arthur motioned to Nicholas, "could forgo pleasuring himself with the damsels until Christmas Day. I believe you have long known of his reputation."

Laughter burst forth from around the table as all the knights nodded to each other.

Nicholas frowned. Arthur seemed to be enjoying himself at Nicholas's expense.

"Sir Nicholas once stood here and told me that ladies meant little to him. That is, until he met the Lady Noelle. At long last, I think Nicholas has fallen under a woman's spell. I believe he has chosen well. Do you not agree with me?"

"Hear, hear," everyone shouted, agreeing with the king.

Nicholas still said nothing as he watched the king, who at this moment reminded him of a sly fox.

"Nicholas once told me that a perfect woman does not exist. I want to know—do you still feel the same, Nicholas?"

"Nay, sire. And, I believe you will not let this rest until I admit I was wrong. So in front of God and King, I do admit I was wrong, perhaps, only once in my life. I have found my woman."

The other knights chuckled.

"And I believe you also said you never lose," King Arthur prodded.

"I did say that, sire. I now say I have lost once, and you know damned well when that was," Nicholas said, letting his irritation show, and then getting angrier because he had done so.

Arthur laughed long and hard. "I wish I could say I am sorry for the fun I have had at your expense, Nicholas, but it would be a lie."

Nicholas furrowed his brow. "I do not understand, sire."

"My brave knight, I have put upon you that which you refused to see," Arthur said. Nicholas's frown was so intense, it was all Arthur could do not to laugh at his knight again. It was plain to see that Nicholas was already angry. "You see, Nicholas. I decided it was time for you to marry. You were wreaking havoc with too many maidens, so I spoke with Sir Gavin and told him I planned to bring a young woman to Camelot to wed you. Sir Gavin pointed out that you would have none of it and would shun the woman the moment you saw her. So he suggested a diversion."

Nicholas turned to Tristan. "Did you know of this?"

"Nay, I was told she would be betrothed to Sir Gavin," Tristan replied honestly.

"Were the banns not posted?" Nicholas wondered if the king thought him stupid. The banns would have been posted and Nicholas hadn't signed anything.

The king interrupted. "If you check, Nicholas, you will see that the banns were posted and filed with your name and Noelle's. So what say you, my brave knight? Have I not given you the best Christmas gift of all?"

The room fell silent as all eyes were cast upon Nicholas, who was sitting back in his chair with his arm propped upon the armrest, glaring at the king.

Nicholas took a deep breath before leaning forward on the table. Then he directed his question to Sir Gavin. "So that is why you seemed so nonchalant about Lady Noelle?"

"Aye," Sir Gavin said with a nod.

"And the joust?"

Sir Gavin cleared his throat. "Our king suggested that you would appreciate your prize more if it were won and not handed to you."

Nicholas's gaze was back on the king. Slowly, Nicholas got to his feet. "It would seem, sire, that you have thought of everything."

King Arthur smiled. "I think so."

"Then there is nothing left for me to do but . . ." Nicholas turned and started to leave. The room was so quiet that Nicholas could hear himself breathe.

"You did not ask permission to leave," Arthur's voice boomed. "Where are you going?"

"To collect my Christmas gift," Nicholas said and turned back toward the king. "And if the rest of you want to see our king's hard work come to an end, I suggest that you all get up so you are not late for my wedding." Nicholas smiled at the stunned faces.

The other knights began to cheer as they all came over to congratulate Nicholas. And then King Arthur stood before him. "You should go ahead and admit the truth, and then I will cease tormenting you."

"One of these days I will return the deed tenfold," Nicholas warned him. He laughed and then he said what he knew the king wanted to hear. "You were right, sire."

"Good, Nicholas." Arthur wrapped an arm around his cousin and gave him a hearty squeeze. "You should always remember those words. Now let us go and find your bride."

"Look out the window," Carolyn said.

Noelle and Isabelle went over and gazed out. The ground was blanketed in pristine, white snow.

"It is beautiful," Noelle said in a dreamy kind of voice. "The day is perfect."

"I cannot believe that you are actually marrying that fierce knight. Did you see how relentless he was against his competitors yesterday?"

"He was magnificent," Noelle said.

"Let me finish your hair," Isabelle said, gesturing for Noelle to sit down. When she had taken a seat, Isabelle continued. "You are so lovely in this scarlet velvet cotehardie that you will stand out in the snow."

"I like the white fur on her sleeves," Carolyn remarked.

"I wonder what Nicholas will give me for the first day of Christmas," Noelle said as Isabelle wrapped the braids around Noelle's head.

"That is easy," Isabelle chuckled. "He is giving you himself."

"Not a bad present," Carolyn commented, and they all laughed.

Noelle got up. "I am ready."

As they made their way down to the Great Hall, Merlin met Noelle in the first corridor. "My child, you look exactly like I have always seen you in my visions."

"Thank you for all you have done for me and especially for saving Nicholas's life."

Merlin chuckled. "Now Nicholas will not only have the title of dragon, he has the dragon within him. Most appropriate, I think."

"And I will have a hard time taming him," Noelle said wistfully.

"But tame him you will," Merlin whispered, "and

those are my last words of wisdom this day. Now, go forth and claim what is yours."

When they entered the Great Hall there were minstrels playing flutes, viols, trumpets, drums, and bagpipes. Everyone was in a festive mood. There was dancing, and a bright fire roared in the hearth. A few people sat around playing chess.

And then she saw him, standing tall and proud, talking to Dirk. It was as if the rest of the world disappeared around them.

Nicholas's back was to Noelle, so he couldn't see her approach. She noticed that he was dressed all in white as pure as the snow. And then she thought to herself, with a wicked grin, what a contradiction that was.

As Noelle moved closer, she saw Matilda approaching Nicholas. The old servant stopped and handed him a scarlet surcoat. "I made this for your wedding, sire."

"Thank you, Matilda," Nicholas said, taking the garment. He removed his coat and slipped the new one over his arms. Maltida had embroidered a small dragon on the bottom of the coat. "This is truly fine work," Nicholas said, then smiled his appreciation to Matilda. "You are coming to my wedding?"

"Of course, sire. You have chosen well," Matilda said with a wink and a curtsey. "And here is your lady now."

Nicholas swung around, then took a step back. Noelle stood before him, her ladies-in-waiting flanking her. But his eyes were only on Noelle. She was so beautiful dressed in red that it took his breath away. She had dressed in his scarlet colors this day and it pleased him well.

He strode to her side. "My lady," Nicholas said with a bow. "You are beautiful."

"Thank you," Noelle said with a blush. Then she looked at Matilda. "I never had the chance to thank you for finding Merlin."

"I was there when Sir Nicholas was struck down, and I knew it was serious. So, I went for Merlin, posthaste."

Noelle ran her hand over the needlework on Nicholas's surcoat. "You do fine work, Matilda. I'm sure that Nicholas will treasure this garment always."

"I only want him to be happy," Matilda said, and Noelle saw tears in Matilda's eyes. "I hope you'll have many children."

Nicholas placed a hand on Matilda's shoulders. "You, of all people, should know why I care not to have children."

Matilda's complexion paled. "Might I have a word with you both before you wed?" she asked and nodded her head toward an empty corner of the room.

They followed the old woman to the quiet corner, and Matilda turned and looked at both of them. "As you know, sire, I have been with you most of your life," Matilda said.

"That is true," Nicholas said. "I can remember many a time that you dried my tears."

"Aye, and I was glad to do so. I hoped never to

tell you about your mother, but I'll not have you worrying about your children when there is no need."

"You know how mad my mother was?" Nicholas said.

Matilda took a deep breath. "Nicholas, she was indeed mad, but she was not your mother," Matilda said in a quiet voice. "Therefore, her blood doth not flow in your veins."

Strange and disquieting thoughts began to race through Nicholas's mind, as well as hope. "If she was not my mother, then who was?"

"It is not important," Matilda said. "I just wanted you to realize that you can have children. As many as you desire."

"It *is* important to me," Nicholas said, "and I believe you know who my mother is."

"I cannot tell you."

"Why?" Noelle asked.

"The truth could cause Nicholas more pain, and I'll not allow anything to do that."

Nicholas took Matilda's arms. "Look at me, Matilda."

Slowly she glanced up at Nicholas, and Noelle wondered what she was going to say.

But it was not Matilda who spoke.

"You are my mother." Nicholas said, softly.

"I am sorry. I've never wanted the truth to cause you trouble. Surely you are disappointed," she said as a tear trickled down her cheek.

Nicholas stared at Matilda for many long moments. Noelle wasn't sure that he was going to move. He seemed frozen to the spot.

And then he did something that brought tears to Noelle's eyes. Nicholas drew Matilda into his arms and said, "How could I not be happy? It is a relief knowing that I was never a part of a woman who hated me. Now I know why she felt as she did. I wish you had told me sooner."

"Then you would have been labeled a bastard. I did not want that for you," Matilda murmured. "I shall go now."

"Nay. You will stay, Mother, and be part of my wedding."

Matilda shook her head. "Nay. I will not shame you and your lady and have others know that I am your mother. But I will be at the church all the same." She didn't wait for Nicholas to say anything else as she scurried off.

"It is not right," Noelle said.

"I agree," Nicholas said as he watched his mother disappear into the gathered crowd. "But at the moment, we are expected at the church. That is, if you still want to marry me."

Noelle swung around and gaped at him. "I have gone to too much trouble to find you and to prepare for this day. Do you think I would beg off now?"

He frowned at her. "Trouble?"

"Aye." She finally grinned. "It was not easy to capture you."

Nicholas bent down and kissed Noelle lightly on the lips. "But I thoroughly enjoyed the chase, my love."

"We will have none of that *until after* the vows are said," King Arthur said as he came up behind them.

"The sooner the wedding occurs, the sooner I can breathe easy again." He chuckled.

Noelle went over and kissed the king on the cheek. "I somehow have an idea that I should thank you for whatever part you played in this wedding."

"You will never know, my dear, how enjoyable you have made this Christmas season. And since this is a very short engagement, and Nicholas had not the chance to gift you with a ring, I hope you do not mind me presenting you with one."

King Arthur handed the ring to Nicholas, who nodded his approval. Nicholas took Noelle's left hand and placed the plain gold band on her finger as he said, "Our names are engraved on the inside. But I didn't forget the most important ring of all. That one, you'll receive during the ceremony."

Noelle looked at the king. "So you knew all along?"

"Guilty." The king chuckled, then motioned for them to precede him. "Your wedding awaits."

The procession to the church was more like a parade led by a troupe of minstrels playing flutes, viols, and trumpets. Behind them came Nicholas and Noelle, and then everyone else.

The snow crunched beneath their feet as they walked to the church. But Noelle was numb to the cold. She glowed in the warmth of her heart. This was truly the wedding she'd always envisioned, and the snow just added to the beauty.

When the grand parade reached the church steps

the knights had formed two lines leading up to the steps. The serfs had gathered also to cheer the couple.

Tristan came over and took Noelle's hand. "I believe it's my duty to give her to you," Tristan said to Nicholas.

Dirk, who was dressed in Nicholas's colors, as were all his men, joined him as best man. "Looks like ye are stuck with me," Dirk chuckled.

Tristan then escorted the bride to the church steps. As soon as they reached the stairs to the church, the doors were thrown open, and the priest came out bearing the wedding ring.

Tristan stood between Noelle and Nicholas with Dirk on Nicholas's right.

Father John asked, "Are you old enough to legally marry?"

"Aye," Nicholas and Noelle answered.

"Do you swear that you are not related in any manner?"

"Aye."

"Have you published the banns for this marriage?"

"Aye," Nicholas said, then added, "Thanks to our king."

"Do you both freely enter into this marriage?"

Nicholas and Noelle looked at each other and smiled as they said, "Aye."

The priest nodded, and the provost stepped forward and began to read aloud the list of dowry arrangements. Noelle was surprised at Nicholas's holdings. When the provost had finished, Nicholas handed Noelle a bag of thirteen gold coins, which would be distributed to the poor.

Tristan relinquished his hold on his sister with a kiss on her cheek. Then he gave her right hand to Nicholas. "I give you the most precious gift you have ever had."

Nicholas smiled and then said when the priest nodded, "I take thee, Noelle, to be my wedded wife, to hold and to have, at bed and at board, for better or worse, in sickness and in health, to death us do part, and thereto I plight my troth," Nicholas said in a voice full of emotion.

Noelle remained silent as was the custom, but she gave Nicholas the most dazzling smile as the priest delivered a short sermon on the sanctity of marriage.

Father John held up the ring and blessed it before giving it to Nicholas, who took Noelle's hand and then slipped it, one by one, on the first three fingers of her left hand. As he moved the ring from finger to finger, he said, "In the name of the Father, and of the Son, and of the Holy Ghost, with this ring, I thee wed."

Tears were brimming in Noelle's eyes as she looked down at the blood-red ruby that now perched on her finger and proclaimed to all that she belonged to Sir Nicholas the Dragon.

Nicholas placed a finger under her chin and nodded to the small bag of coins that she still had in her hand. Noelle nodded. She turned and walked down the steps to the crowd and distributed the coins to the poor before returning to her husband.

The wedding had been sanctified, but now it was time to enter the church. The bride and groom followed the priest to the front of the church while everyone took their places. Isabelle and Carolyn stood on Noelle's left, and Dirk stood on Nicholas's right. As the couple knelt in front of the priest, Isabelle and Dirk opened a large cloth over their heads.

When the Mass was finished, the canopy was removed, and the priest gave the groom the "kiss of peace," which Nicholas then transferred to his wife, but the kiss to his wife was not on the cheek.

Nicholas gathered Noelle in his arms and kissed her long, to the cheers of his men. When he lifted his lips, he asked her, "Are you happy, my love?"

"Aye," she said with a smile, "for you are mine, Nicholas the Dragon, and never forget that it is true."

"I doubt that you would let me, my love," he said with a grin. "Now let me do one more noble thing this day."

They both turned and faced the gathered crowd, and received their loud cheers. Then Nicholas held up his hand to quiet the crowd. "We appreciate your best wishes," Nicholas said. "As you know, I have no parents to help me celebrate, or I thought I did not until his morning when I found out that my mother still lives."

There was a gasp throughout the gathering. "I am so happy that my mother is not who I thought she was when I was small. My mother is Matilda, and I would like all of you to join in rejoicing with me. Mother, please come forward."

One of Nicholas's men took the reluctant Matilda's arm and escorted her to the front of the church amongst a lot of whispering. When red-faced Matilda reached Nicholas, he put his arm around the weeping woman.

"Do not do this, Nicholas," Matilda whispered to her son. "It will bring you nothing but shame."

"From this day forward, let there be no doubt that I recognize this woman as the mother I never knew when I was small. And I shall honor her until the day that I die," Nicholas said. He reached down and kissed Matilda on the cheek.

The crowd cheered, and Noelle had never been prouder of her husband. He was truly a very special man. And, thank God, he was now hers. She moved over and gave Matilda a hug, too. "I always knew that you cared a great deal for Nicholas, and now I know why."

Back in the Great Hall, there was feasting as they celebrated not only Christmas, but the wedding as well. There were two roasted wild boars on each end of the table, and the Yule log burned brightly in the hearth as children gathered around and sang Christmas carols.

King Arthur strode across to the couple. "You know, I have yet to give you my wedding gift."

Nicholas laughed. "You probably gave us the greatest gift of all, sire. If not for your meddling, we would never have married."

The king chuckled. "I like to think it was *guiding,* not meddling, which I must admit gave me great pleasure. However, I want to give one other gift, a gift that Nicholas was willing to give up for you, young lady," Arthur said as he smiled at Noelle.

"From this day forth, consider Briercliff yours. I do expect that the firstborn be named for me, of course."

"Of course, sire. And we will have him blessed on Christmas Day as we will once again spend Christmas in Camelot," Noelle said.

"This is one Christmas I shall never forget," Arthur said as he bent down and kissed Noelle on the cheek. "Go forth and be happy."

Nicholas pulled Noelle into his arms. "We will be happy, my love?"

"Aye."

"And what Christmas gift do you present to me?" Nicholas asked.

"I give you the greatest Christmas present of all. I give you my love, Nicholas," she said with a sassy smile. "Now let us join the others and celebrate Christmas in Camelot."

Nicholas still held his lovely bride in his arms, reluctant to let her go. He rubbed his thumb across her chin and said in a very husky voice, "And tonight we will celebrate a beginning of love . . . of life . . . of happiness.

"I love you, Noelle."

AUTHOR'S NOTE

Merry Christmas! Thank you for spending Christmas with me in my magical kingdom of Camelot. I hope you enjoyed the story as much as I enjoyed writing it. I really hated to say good-bye to Sir Nicholas the Dragon.

Thank you for all your letters and e-mails. I do answer all fan letters. Please check my web pages for contest information. And as always, the first fan who writes a letter about this book will receive a special gift from me, and the first five will receive an autographed cover. So keep those cards and letters coming. A legal-sized SASE is appreciated.

May Christmas bring you the greatest gift of all . . . LOVE.

Best wishes,
Brenda K. Jernigan
80 Pine St. W.
Lillington, NC 27546
e-mail: bkj1608@juno.com
web sites: www.theromanceclub.com
http://www.members.tripod.com/brendajernigan/
http://www.bkjbooks.com